CANDLELIGHT
Supreme

"I WANT TO SEE MY BROTHER AND I WANT TO SEE HIM NOW!" AMELIA CRIED.

Colt quirked an eyebrow, causing his long scar to stretch out into a thin line. "You're not in any position to be giving orders, Miss Stowaway. And you'll do exactly as you're told."

"Who's going to make me?" she shot back defiantly.

He suddenly pushed away from the post and advanced toward her. "Is that a challenge?" he asked, his deep voice full of sensual threat. "Or an invitation?"

"Colt, there's no need to get into this now," she cautioned, not liking the gleam in his eye one bit.

"Maybe not right now, but soon. Very soon," he said in a low, velvety voice. "And what I have in mind is a very leisurely and thorough exploration, just the way it should be for our first time."

CANDLELIGHT SUPREMES

LOVING CHARADE

Linda Vail

A CANDLELIGHT SUPREME

Published by
Dell Publishing Co., Inc.
1 Dag Hammarskjold Plaza
New York, New York 10017

ISBN: 0-440-15103-1

Printed in the United States of America

July 1987

10 9 8 7 6 5 4 3 2 1

WFH

To Our Readers:

We are pleased and excited by your overwhelmingly positive response to our Candlelight Supremes. Unlike all the other series, the Supremes are filled with more passion, adventure, and intrigue, and are obviously the stories you like best.

In months to come we will continue to publish books by many of your favorite authors as well as the very finest work from new authors of romantic fiction. As always, we are striving to present unique, absorbing love stories —the very best love has to offer.

Breathtaking and unforgettable, Supremes follow in the great romantic tradition you've come to expect *only* from Candlelight Romances.

Your suggestions and comments are always welcome. Please let us hear from you.

Sincerely,

The Editors
Candlelight Romances
1 Dag Hammarskjold Plaza
New York, New York 10017

CHAPTER ONE

"I beg your pardon?" Amelia Drake asked, staring in disbelief at the distinguished white-haired stranger sitting across the table from her.

"I want you to have my great-grandchild," he replied, casually sipping his coffee.

Amelia's dessert fork clattered loudly as it hit the delicate glass plate in front of her, the remains of an incredibly rich chocolate mousse cake completely forgotten. She glanced nervously around the crowded restaurant to see if anyone else had noticed she was having lunch with a crazy man. Apparently no one had, so she turned back to stare at him incredulously.

"You're kidding me, right?"

He shook his head, a placid, comforting smile still upon her. "I'm quite serious."

A red-hot blush suffused her face and neck as Amelia realized he meant every word. "I'm afraid—"

"Oh, I doubt that," the suave older man interjected. "Confused, certainly, perhaps even a tiny bit worried about my sanity. But afraid?" His smile broadened. "I wouldn't have picked you if I thought you were a woman who scared so easily."

Amelia continued to stare at him, his assessment of her personality leaving her speechless. Picked her? She wasn't aware she had entered a contest.

Despite his gentle manner and smiling countenance, she did in fact feel an uneasy prickling sensation at the back of her neck. Not fear, exactly, but a definite warning signal. Just how well did she know this Michael Colt?

Not well enough, obviously. They had met at the hospital where her brother was recovering from surgery for a gunshot wound. Their paths seemed to cross so often in the halls that it would have been impolite not to speak to one another.

He was always dressed impeccably, in snow-white shirts, conservative suits, and silk ties, the kind of older man one immediately recognized as a member of the upper echelon of Austin, Texas, society. He was rich and charming, and had become a friendly familiar face in the sterile hospital halls.

Amelia realized—belatedly—that she had simply made the assumption that he was visiting a sick friend at the hospital. Assumptions could get you in trouble. They could lead you to believe your brother traveled a lot because of some normal occupation, for instance. Or that two people who had chatted several times in a hospital corridor were having lunch together to share a pleasant hour of respite from a worrisome vigil at the bedside of a friend or relative.

Not to discuss the conception of great-grand-children.

And the worst part was, Michael Colt hadn't appeared crazy to her when she accepted his kind invitation to dine with him, nor did he appear crazy now. His blue eyes were full of intelligence and a glimmer of amusement. She could only guess that he was pulling her leg.

But he wasn't. "Amelia, my dear," he said softly, waiting for her full attention, "I realize how this must sound to you. I assure you I have neither taken leave of my senses nor am I making some kind of joke. I am making a business proposition. You do your best to present me with a great-grand-child in the near future, and I'll do my best to keep your brother safe."

Shocked, Amelia's whole body seemed to sag at his words. The blood drained from her face, leaving it chalk-white. She closed her eyes, took a few moments to calm herself, then looked at him in amazement.

"How do you know about my brother?" Her voice was barely above a whisper.

Michael gazed back at her appreciatively, feeling her strength as she pulled herself together and confronted him head on. Healthy color was returning to her face already. He hadn't been wrong about this girl, she had guts.

"Did you happen to notice any of the names on the hospital wings?" he asked, evading her question.

Her brow furrowed in concentration as she tried to remember the plaques on the red brick walls she had come to know so well. She nodded slowly as her mind's eye focused on one, big block letters on a shiny brass background.

"The Margaret Colt Research Wing." Amelia paused as a wide smile crossed his face, revealing almost perfect teeth. Were they his own, she wondered abstractedly. Had any of this past week been real? Maybe she'd wake up soon and find out it had all been a bad dream. "A relative of yours, of course."

He nodded. "My first wife."

Amelia waited, but apparently he wasn't yet going to tell her the story of his first wife or even more about her brother. He was waiting to be coaxed, hoping to draw her into whatever scheme he had planned for her. She didn't have much choice at the moment but to play his game.

"Didn't you say wings?"

"There is another." His pale blue eyes twinkled back at her. "An area you haven't been in need of yet," he said in a teasing voice. "But soon will. Maternity."

She ignored his taunt and took a direct approach to get her questions answered. Forget the coaxing. "That still doesn't tell me how you found out about my brother."

"Easily." Michael had been appalled at how easy it had been to gain access to such information. "It was, in fact, so simple that I took it upon myself to implement a few policy changes, pull a few strings." He grinned and added, "As a show of good faith on my part, Amelia. No matter what your decision concerning my proposition, your brother is safer now than he was before, thanks to me."

"Before you start totaling debts," she objected, "may I point out that he is already under protection?"

"Supposedly he was. He most assuredly is now." With those few words he seemed to change and become someone else. Hard, almost bitter, stronger and very much in charge. "Again, thanks to me."

Amelia glared at him. "And just who are you?"

The smile returned smoothly to his tanned face. "I am Michael Colt. Head of Colt."

"I've never heard of it," she announced flatly.

"Good. We're a very private, family-owned company."

"The better to sneak up on unsuspecting women?"

He laughed. "Hardly."

A truly baffled, charming face glared back at him. Amelia Drake wasn't a breathtaking beauty, but there was something very appealing about her nonetheless, and Michael knew quite well that she would fit his grandson's preferences.

Her face was almost a perfect oval, a pert nose marring the otherwise classic lines of her high cheekbones and delicate jaw. Warm brown eyes the color of aged sherry were surrounded by long, lush lashes, her dark eyebrows shaped into graceful, arching curves. Her thick brown hair was streaked by lighter shades and swirled around her shoulders with each movement of her head.

Another point in her favor was that she dressed

11

well and seemed to know what styles suited her, such as the navy-blue-and-cream shirtwaister dress she wore today. It added delightfully to her feminine appeal.

Amelia blinked, realizing that she was being sized up. But whom was she supposed to fit? In view of Michael Colt's obvious determination and the powerful connections he was hinting at, she had an uneasy feeling she would find out soon enough—whether she wanted to or not.

"What do you want with my brother?" she asked suspiciously.

"Not a thing. It's you I want."

The directness of his words jolted her and she tried to think of something else to say, anything to avoid discussing his absurd proposition. "So, you head a mysterious company and have a penchant for contributing to hospitals. Research and development seems a logical investment, I suppose, but why a maternity wing?" she asked, then groaned aloud. What a stupid choice of conversational topics!

Michael refrained from showing too much glee. His plan was going to work. He wasn't really surprised. He'd never had one fail yet. "There was a need, and I filled it, though I suppose you could say it was an investment too. An investment in the future. My son's wife came close to losing her life when she gave birth to my grandson, Colt."

"Colt Colt?" Amelia asked, incredulous.

"No," he assured her, chuckling. "His name is Michael, like my son and me and my father before me. We've all been called by our last name, of course, like a nickname, but with Colt it stuck."

"At least it saves some confusion, what with all the Michaels in your family," Amelia observed. She was starting to relax, probably not a good idea. For all his manipulative ways, however, there was something about this man she liked. "And it's certainly a colorful name."

"It's appropriate." His eyes twinkled as he looked at her. "You'll see. He's one of a kind. Literally. There were so many complications, my daughter-in-law couldn't have any more children after Colt."

"I'm sorry," she offered sympathetically.

"No need, girl. It's all in the past and I was too busy back then to enjoy more than one anyway."

Amelia was watching him carefully. The look that came into his eyes was almost tangible. A queasy fear leapt back into the pit of her stomach. This was a man who was used to getting what he wanted. Right now, he wanted a great-grandchild. And he wanted her to do the honors.

"But now," he continued pointedly, "I'm slowing down and ready to enjoy them."

"Adopt a few," Amelia retorted.

"I want my own flesh and blood."

A wicked thought suddenly flashed in her brain and she couldn't resist the taunt. "What if your grandson isn't virile enough to make that possible?"

"What?" Michael sat up straight in his chair. The thought had never once occurred to him.

"Anything is possible," she quipped, enjoying

13

herself immensely for the first time in this crazy conversation. It just didn't seem possible he could be serious about this.

"Balderdash. I'll worry about that when and if the time ever comes, maybe endow a fertility research unit or something," he mused, then returned to his train of thought unperturbed. "Anyway, I don't want them full time, just now and then."

"Them?" Her eyebrows arched.

"One to start. I won't be greedy."

The innocent expression on his face didn't fool her for a minute. She was definitely starting to worry. It was crazy enough to sit here discussing a baby-for-hire sort of arrangement in which she would bear him a great-grandchild in return for his help protecting her brother.

But Amelia was getting the distinct impression he was after much more than great-grandchildren. He had picked her with a full-time position in mind. Though he hadn't come right out and said it yet, Michael Colt wanted her to marry his grandson!

"Don't you think Colt might have something to say about all this?" she asked.

"Bah!" He gestured sharply with his hand, slicing through the air as if cutting something up. "I'm sure he'd have a great deal to say on the subject. My grandson is an intelligent man, mind you, but he simply doesn't know what's good for him. He's thirty-two and in no hurry to settle down."

14

She laughed out loud, relief swirling through her. "I guess that sort of spoils your plans."

"No," he told her softly, placing his tanned, wrinkled hands squarely on the starched white tablecloth. "I am a very thorough man, Amelia. I've taken Colt's reluctance into account. That's where you come in."

"Me!"

He nodded sagely at her. "You."

"Not that I'm taking any of this seriously, mind you," Amelia said, trying not to squirm beneath his determined gaze, "but for the sake of argument, how am I supposed to convince your grandson to settle down with me and raise a family?"

"Seduce him."

"What? Of all the ludicrous, impossible . . ." She trailed off, stunned. "I don't even know him!"

Michael sat back comfortably in his chair. "I'll arrange for you to meet."

"You will do no such thing!" Amelia stood up and grabbed her purse, glaring at him. "This whole preposterous conversation has gone far enough. Thanks for lunch," she said brusquely, then turned and strode out of the restaurant.

Michael quickly followed her, quite pleased with the outcome. He was sure now; she was the one. His grandson was hardly the easiest person in the world to get along with. For all her calm, regal air, Amelia had a lot of fire in her, and she would need every ounce to hold her own against Colt.

She was fast on her feet, too, another quality that would undoubtedly come in handy in her dealings with his grandson. "I'll escort you back to

15

the hospital," he said, cradling her elbow gallantly when he finally caught up with her at the street corner.

"Mr. Colt," she warned, resuming her brisk pace the moment the light changed, "I have listened to as much of your so-called business proposition as I am going to. Now would you please—"

"Call me Michael," he interrupted. "And could we please slow down a bit, my dear. I am an old man."

"Hah!" she exclaimed, thinking he was just devious enough to use ill health as a way of getting her to listen to more of his ravings. But she noticed his breathing was indeed labored and cut her stride in half. "All right. But I meant what I said, Michael. I've heard enough."

He gave her an understanding but noncommittal smile as they stopped at the cross street in front of the hospital, waiting for the light to change. She scowled at him, then turned to stare irritably at the imposing red brick building in front of them.

"They did a nice job with the new landscaping," Michael commented, breaking the silence as they crossed the street to the hospital.

"Yes," Amelia agreed warily, suspecting yet another ploy. Before them, small ground-hugging evergreen and fall-flowering shrubs were surrounded by jagged rocks. "It's nice for the patients to be able to look out and see a ray of hope, of new life and growth."

"My Margaret Mary always did like flowers." He stopped walking, gazing at the hardy yet beautiful Tyler roses in full bloom beside the concrete pathway. His voice had gone soft, choked with emotion as he seemed to drift back in time. "I used to tease her, the more the Mary-ier."

"Margaret Mary?" Amelia frowned, then remembered that this wing of the hospital was dedicated to his first wife, Margaret Colt. He must have had this garden walk built in her memory as well. She looked up into his shimmering, pale blue eyes and felt his sadness. "You loved her very much."

"Yes," he whispered. "She was so young when she . . ." A single tear slid down his sun-wrinkled cheek. "Excuse me."

Amelia couldn't be sure this wasn't all a ruse to soften her up. Then she was suddenly cross with herself for being so cynical. He didn't even seem to be aware of her presence anymore. Whether real pain or an act, it was working.

She slipped quietly into step with him as he slowly walked toward the enclosed inner courtyard and the bright, flower-laden planting beds. Smooth, flat stones formed a pathway through the richly jeweled hues of glorious flowers and small green trees. The small dated plaque at the outside entrance explained his earlier emotionalism. His Margaret Mary had passed away almost fifty years ago this week.

They walked in companionable silence along the winding paths, Michael Colt lost in the past, Amelia trying not to dwell on the unsettled futures of her brother and herself. Instead, she pondered the problem presented by this man walking beside

17

her, with his odd mixture of hardheadedness and gentle sentimentality.

Michael was evidently a powerful, wealthy man. He could help them, she sensed that much. But could he be persuaded to do so without insisting upon his outrageous fee?

"For you," he said, plucking a brilliant orange bloom and handing it to her.

"What is it?" she asked, inhaling the sweet scent.

He winked at her. "Damned if I know! I just like the way they look."

Amelia smiled back at him. He had returned from his sad walk down memory lane. "Thank you, but you shouldn't pick the flowers."

"Do you see a sign anywhere saying you can't?"

"Well, no," she agreed, glancing around.

"Nor will you. Ever. I help pay for this, and they're meant to be enjoyed. Nothing lives forever, including me." He looked at her slyly. "Which reminds me . . ."

"No!"

"Just meet him."

"Absolutely not."

Amelia was beginning to like this old man— though she was at something of a loss as to why. She didn't want to hurt his feelings. But he was simply going to have to get rid of this ridiculous, harebrained idea.

"All right," he said amicably. If there was one thing Michael had learned a very long time ago, it was when to back off and when to pursue. That didn't mean, however, that he had any intention of giving up one facet of his plan. "Let's go check on that brother of yours, shall we?"

"We?" Amelia didn't like the sound of that. She could practically hear the mischievous little gears grinding away beneath that head of white hair. "Now, you wait just one minute, Michael. I've told you I'm not interested. Your price is too high."

He chuckled, took her arm, and led her toward the elevators. "Don't you think you should check the quality of the goods before deciding that, Amelia?"

"What's that supposed to mean?"

"You'll see."

She gave him a puzzled look and opened her mouth to object, but the elevator arrived. They squeezed into the crowded cubicle, shuffling and moving aside as they stopped at each floor, Amelia carefully protecting her orange flower. She continued to eye Michael warily. The elevator bumped to yet another stop.

"Excuse me, this is where we get off," Michael said politely, stepping through the crowd and pulling Amelia out of the car with him.

"This is the wrong floor," Amelia protested. "The colors are different."

"Shh!" Michael Colt silently led her past the busy nurses' station and off down another corridor with no one in sight. "This is a hospital, remember?"

Amelia went with him reluctantly, totally confused. Then a startling thought shot through her. She didn't really know anything about this man! Everything he'd told her could be a lie! It hadn't occurred to her that she should have asked for some kind of identification the minute he mentioned her brother, just as it hadn't occurred to her that this nice old man could be part of some conspiracy.

She could be excused for her ignorance. This whole game of skulduggery her brother had gotten her involved in was completely alien to her. But a fat lot of good her excuse would be should her trusting nature get her brother killed.

Good Lord! How could she have been so stupid? Having failed in their attempts to get to him directly, they were going to use her as a hostage to bring him out in the open!

"Let go of me!" she said in a horrified whisper, jerking free of his hold.

"My dear! What ever is wrong?" Michael asked.

He took a step toward her. She started to slide along the wall away from him. The next thing she knew she had bumped into a large, muscular man standing behind her. *Scream!* she thought, trying to make her throat obey. All that came out was a weak, raspy "Help!" She began struggling to break free of the strong, firm hands that held her shoulders.

CHAPTER TWO

Adrenaline, Amelia thought wildly as she yanked on the big man's arms and managed to twist out of his grasp. *I've got so much adrenaline in my blood that I'm stronger than he is.* She turned to look at her attacker, ready to fight for her life, and saw that he was wearing a police uniform.

"Oh, no!" She gasped. "You've bought off the police." All hope for escape vanished. Michael Colt was too powerful for her. She and her brother were finished!

"What's wrong with her, Mr. Colt?" the burly policeman asked, quickly stepping away from Amelia as if whatever she had might be catching.

"I haven't the slightest idea," he murmured, looking in astonishment at the terrified woman before him.

Amelia, eyes wide, took a closer look at the policeman and the name tag pinned to his crisp blue shirt. Then she closed her eyes and wished she could sink straight through the floor.

The bewildered policeman was none other than Sergeant Jerry Enger, the man responsible for protecting her brother. He and his wife had insisted

Amelia stay with them this last week and she'd gotten to know and like both of them. However, she had never seen Jerry in uniform. Jeans, tennis shoes, and casual shirts appeared to be his normal garb. She had made an understandable mistake.

She had also just made a complete fool of herself. "Jerry"—Amelia groaned—"I'm sorry. And if you ever breathe one word of this to Nathan, I'll—"

"John," the big redheaded man interrupted sternly. "His name is John Smith here. You have to remember that." Then he patted her gently on the shoulder and smiled. "Don't worry, Amelia, I'll never tell. But you're perfectly entitled to be jumpy, you know."

Amelia sighed gratefully. "Thanks. Now, would you mind telling me what's going on?" she asked him, turning to look at Michael. He was standing there with a bemused smile on his face. "You obviously know this man."

"Mr. Colt?" The stocky, rough-featured police sergeant nodded his head in agreement. "Sure. He's been quite a help to us in the last twenty-four hours."

"Are you sure he's who he says he is, Jerry?" she asked, still doubtful even though she could tell he not ony knew but respected the older man.

A broad grin split Jerry's face from ear to ear, the tanned skin around his eyes crinkling deeply. "Amelia, you've been reading too many of those mystery novels again, I can tell," he teased. "But, yes, I'm sure. Even though Mr. Colt is well known around the hospital I checked him out thoroughly myself. He is who he says he is."

Her brother, Nathan—John, she reminded herself with a bitter smile—trusted Jerry Enger implicitly. She had come to trust him too. If he said Michael Colt was all right, then she had to believe him.

If anything, however, Jerry's faith in the older man only made her more nervous. He was legitimate. He was wealthy, had connections, and had been of service to her brother. In other words, Michael Colt was capable of upholding his part of his bizarre proposition. And the time was fast approaching when Amelia would have to decide whether the help he was offering was worth the price.

"Where's my brother?" she demanded, crossing her arms defensively over her breasts. Standing between the two men, she glanced at Michael, then settled her gaze on Jerry. "You had him moved, didn't you? Why?"

"I'll handle this, Jerry," Michael said with calm assurance. He slipped his arm through hers and patted her hand. "Let's find a nice quiet place to talk, then we'll visit with John."

Jerry cleared his throat. "Um, he's no longer on this floor, Mr. Colt," he informed the older man quietly.

"No longer . . ." Michael took one look at the policeman's eyes and immediately understood. "I see." Things were far more serious than he'd imagined. John Smith would have to be quietly moved to a safer place than a hospital—and soon.

"What is it?" Amelia demanded. "What happened?"

Jerry walked over to the nearest door and knocked loudly. When no one answered, he ushered them inside with a motion of his head and closed the door behind them, inspecting the stripped room. Painters had been in here recently, you could still smell fresh paint fumes lingering in the air.

"Well?" Amelia paced around, unable to sit still, while Michael removed a plastic sheet and settled in a padded armchair. "Are you going to tell me or not?"

"Calm down, Amelia," Jerry told her in a stern but gentle voice. "John is safe." He turned his steady gaze to Michael. "We had to move him again, sir. There was another attempt on his life."

"He was supposed to be safe here!" Amelia cried. "You promised, you—"

"How?" Michael asked, the sudden hardness in his voice cutting Amelia.

"Someone tampered with his IV."

"Who discovered the tampering?"

A wry, appreciative smile lifted one corner of Jerry's mouth. "That private duty nurse you hired, that's who. She's really something. Where on earth did you find her?"

"I'd rather not say," Michael replied with a thoughtful nod. "Good to know she's worth her fee."

"It was like something out of one of those mysteries you read, Amelia," Jerry said. "Somebody got into the medical stores and used a syringe to inject a foreign substance into the intravenous solution John's doctor prescribed."

Amelia's face went white. "Poison?"

"We don't have a report back yet, but when we do I imagine it will prove to be some kind of toxic agent, yes," Jerry replied. "I repeat, John is fine. The nurse spotted the tampering and brought it to our attention before the IV was administered."

In the back of her mind Amelia realized that she now owed Michael Colt a very large debt. The nurse he had hired had saved her brother's life. At the moment, however, she was too frightened and outraged to think about what she might have to do to repay that debt.

She stroked the soft, velvety texture of the flower Michael had given her, drawing solace from its beauty. "I don't understand how any of this could happen," she said, her voice trembling with angry accusation. "He was supposed to be safe here, Jerry."

"Don't you think I know that?" he returned sharply, then put his big hand on her shoulder, his eyes full of regret. "Sorry."

She sighed, calmed herself, and patted his hand. "No, I'm sorry. It's not your fault."

"Yes, it is." Jerry ran his hands through his short, bright-red hair, tugging it backward. "Amelia, they didn't move him to Austin just because they thought he'd be safe here. They did it because he trusted me," he said dejectedly, straddling a covered wooden chair and sitting down with a heavy sigh, ignoring the splatters of paint on the dropcloth.

25

"Amelia is correct, Sergeant Enger," Michael pointed out, his voice surprisingly sympathetic. "It's not your fault. You were in charge, it's true, but neither you nor anyone else had any idea just how determined the people who are after your friend could be."

Jerry didn't appear comforted. "We sure know now, don't we?"

"Yes, we do. We won't underestimate them in the future. And the main point is that John is all right," the older man reminded him.

"Thanks to you," Jerry noted.

Michael smiled. "Pleasure to be of service."

Rather than think about the bill Michael had in mind for those services, Amelia said, "I still don't understand how they found him in the first place. Who knew he was coming here?"

"A very select few, but obviously one too many," Jerry replied, leaning his chair back and looking at her sheepishly. "I didn't tell you this before, but someone included the name he worked under on his hospital records, deliberately setting him up." He banged his chair to the ground. "In fact, that's how Mr. Colt introduced himself. He was the one who informed us of the discrepancy hidden deep in John's numerous charts."

The debt was growing too rapidly for her to ignore any longer. Amelia looked at the elderly gentleman. "Thank you, Michael." The depth of her gratitude came through with those simple words. But would words be enough? From the way he was smiling at her, she feared not.

"Again, my pleasure. I also made the suggestion

John be moved to another room, but evidently that didn't throw them off the trail," he explained, frowning thoughtfully. "Moving him to yet another room will help keep them off balance, but I fear stronger measures are in order now."

"Such as?" Amelia asked.

Michael looked at Jerry, giving him the opportunity to speak his mind. The alternatives were obvious, but both he and Amelia would have to come to them on their own before Michael took control. Amelia in particular had to understand the realities of the situation.

Jerry stood up and went to look out the narrow hospital room window at the city below. "Hell, I don't know." He shook his head in disgust. "This has been a mess from the start. He'll have to be moved again, out of this hospital, maybe to another city. And since we don't know who we can trust, any action we take is going to be tricky. I just don't know."

Amelia slumped against the unmade bed, unable to stand any longer. The value of the help Michael had offered at lunch was starting to sink in. "Can I see him?"

"I don't think so." He glanced over his shoulder at Amelia. Her crestfallen expression made him relent a little. "Maybe later, but we'll have to smuggle you in and it'll be risky. We have to assume that whoever tampered with his records and his IV is still around, watching," he explained. "If they link you to him it will place you and your parents in danger too."

She nodded her head miserably. "You're right."

27

"For a change." Jerry turned from the window, his face clouded with self-contempt. "I'd damn well better start doing something to earn the trust he has in me."

"Stop beating yourself up, young man," Michael said curtly. The tone of command was back in his voice. "There are plans to be made. What is the situation now?"

"I've assigned men to his room around the clock," Jerry replied. "Even they don't know who he really is. And I've set it up to make them look like close family friends keeping vigil with him. No uniforms and no set hours."

Michael smiled, got up, and patted him heartily on the back. "I think your friend's trust in you is well placed. You can't blame yourself for being unprepared for the unthinkable. And you've learned from your mistakes, the sign of a truly wise man."

"Thanks. I appreciate the support, Mr. Colt."

Amelia appreciated his support, too, more than she could say. Unlike Jerry, however, she knew Michael had his own personal reasons for taking such a decisive part in her brother's affairs. She also knew he would be discussing those reasons with her again very soon.

"All right," Michael continued, a hard glint in his eyes now that the time had come. "Can he be moved somewhere with twenty-four-hour care, preferably not a hospital?"

"I don't know, Mr. Colt. According to the doctors he's out of the woods as far as the surgery is concerned. He just needs rest and time to recuperate. But we don't have the resources to do what you're talking about in any case."

The older man's smile broadened. "I do."

Yes, he did, as Jerry knew for a fact. "It's an idea, and a good one. I'll check with his doctors, Mr. Colt."

"Thank you. And please, call me Michael. 'Mr. Colt' makes me feel old."

"You are old," Amelia interjected, feeling the need to rattle Michael's cage a bit. He was so much in control that she felt she was being swept away. "You told me so yourself."

"Such brash young people today," Michael commented, shaking his head. But he was pleased. She was a fighter. This was going to be an interesting contest right down to the last bell.

Jerry placed his hand on the door pull and glanced at his watch. "I need to go check on things." He turned toward Amelia. "It would really be better if we didn't try to smuggle you in this late in the day, Amelia. He's been heavily sedated because of all the fuss. Maybe tomorrow."

She knew that Jerry had never intended to let her visit—he had just wanted to ease her mind earlier. "Whatever's best for him."

It was an ominous thought. Doing what was best for her brother was the main thing on her mind right now, and it was going to put her smack in the middle of Michael Colt's plans.

"We'll keep him alive while he's here, Amelia," Jerry said quietly as he left the room. "That's a promise."

When he was gone, Amelia turned to face her

white-haired benefactor squarely. The nightmarish feeling that had descended upon her at lunch was back again. He was definitely serious about wanting great-grandchildren, and maybe he was even serious about considering her a likely candidate to marry his grandson. She could not, however, bring herself to believe he was actually serious about his so-called business proposition. Words would simply have to do.

"Thank you, Michael," she told him.

Michael took her hand, squeezed it, and chuckled softly. "You're welcome, my dear. Now tell me. Does the price fit the merchandise?"

Amelia's eyes widened. "You really are serious?"

"Never more so," he informed her amiably as he walked her out of the room and down the quiet hallway. "I am not, however, an unfeeling beast. A part of me is helping your brother because that's just the way I am."

She breathed a deep sigh of relief. "I knew it!"

"But never doubt for a moment that I have my mercenary side, too, Amelia," he added, the hard edge back in his voice. "While you are considering my proposal, I will be going ahead with my plans. But there will come a time when you and I will have business to discuss."

She didn't doubt it. Not now. Not for an instant. "All right," she said decisively. "I'll meet Colt. And then we'll see. I propose a compromise, Michael. You go ahead with your part of the deal, I'll go ahead with mine—up to a point. I won't bargain for more than a day at a time."

"Spendid!" He beamed at her. "I like your style, Amelia. Colt will, too, you'll see. There's just one thing."

Amelia looked at him warily. "And that is?"

"While we're doing this day-to-day bargaining, you will of course stay under my roof. That will make it so much easier for us all to get to know one another better."

And keep her right where he wanted her, she thought with a sudden surge of panic. "No," she replied flatly.

"Be reasonable, Amelia. It will be safer for both you and your brother if you are kept out of harm's way while he recuperates."

Amelia glared at him. "Why don't you just come right out and say it? You want me under your thumb."

"I admit I want to keep an eye on you, but—"

"So that if I don't appear to be going along with this scheme of yours," she interrupted heatedly, "you can pull the rug out from under my brother. Right?"

Michael's eyebrows shot up and he glared right back at her, apparently wounded to the quick. "Have I made that threat?"

"Well, no, but . . ." She trailed off in confusion.

"I am doing you and your brother a favor. I have requested a favor in return. The decision to keep your part of the bargain is yours and yours alone." His eyes seemed to bore right through her as he added, "I am depending upon the kind of person you seem to be—your character, if you will.

31

Not threats. In other words, let your conscience be your guide, young lady."

Her conscience? Now he really was joking, wasn't he? "I don't understand. Are you saying you actually expect me to do this out of gratitude, because it's the right thing to do?" Amelia asked incredulously. "Like the honor system in school where you don't cheat on a test when the instructor leaves the room or something?"

The smile returned to his lips and he nodded. "That is precisely what I am saying, my dear," he agreed happily.

"You really are crazy!"

"What I am, Amelia, is an old man who wants to bounce great-grandchildren on his knee. I am also a very shrewd judge of character, and I have every faith in you." He was practically pulling her along, his step spry now that his plans were taking shape. "Come along. We must get you settled in at the house and then I shall make arrangements to move your brother."

"All right! I'm coming!"

They left the hospital, Michael whistling merrily, Amelia fuming. She was suddenly so irritable and confused she could barely stand it, her thoughts one big jumble. The bright sunlight made her feel only slightly better.

This was crazy! She would stay at his house, meet his grandson, maybe go through the motions of agreeing with his wild schemes. But surely he realized his position was untenable. He probably just thought he'd throw the two of them together and see what happened.

32

Well, nothing would. She'd see to that. And day by day her brother would get stronger until Michael would no longer have any hold over her and she would leave. She would be grateful, would offer to pay him the debt she owed some other way, but she was most assuredly not going to seduce a man she didn't even know!

A part of her felt relieved and happy, knowing that her brother was going to get some real protection at last. Then she thought about disappointing —cheating—the man responsible for providing that protection, and another part of her, deep inside, felt absolutely awful. *Let your conscience be your guide!*

CHAPTER THREE

Michael kept up a running commentary on the new growth and future of Austin all the way to his home. The influx of high-technology businesses, mainly electronics firms, had some people calling this city the new Silicon Valley. A San Antonio resident herself, Amelia was well aware of how fast the Texas state capital had grown, but she nevertheless found herself hanging on Michael's every word.

He was a good conversationalist, and his intimate knowledge of the political and economic forces at work in the city interested her. More importantly, however, she was gaining insight into his character, getting a better idea of what kind of man he was. Since his grandson was in the same business, Amelia imagined she was also getting a small preview of what Colt might be like as well.

As she listened, she realized she was going to have to stay on her toes. These men were venture-capital investors, and as such natural-born risk-takers, but they were also sharp as tacks; the risks they took were carefully calculated. Michael was taking a risk on her, gambling that her feelings of gratitude for his help would cause her to repay him with the favor he was after.

He was planning to use guilt as a weapon, and Amelia knew she was anything but immune to that approach. She had no intention of giving him what he wanted; therefore every nice thing he did for her and her brother would weigh heavily upon her conscience.

Was what he wanted her to do so very wrong? After all, the only thing she had agreed to so far was to meet his grandson, sort of like a blind date. But what if she liked him? What if they hit it off? Would she then be tempted to go along with the rest of Michael's plan?

Her mind clamped down on the thought. The courage of her own convictions would be the only shield she had, and right now that courage was wavering in the wind like a sail striving to break free. There had to be another solution to this problem, another form of payment, she just hadn't found it yet.

Michael's house was immense, the sight of it as he pulled up the tree-lined drive giving her a brief respite from her confusing thoughts. The sprawling, multilevel mansion was situated on a hilltop overlooking Lake Austin, with a view that was nothing short of spectacular. It combined the best of modern architecture with an aura of homespun charm.

"You see?" Michael commented as he escorted her inside. "Hardly a prison."

Amelia laughed in spite of her nervousness.

"Hardly," she agreed, thinking she could be quite comfortable here while her brother recuperated.

Maybe too comfortable. She reminded herself to remain on her guard no matter how gracious the company or beautiful the surroundings. It was a losing battle, however. Amelia was already starting to relax, her raw nerves giving in to the feeling that a great weight was about to be lifted from her shoulders.

Collecting the small overnight bag she had recently gotten into the habit of taking with her everywhere, Michael showed her to the second-floor bedroom that would be hers for the duration of her stay. She decided it would be better not to think about how long that might be. And the accommodations would be anything but a hardship.

The room was as lovely as the rest of the house she had seen so far. It was elegant yet cozy, and tastefully decorated in peaceful shades of yellow. A sliding glass door gave onto a balcony with a breathtaking view of the landscaped grounds and lake far below.

Promising her a tour of the rest of the house after they had a chat, her host then showed her to a richly appointed study with full bookshelves lining the walls. He took a seat in a leather wing chair behind a beautifully carved antique mahogany desk, while Amelia settled into another, equally comfortable chair in front of him.

A chat? A carefully disguised inquisition was more likely! Instead of battling with him head on right away, Amelia decided to beat him to the punch by drilling Michael on his own life. Hopefully she'd regain some of her usual fortitude in the process. It was just possible he might leak some information that her logical mind could use to help her find a way out of this mess.

"Are you married?" she asked in her best conversational tone. He wore a narrow gold band on his left ring finger, but that didn't signify anything. He had already told her about his first wife, Margaret Mary. "I mean currently."

Michael shot her an amused glance. "Yes, happily, for almost forty-nine years."

It was an opening, and Amelia grabbed it. "Does she know what you're planning?"

"Helen? Heavens no!" he exclaimed, shaking his head vigorously. "The woman would definitely interfere."

His expression was fierce, stubborn, but Amelia observed with a thrill of hope that at the mention of his wife Michael seemed to become a different person. A worried tenderness showed through his blustery exterior.

"That's interesting," she said, looking at him intently. "Are you saying she wouldn't approve?"

Amelia expected him to demand that she not mention the matter to his wife. Instead, his gruff frown gave way to an open grin and he laughed heartily.

Nonplussed, Amelia glared at him. "What's so funny?"

"I wouldn't look for an ally in Helen if I were you, my dear," he informed her, still chuckling. "When I said she would interfere, I didn't mean she would come to your aid."

"No?" she asked, trying to sound threatening.

"No." He shook his head and laughed again. "Helen's methods are quite different from mine, but concerning Colt, his bachelor status, and the subject of great-grandchildren, our goals are the same." Michael gazed at her, something akin to pity in his eyes. "Tell her anything and I'm afraid you'd find yourself in the middle of a whirlwind. You'll see what I mean when you get to know her."

Amelia reminded herself that this man had more twists and turns than a country road. She would indeed get to know his wife, and judge for herself whether Helen would help her dissuade Michael from this devious scheme.

"Where is she?"

"Visiting our grandson, shopping, gossiping. Who knows?" he replied, his tone growing petulant. "She just announces she's taking off for a week or two and away she goes, leaving me to fend for myself."

Probably to get away from him and his manipulating ways, Amelia thought vindictively. It was nice to know he was married to someone who stood up to him. Helen might still turn out to be an ally of sorts, even if she and Michael did share the same matchmaking goals.

It was also nice to see his soft side again. From his wounded expression it was obvious that he missed his wife terribly. "Why didn't you go with her?" she asked curiously.

"Bah," he grumped, gesturing wildly with his

hands in frustration. "I'm glad to get rid of her for a while."

How many sides were there to Michael Colt? Tough one moment, kind the next, and right now he reminded her of a little boy who couldn't have his way. Amelia tried hard to hide the laughter bubbling inside of her, but lost the battle and giggled helplessly. She couldn't remember the last time she'd actually giggled at anything.

It felt good to laugh, and once she got started she couldn't seem to stop. She deserved a break. The past few weeks had been fraught with tension, what with the intrigue surrounding her brother and the attempts on his life, the surgery, and now the knowledge that the people who were after him were closing in on him. If she didn't laugh she might drown in her own tears.

"What's wrong with you, girl?"

Amelia slowly began to bring herself under control as Michael sat scowling at her. But all it took was just one good look at the stern, disapproving expression on his fatherly face and she started laughing all over again.

"Women!" he muttered in disgust, removing his tie and camel-hair suit coat.

"Face it, Michael," she quipped once her fit of the giggles had subsided, "you can't live with us and you can't live without us."

"I am painfully aware of that fact, young lady," he grumbled. "Oh, well. At least my life isn't dull. I never know what that woman is going to do next."

Eyes shining with good humor now, Amelia was

reveling in the opportunity to see Michael disarmed of his usual control. "But you love it."

"Yes. I've been very fortunate in my life, to have found two such wondrous creatures to love," Michael said, his voice dropping to a hoarse whisper as he added, "one I lost and one I got to keep."

Amelia didn't know what to say. She'd never met anyone quite like him. His moods and emotions changed with such mercurial quickness—like an actor, she reminded herself. He seemed to be two different people, a lonely old man and a strong stubborn ox who always got his own way.

"You deserve a marriage like mine," he announced suddenly, as if bestowing a gift on her.

"I'd have to find a man first," she returned dryly.

He looked pleased with himself. "See all the hard work I'm saving you? I've already found you one."

"I meant one who's willing to marry me," she pointed out. "Or are you planning to have a traditional shotgun wedding?"

"I doubt it will come to that," he said, rubbing his hands together in anticipation. "You underestimate yourself, Amelia."

Amelia let out an exasperated sigh. For a few moments she had managed to forget what he wanted of her. Come to that, she still wasn't exactly sure what all he had in mind. But she doubted that a conservative older man like Michael would consider anything so avant garde as surrogate motherhood. It was reasonably certain he wanted her to do things the old-fashioned way, but she supposed she had better find out.

Perhaps she could even shock him into seeing how insane this was in the bargain. "Speaking of weddings, aren't you changing the rules on me in the middle of the game, Michael?" she asked. "You didn't mention marriage before."

Michael did look startled. "Well, I—"

"I thought you wanted a great-grandchild?"

"That too. I'm not picky," he said magnanimously. His grin was sly as he pinned her to her seat with his eyes. "Nor am I that easily shocked, my dear. Just because I'm old doesn't mean my mind is set in concrete. Children or marriage, whichever comes first is fine with me."

Amelia closed her eyes, barely managing to suppress a groan. "In case you didn't know, Mr. Colt," she said, opening her eyes again to glare at him accusingly, "arranged marriages are no longer in fashion, at least not in this country."

"Maybe I'll start a trend. You young people these days don't know what's good for you anyway. Most of you seem to avoid marriage like the plague." He settled back comfortably in his leather chair. "That's why I didn't mention it at first. I didn't want to scare you off."

Her eyes widened. "And having a baby wouldn't?"

"You're here, aren't you?" he asked, bushy white eyebrows raised in dramatic triumph.

"You know darn good and well why I'm here, Michael, and what I'm afraid of. I heard Jerry. The police don't have the resources to give my brother the kind of protection he needs now. You do." Someone had already betrayed him once. In all likelihood it would happen again. Michael was her best chance and he knew it. "I'm still hoping you'll come to your senses and forget this match-making stuff."

"And I'm hoping you'll realize how very much this means to me and do what you know in your heart is the right thing," he returned calmly. "We're bargaining, remember? One day at a time. It should prove to be an interesting process."

That was an understatement! Amelia looked up at him, proud and determined. "I've agreed to meet him, but I'm not promising anything."

"Done. Your word is contract enough for me, Amelia."

They sat there staring at each other warily for a minute or two. Their bargaining was over with, at least as far as today was concerned. Amelia debated with herself as to whether she should feign disinterest or ask the one question that had been bothering her about the man she was going to meet soon.

Her curiosity won out. "Is he that ugly?"

Michael threw his head back, his open, hearty laughter filling the room once again. "No, I can guarantee you he isn't," he told her. "He's not a pretty-boy model type, mind you, but women seem to find him pleasing."

"Is he anything like you?" she asked, letting his remark about other women slide by without comment.

"Mmm, I think so, a lot like me. A grandson to be proud of," he said fondly.

"Then the deal's off."

"What?" He straightened in his chair and fixed her with a ferocious look.

She grinned back at him. "I'm not sure I'd like to live the rest of my life with someone as contrary as you."

"Now you listen here, young . . ."

His voice trailed off and he frowned at the odd sort of thumping whine that suddenly broke the quiet solitude of his study. As the noise grew louder and closer, Amelia recognized it as a helicopter. It sounded—and felt—as if it was going to come down right on top of the house.

"What's wrong?" she asked, following him when he sprang from his chair and hurriedly left the room.

"Damn that boy! How many times have I told him not to land that thing in my backyard?"

They went out onto the redwood deck, the clear, fall afternoon sunlight making them both blink. Amelia looked out over the balcony railing, past the full-grown trees dotting the yard to where a huge machine sat, the long, shiny blades atop it winding down.

"Look at all those leaves!" Michael roared, pounding the railing with his fist.

"I think they're very pretty," Amelia told him, watching the splashes of autumn color blowing around the yard.

"They belong on the trees!"

She laughed. "Not even you can make leaves

stay glued to the trees, Michael. In case you hadn't noticed, they fall off about this time every year."

"Eventually! I see no need, however, to give Mother Nature a helping hand," he fumed. "That boy had better rake every last one of them up, that's for sure."

Amelia could just make out two shapes moving behind the helicopter's windscreen, but the glare of the afternoon sun made it impossible to see details. "Who's here?" she asked, frowning.

"Helen."

"Is she the passenger or the pilot?"

"Don't give her any ideas," he ordered, a pained look on his face. "She's got plenty of her own. That thing belongs to Colt and luckily he doesn't allow anyone else to fly it."

"Colt?" she asked quietly, one eyebrow arched. "Your grandson?" He nodded and she stared at him in accusation. "You knew he was going to be here today?"

"I called him yesterday, it was high time Helen came home. I had figured that you would at least agree to meet him."

It made her angry to think she had been so predictable. Her anger, however, was nothing compared to the sudden attack of nerves she was having. She thought she would have time to prepare herself mentally for this meeting. Shielding her eyes with her hand, she tried again to see into the helicopter, to no avail.

"Well?" she asked, her throat dry. "Are they planning to come in?"

"She's waiting for the blades to come to a complete stop," he explained. "That means she has a new hairdo."

With something approaching dread Amelia watched as one of the doors of the aircraft opened. A tall man stepped out, walked around to the other side, and graciously helped his female passenger out. Then the man climbed back inside.

Feeling a surge of hope, Amelia said, "Look's like you were wrong about his staying."

"No, he's collecting her purchases," he murmured, fondly watching the silver-haired woman walking toward them.

Her hair was swept sleekly up and off her perfectly made-up face, giving her a very sophisticated look. Somehow the black jumpsuit and white tennis shoes she wore didn't fit in with the modern hairstyle or her short, chunky figure.

"Does she always . . ." Amelia began, then stopped when she realized she was now alone on the balcony. Michael came into view down below and walked into his wife's open arms.

Feeling like a Peeping Tom, Amelia quickly turned her gaze back to the helicopter, but all she could see were dress boxes in various sizes, stacked in neat piles on the leaf-strewn lawn. At last a dark head poked out of the cockpit, but the man moved too quickly for her to see his face before it was hidden behind the stack of boxes he carried. The top of his head and his legs were all that showed as he came toward the house.

Great. How was she supposed to know what to expect when her only glimpse of the man was black hair and lean thighs? His stride was swift and businesslike, covering the distance rapidly. Maybe he was in a hurry to leave. For a moment Amelia wondered if she could hide somewhere until he was gone, but knew Michael would never allow that. She leaned over the railing, hoping for a better look, but the boxes blocked her view of his face as he walked under the balcony.

"All right, you two, cut it out," a warm, masculine voice teased with obvious affection. "Plenty of time for that later."

"Too much for you to handle?" Michael asked, his arm wrapped around his wife's waist.

"No, but I'm a doer," Colt returned, "not a watcher. You wouldn't want to give someone as young as me ideas, would you?"

Amelia could hear their laughter, the soft, feminine sound of Helen's voice almost drowned out by the two men. She didn't want to stand there and eavesdrop on their family conversation, didn't want to be there at all as a matter of fact. But she couldn't seem to make her feet move.

"I can remember a time, Colt, when you hid your eyes at the slightest sign of any mushy stuff," Helen teased.

"I couldn't seem to get away from it, had to live with it at home and here too. Is it any wonder I eventually developed such a liking for it?" Colt asked.

"A liking for it?" Michael returned. "I'd say you're pretty well obsessed with mushy stuff, boy."

Michael's comment came through loud and clear, and Amelia realized he was well aware she was listening in. He had already hinted that his

46

grandson was a playboy, something along the lines of his being pleasing to women. Maybe he thought she would find that an exciting and attractive quality in a man.

He was wrong. Perhaps it wasn't going to be so hard to convince Michael this was a mistake after all. If Colt was a lady killer she would make it clear that was the last thing she wanted or needed in her life. Michael would have to see his plan wasn't going to work.

Colt's deep, teasing voice interrupted Amelia's hopeful thoughts. "Come on, old man. Help me unload the rest of her stuff."

"What's your hurry? Didn't you two have a jolly time?"

"You can have her back, Pop," his grandson replied with a long-suffering sigh. "I'm going to have to take a vacation to recover from her visit."

"Wore you out, did she?"

Amelia couldn't hear his answer. They were heading back out to the helicopter, Michael walking beside his grandson, the two of equal height. Colt had a nice build, she noticed with reluctant interest, tall and lean, broad shoulders beneath a white button-down shirt, his thick black hair brushing the collar. His muscular thighs were defined by his tight blue jeans.

"They're striking men together, aren't they?" a soft voice murmured beside her.

Amelia jumped, then turned to see a gentle face, surprisingly lined with age. Somehow she hadn't expected to see a single wrinkle, but instead this

47

woman wore her years openly. Her dark eyes were warm and welcoming.

"Hello. I'm Amelia Drake."

"Yes, I know. Helen Colt," she said, shaking Amelia's hand. Her voice was pleasant, almost lilting. "Michael told me all about your situation."

"He did?"

Helen nodded. "Not without some wheedling on my part, naturally. Michael tends to be modest about these little projects of his," she confided in a you-know-how-men-are tone. "He puts up a good front, but he's just an old softy. I think his desire to help people is wonderful."

"Yes." What else could she say? Helen obviously adored her husband.

"I hope your brother is recovering nicely."

Amelia fought off the usual stab of paranoia she felt when anyone she didn't know mentioned her brother. Helen was no threat. "He's doing fine."

"Good. Come on downstairs, let's have a cup of tea. I've brought the most delicious pastries for us to enjoy," she said, leading the way down the short flight of carpeted stairs. "The men will be a while, they'll have to argue over Colt's landing in the yard again."

Already they could hear raised voices drifting in through the open kitchen window, snatches of the loud conversation clearly audible even at this distance.

"I could always land in the front yard."

"Don't you dare! It took me weeks to get the grass looking right from the last time."

"I like natural landscaping myself."

"Bah! Pure laziness."

"Don't worry," Helen informed her, "this is their usual routine. Neither will give in. They're too much alike."

Wonderful, Amelia thought. Just what she wanted. A bossy, domineering, uncompromising husband. Her thoughts stopped her cold. For a moment, standing in this cozy kitchen with a kindly grandmother type busying herself at the stove, she had actually found herself wondering what it would be like to be a part of this family.

"What do you like in your tea, Amelia?"

"Hmm? Oh. Sugar, please," she replied distractedly, sitting down at a heavy, circular oak table which could easily seat six or eight people. How could she think about tea at a time like this? For a moment she had actually been thinking about taking Michael up on his offer.

"Oh, rats," Helen muttered, gently releasing her hair from a low-hanging plant over the counter. "I pay oodles of money to get my hair done this way and it doesn't last a day," she complained, patting the coiffure back into place.

"It looks wonderful."

The older woman cast her a look of mock annoyance. "You don't have to lie, dear. This style just isn't me." A cheerful, mischievous smile appeared. "Michael hates my hair this way," she whispered like a conspirator, "so I make a point of always coming home with it like this. That man of mine gets his way far too often."

"If I'm not careful," Amelia muttered under her breath, "he'll get his way this time too."

Helen didn't notice her comment. "It does him good when someone stands up to him now and again. But if you're still here in a few days you'll see the real me," she promised.

Amelia watched as she flitted around, arranging things in the big, old fashioned kitchen to her satisfaction. The room was large and airy, with plants hanging everywhere. Natural wood beams were exposed in the ceiling, and light filtered in through evenly spaced skylights.

"We'll start without them," Helen declared, gesturing at the luscious plate of small pastries as she poured their tea. "Better take more than one now, there won't be any left once they start. They both have an incurable sweet tooth."

There was no doubt about it, Helen was definitely what one would call a whirlwind. Recalling Michael's warning to that effect, she decided she had best keep her mouth shut about his plans concerning her and his grandson. If this woman did put her mind to matching her up with Colt, Amelia would be in more trouble than she was already.

"Don't these plants make everything homey?" Helen asked, continuing on without pausing for an answer. "I started with a couple and they kept growing. Now every time I go to a garden shop I find a new variety I want. I even start shoots off some of my more unusual ones for a shop nearby. Oh, my, I can't decide between a Napoleon or an éclair," she said, pursing her lips in indecision, changing the subject at will. "What do you think, Amelia?"

"I—"

"I'll have both," a masculine voice announced.

The moment of truth had arrived. Amelia was about to meet the mysterious stranger Michael wanted her to seduce. And the moment they made eye contact, she had the strangest feeling, like a cross between an ice cube sliding down her back and being struck by lightning.

Would she mind seducing this man? No, she suddenly realized, she wouldn't mind that too terribly much at all.

CHAPTER FOUR

Finally Amelia's mind cleared, her reason and caution returned, and she looked warily into the deepest, greenest eyes she'd ever seen. He wasn't ugly by a long shot, but as Michael had said, Colt's face definitely wasn't model material either.

There was a long, thin scar curving from the edge of his brow to halfway down his cheek, a barely noticeable mark she had to look closely to see. Not frightening or repulsive, it gave him a rather rakish air, like those to-die-for jet fighter pilots Hollywood was so fond of these days. The rest of his face looked chiseled in dark stone, a determined chin, broad forehead, strong patrician nose and gleaming white teeth, of which one was a little bit crooked.

Perfect-looking men had always bothered Amelia. The pretty-boy types, as Michael had referred to them, always seemed a bit too vain, more concerned with how they looked than a man should. Of course, it might have been sour grapes on her part; that kind of man didn't haunt her doorstep. Her looks weren't perfect, either, after all.

Still, on those blue days when she found herself wondering if there were any eligible bachelors left in the world, she had often imagined that the sort of man she could fall in love with would have a few flaws. He would probably be a bit rough around the edges, a guy who obviously led a full, well-rounded life. A man like Colt, for instance.

Stop! Danger! A little voice inside Amelia's head was yelling at her. She averted her gaze from the man standing in the middle of the kitchen and contemplated the bottom of her teacup. The voice dropped to a whisper. *That's better.*

"Sit down, Colt," Helen said, passing him a cup of tea.

"What did you do, Helen, buy out a store?" Michael asked as he joined them and sat down in the chair next to hers.

"I didn't even come close," she answered loftily. "And if you aren't nice, I'm hiding your present."

Amelia risked a glance in Colt's direction and noticed with some relief that he wasn't gazing at her fixedly or even covertly. He did glance at her and nod politely.

"Could you introduce us?" he asked his grandparents, politely cutting into their repartee.

"Amelia, Colt, Colt, Amelia," Michael said, then turned back to his wife. "What did you bring me?"

"Later."

"Give me a hint."

Amelia listened to their playful bantering, trying not to look directly at Colt and finding herself wishing—rather incongruously—that she had known her own grandparents better. They were nothing like Colt's, or at least from her brief exposure to them over the years she didn't think so. Her grandparents on both sides had always appeared so cold and remote. She felt as if she'd missed out on a very important part of her life, and that maybe they had too.

What would Colt think of his grandfather's plans for them? It occurred to her that she might be taking this whole thing too seriously. With a pair like this around, she imagined Colt had endured plenty of attempts to match him up with a wife. This was quite possibly just another in a long line of such attempts, and from the way he was practically ignoring her it looked as though she didn't have a thing to worry about.

Try as she might, however, she couldn't forget the man next to her, sneaking furtive glances at him when she could. He appeared to be thoroughly engrossed in his grandparents' lively discussion. A perverse little flare of annoyance made her frown. Who did he think he was?

He wouldn't be able to remain so smugly aloof if she decided to carry out Michael's request, that was for sure! She could show him a thing or two, she . . .

She'd never tried to seduce a man. Just the thought of it sent tidal waves of tingling sensations throughout her body, pooling warmly in her lower abdomen. Suddenly Amelia was completely aware of him, of his long fingers pulling apart the chocolate-covered pastry, his firm hand cradling the warm cup of tea, the almost tangible male signal his body seemed to be emitting in potent waves. Was she more aware of him because of what they might eventually do together?

Oh, Lord, her crazy imagination was starting to run away with her again. Next she'd be imagining his hands caressing her curves instead of those of the teacup. She could feel a delicate wave of pink wash across her face and hoped no one noticed.

"Now, don't you start in on that, Michael Colt!" Helen's sharp tone brought Amelia back to the present, and she spilled some of her tea. "Excuse me," she said, blotting it up with her napkin.

"Never mind, dear," Helen said, patting her hand. "And wipe that smirk off your face, Colt. I wasn't speaking to you." She turned toward Amelia. "You'll stay to dinner of course. You must be dead on your feet, you poor dear. Hospitals are so tiring. A nice nap is what you need."

Helen was halfway to the kitchen door, looking at her expectantly. Amelia didn't know if she was coming or going. "Well, I suppose I—"

"Come along, we'll leave these men to make pigs of themselves," Helen said, waiting for Amelia to join her. "Did Michael give you a tour of the house? Of course he didn't, what am I saying? Men never think of these important details," she declared. "I'll show you where everything is first. A girl can't wander around a house she doesn't know, now, can she? In the first place you might get lost, and in the second you don't know where all the bathrooms are."

Colt watched as Amelia and Helen left the kitchen, their pretty visitor about five inches taller than his grandmother. The gentle curve of her hips under her dress as she walked was quite appealing. Amelia. It was a nice name, he decided, sort of old-fashioned and exotic at the same time, like the woman herself.

It had been something of an effort not to stare at her as they had their tea. He had been wishing she had left just one more button at the neck of her dress undone; he could have gotten quite an eyeful. She was not overly buxom, but through the lacy, navy-colored brassiere beneath the thin blue material of her dress had shone pale skin, tantalizing him each time she moved.

Who was she? He would definitely find out, but he had learned from previous experience that it was best not to show too much interest in a woman under the watchful, ever-hopeful eyes of his grandparents.

It was, in fact, an even bet that this was some kind of setup, yet another of Michael's or Helen's attempts to marry him off. But the reasons behind the very becoming blush that had washed over Amelia's skin when their eyes met would have to be explored further. Later, he promised himself.

At the moment, his mind was zeroing in on another problem. His grandfather was watching him pointedly. Colt knew the look well, and it didn't have anything to do with matchmaking.

"I have this feeling I'd rather not know," he said

with a wry grin, "but are you going to tell me what's wrong or am I supposed to guess?"

"Young pup!" Michael scowled. "I need you to fly an injured man somewhere for me."

Colt's craggy face showed no surprise at the request. He was well acquainted with his grandfather's missions of mercy. "When?"

"As soon as possible. How about tonight?" he asked.

"The weather should hold," Colt replied thoughtfully. "Which side of the law is he on?"

Michael didn't even try to look indignant. A smile quirked his lips. "The good side, naturally."

"Naturally." His grandfather had always believed in helping out innocent people, no matter what others thought they might have done. He always said that innocent people could be proven guilty all too easily, and Colt knew that was true. He helped himself to another small éclair and asked, "What's his name?"

"John Smith."

"Convenient." Colt savored the last bite of the pastry, licking the chocolate from his fingers. "She his sister?" he asked with studied nonchalance, pointing toward the ceiling.

Michael wasn't fooled by his grandson's apparent disinterest. He had seen the light in Colt's eyes when he first saw Amelia. But he had played enough poker with the younger man to know better than to tip his hand.

"She is. You always did see more than what was right in front of you, boy." It wasn't necessary to tell him not to spread such information around, though. His trust in Colt was complete. "I'll also need the use of your ranch."

"So it's like that, is it?"

"Yes."

Colt nodded his head in agreement. "It's fine with me, and Molita will be in seventh heaven."

Molita, his fiery Latin housekeeper, liked nothing better than to have someone to fuss over like a mother hen. This stranger would keep her busy and happy for a while. As an added bonus it would also gain Colt a reprieve from her sly, insinuating comments about his advancing age and lack of either a wife or heirs. Everyone, it seemed, was concerned by his bachelorhood, and it was about to drive him crazy.

"Amelia won't be going with you," Michael went on, answering Colt's next question before he could ask. "They don't want to have her connected to him in any way. He's single, so we don't have to worry about that, but there will be a nurse accompanying him. You remember Teri?"

"Teri? What did this guy do to warrant her special talents?" he asked, clearly surprised this time. "Or does that fall under the heading of minding my own business?"

"To be perfectly honest, Colt, that is precisely the kind of answer I got when I started digging into his background," Michael replied, obviously irritated.

Knowing his grandfather's connections, that struck Colt as rather ominous. "I thought you said he was on the good side of the law, Pop."

"You know how hazy that line can get at times,"

he replied. "But I do know that the people who are after him are one heck of a lot nastier than he is, and that he doesn't stand much of a chance with the level of protection the police are able to provide."

It was a serious matter, all right, but Colt still had to laugh. "No wonder your eyes have that certain sparkle today," he teased. "This is just the kind of situation you can't resist."

Michael chuckled too. "That's me, the defender of the underdog. Anyway, he needs our help. Teri has already aborted one attempt on his life. I'd like to get him out of the city before she or anyone else has to do it again."

"How bad is he?"

"He can be moved safely, if we're very careful. And Teri is first and foremost an excellent nurse, so we're covered on that end of things."

Colt nodded, deep in thought. "Then let's take him out to San Angelo first," he said finally. "We can set up a trap there to take care of any future problems."

"Fine." That decided, Michael reached for the last éclair and changed the subject. "How'd the Cisco deal go?"

"How badly do you want to know?" Colt asked.

Michael looked up and noticed that his grandson was gazing at him pointedly. "I suppose you're going to refuse to answer me unless I split this with you, right?" Colt nodded. With a forlorn sigh Michael pulled the pastry apart and gave him the smaller piece, holding the other out of reach.

"Your generosity astounds me," Colt taunted as

he quickly devoured his share. "Cisco went well. Thirty-eight percent of the stock, enough for a controlling interest."

"How's management?"

"Good, we shouldn't have to make any changes. How about you?" the younger man asked. "Were you able to dig up anything on SynSystems?"

"Not enough. They're undervalued, which is promising, but your lawyer father is checking into possible future lawsuits over one of their products." Michael looked at him intently and asked, "What about Lakes?"

Colt braced himself for a fight. "I sold the stock."

"What?"

"You heard me," he said, his eyes locked to Michael's with grim determination.

"I thought we agreed to wait!"

"You wanted to wait, Dad and I wanted to sell. That's two out of three, Pop. Majority rules, remember? In fact, it was actually four out of five," he added with a cheerful smile. "Mom and Helen were on our side."

Michael stood up and wagged his finger at him. "Now, you listen here, you young scalawag. I'll have you know I'm the most experienced person in this group and—" He stopped, his eyes practically bulging. "Helen! How dare she go behind my back!" he shouted.

"It's the only way to go with you, you wily old fox," Colt shot back, unperturbed by Michael's wounded expression. The man should have been an actor. "If we try to do anything in front of you we might get bitten, and rabies shots aren't any fun."

Michael glared at him, but there was a dancing spark of amusement in his eyes. "I hope you're wrong," he said spitefully. "Teach you all some respect."

"We already respect you so much, we run when we see you coming." Colt suppressed a grin, knowing it would only enrage him even more. "And you know you don't want us to be wrong. You'd lose money."

"It'll be worth it just to hear your apology!"

Helen's lilting voice interrupted them. "Michael, dear," she called sweetly from somewhere upstairs. "Aren't you going to come see what I brought you?"

"I should let her stew for going against me like that," he muttered under his breath.

"Oh, I don't think you should," Colt informed him, a twinkle in his green eyes. "I saw what she bought. Very sexy!"

Michael straightened with comic abruptness and his eyebrows shot up. "Like I said, a little business disagreement is no reason to hold a grudge. I'll go forgive her." He pointed at Colt. "You go take care of the details concerning Amelia's brother, but be back in time for dinner," he ordered before leaving the room.

"Yes master," he called after him.

"Rot!" his grandfather returned. "And while you're at it, get a haircut!"

* * *

Though her exhaustion was more emotional than physical in nature, Amelia wasn't about to disobey a direct order from Helen. So, after her tour of the house, she did her best to take a nap. Her bedroom, all done up in shades of yellow with its soft, butter-cream-colored walls, was actually quite soothing. It was her mind that kept her restless and turning, relentlessly tossing around all the possibilities of her predicament.

She thought back to the bit of conversation she had overheard as she and her hostess had left the kitchen earlier. Evidently, Colt was going to be the one to fly her brother to safety. Wonderful. Just one more reason to feel indebted to both of them.

Amelia rolled over, burying her face in the down pillows. What was she going to do? She loved her job in San Antonio, where she had worked hard for her present position as a floating supervisor. The management had been sympathetic to her request for time off to attend to a family emergency, but their understanding had its limits. So did the company maternity policy. Should she find herself coerced into going along with Michael's plans for her, she might have to pay the added price of losing a job she really enjoyed.

If only her parents were here. They were in Europe, her father on a two-year exchange program for professors, her mother having opted to take a leave of absence from her job as a first-grade teacher to go with him. She remembered how thrilled her mother had been at the chance to spend that much time over there, a dream come true.

But then again, what could they do? Nathan would still need protection, Michael would still be the one who could provide it, and she would still be faced with dealing with the white-haired manipulator alone. She couldn't even call and tell them what was going on.

Nathan had sworn her to secrecy. As far as her parents knew, her brother worked for a large corporation and traveled all over the world. They had accepted his infrequent cards and phone calls as their only contact with their son because he moved around too much for a phone number or permanent address. Who was she to burst their bubble?

Amelia had found out about his real occupation completely by accident herself, more than a year ago. She had taken a spur of the moment trip to her aunt's vacant summer home in the country, intending to spend a long weekend alone. To her astonishment she had waltzed in and found her older brother recovering from a nasty bullet wound in the thigh. Even then he hadn't told her everything, just enough to keep her quiet.

Her three-day weekend had turned into a full week of vacation during which she got to know Nathan all over again. In many ways they were like strangers meeting for the first time. They hadn't spent much time together as kids. He was five years her senior and had left home for college when she was thirteen. She only saw him on holidays, since he mysteriously spent his summers working elsewhere, and his visits dwindled to once a year or less after he graduated. Now she knew why.

Nathan worked undercover. The people he worked for had recruited him as a college freshman, guiding his studies and preparing him in other ways for his chosen career. Who those people were, he would never say, but Amelia had her suspicions. Nothing so dramatic as the FBI, but something similar and just as governmental.

Danger and bullet-wounds notwithstanding, he loved his job. He had told her that and as much more as he could, when he awoke that morning to find her sitting in a chair by the bed in their aunt's house, staring at him in shock and horror. His explanation helped some—at least he wasn't an outlaw—but she couldn't mask her sisterly concern over what he was doing with his life.

For the next ten days they talked and laughed and cried together while she nursed him past the worst phase of his injury. For the first time in years Amelia felt like she had a brother. He reminded her of all the cloak-and-dagger games he had masterminded when they were kids. Even at that age Nathan had worked at being a master of disguises, occasionally even fooling their surprised parents. What he had so loved as a boy had become his career as a man.

Amelia flopped restlessly onto her back, looking up at the yellow ceiling of her bedroom. Nathan's bullet wound a year ago had been bad, but the one that had put him in the hospital last week was worse. His career had almost killed him for the second time. The third time, actually, considering the attempt on his life at the hospital.

It was Jerry Enger who had alerted her to Nathan's latest brush with death. She had known something was wrong the instant Jerry had identified himself over the phone, because Nathan had given her his name on the last day they were together. Other than Amelia, he was the only one Nathan trusted with his secret.

Until that phone call she had almost managed to stop worrying about her brother. Now it was possible that one call would change her entire life.

There were so many decisions to be made! She didn't really trust Michael, had the uneasy feeling she would actually have to seduce his grandson to ensure his continued help. Amelia loved Nathan, would do anything for him, but she didn't know if she was prepared to have a stranger's child to keep her brother safe. What should she do?

Amelia struggled to stay awake, but the heavy weight of her eyelids seemed to be winning out, her week of missed sleep catching up with her. "I'll just close my eyes for a few minutes," she told herself in a groggy voice.

CHAPTER FIVE

Catnaps usually left Amelia feeling cranky, and this one wasn't any different. It didn't help that she awoke with the important decisions regarding her future unresolved. She wasn't going to be able to put them off forever. Still, there was dinner to think about, a pleasant prospect in more ways than one. Helen was probably a very good cook, and Michael couldn't very well discuss his plans in front of his wife.

She squinted at the oval mirror atop the pale yellow dresser, unable to see what her hair looked like from this distance. Her contact lenses were safely stored in a case on the bedside table and would remain there the rest of the night. Delving into her oversize leather purse she found her hairbrush and the much-needed glasses.

After running the brush briskly through her hair she slipped on her red-and-black thin-framed glasses and everything came into focus. Not bad, she decided as she studied her reflection, considering the day she had had so far. After a moment of befuddled searching she spotted her errant shoes, half hidden under the yellow bedspread.

"Dinner is served," a masculine voice announced through the closed door.

Amelia groaned. It was Colt's voice. She thought she had seen the last of him for today. "All right. Thanks."

"Do you need any help?"

"What?" she squeaked out, her voice sharp and at a high pitch. What kind of help did he have in mind?

Colt's answering chuckle sounded amused, slightly evil, too, unless she was imagining things. "It's a big house. I thought you might need some help finding your way."

"Oh. I, um, don't think so."

"I'll wait for you anyway."

"Suit yourself," Amelia said, then inwardly groaned again at how terse her reply had been. He was just being helpful.

She had to get a grip on herself. There wasn't any reason to take her confusion out on Colt. He didn't even know what was going on, and that made him even more of a pawn in Michael's game than she was.

The real trouble, she knew, was that she was very much attracted to Colt, and it worried her. Thoughts of what their future relationship might be had her body almost buzzing, a feeling she would have enjoyed under other circumstances. Because it was exactly the feeling Michael wanted her to have for his grandson, however, she was fighting it, and it was making her terribly irritable.

Her heart and pulse were fluttering wildly as she opened the door and found him waiting for her.

Colt hadn't changed his clothes and yet still looked fresh and inviting in his jeans and white shirt. Inviting! What was wrong with her?

"Thank you for waiting," she told him politely. "I didn't mean to bite your head off. I'm not very sociable when I first wake up, I'm afraid."

"No problem. I'm used to being bitten." He looked at her, the faint lines around his bright green eyes crinkling at the edges when he smiled. "Did you want to wear shoes?"

Amelia looked down at her stockinged feet. No wonder he seemed so tall. "Yes," she said, going back to the bed and stepping into her pumps. "Is anyone else coming to dinner?" she asked to cover her nervousness.

"No, the two of us will be enough of an audience for them," he replied. He studied her for a moment, a rather exciting gleam in his eyes, then turned abruptly and led the way down the hall. "This way."

He was an odd mixture, just like his grandfather. The way his eyes had roved over her before he turned away told her he found her attractive, too, and yet he still had a cool air about him, as if he wanted to keep his distance. Amelia realized he knew something was up, not the particulars of Michael's plans, certainly, but the general idea. Apparently, Colt didn't like his grandfather playing Cupid.

The thought troubled her. Should she tell him what was going on? That would fix Michael's wagon. If Colt was wise to the game, that would be the end of it, right?

Then again, with his helicopter and his strong, capable character, he probably figured prominently in the protection of her brother. There was no telling how he might react if she informed him of his grandfather's nefarious scheme, and she couldn't risk losing his help. She decided she'd better wait until she knew him better.

Then another, even more disturbing thought occurred to her. Suppose she couldn't tell him, couldn't find a way out of this mess no matter how hard she tried? Given the cool way Colt was behaving toward her now, Amelia doubted he would allow her to get close enough even to get to know him, let alone carry out Michael's wishes.

What if she had to seduce him and couldn't? Where would she be then? She almost tripped on the stairs just thinking about it, barely managing not to fall on top of him. Colt appeared not to notice and she followed him into the dining room, feeling clumsy and even more irritable than before.

"Sit down," Helen commanded as they entered the room. "Everything's on the table. I love your glasses, Amelia, they're darling on you. Maybe I'll get some like that for reading."

Helen chattered on and Amelia managed to put portions of food on her plate without splattering anyone else. As she ate she listened to the conversation swirling around her and answered the friendly questions directed toward her. There was such an air of domesticity about the whole meal, the way family dinners had been at her own home when she was younger.

Amelia realized then that there was more to Michael's offer of help and protection than she had first thought. She was getting the chance to think, to recharge her batteries and feel almost normal. The whole experience was comforting, and she knew by the twinkle in the old man's eyes that he had planned it this way all along.

"Why aren't your parents here with you?" Helen inquired when they were almost finished with the meal.

"Helen!" her husband admonished.

Amelia wasn't bothered by her question. "They're in Europe. Dad had a chance to take part in a new exchange program for professors, something like the student exchange program, only he teaches over there," she explained. "Right now they're on vacation and traveling around the various countries, so I can't get in touch with them." The little lies were getting easier to tell all the time. Maybe she should go into Nathan's line of work.

"Well, dear, if you need anything at all, you have us here to help you out. Think of us as your temporary mother and father," Helen suggested. The phone rang. "Since you're finished eating, would you get that, Michael?" she asked, pausing until he had left the room before continuing her sly interrogation. "Are you married?"

Oh, Lord! Amelia could see it coming; the whirlwind was about to blow. So much for the notion that Helen might be willing to help her out without the terms her husband was requiring. What was this, a conspiracy?

"No, I'm not."

"Marvelous."

Colt made a choking noise as he sat down and turned away for a moment. When he turned back, his eyes were bright. "Excuse me," he croaked. "Something went down the wrong way."

Helen looked at him, frowned, then returned her gaze to Amelia. "Did Michael tell you how we met?" she asked, the sparkle in her dark eyes heightened by the high-necked pale-peach blouse she was wearing.

"No, he didn't."

"It's a very romantic story," Helen informed her, "one I'm sure a pretty, unmarried young woman such as yourself will enjoy."

Colt cleared his throat again, and this time Amelia could see the wry, amused look on his face. He was aware there was matchmaking afoot, all right, but he didn't appear to take the matter seriously. It was a good sign; he might be a man she could deal with after all.

"I'd love to hear it," Amelia assured her.

"Good! Just let me get the tea," Helen said, bouncing up from the table, "and then we'll relax in the sitting room while I tell you all about it. Isn't this fun?"

When she had disappeared into the kitchen, Colt leaned closer to Amelia and whispered, "You're in for a treat. She only tells this story to a select few." That select few included every woman his grandparents had deemed appropriate wife material for him. Colt was now positive they viewed Amelia that way. "But first you have to eat everything on your plate, or no happily-ever-after fairy tale for you."

"But I already . . ." Amelia trailed off and looked down at the offending vegetable. She hated Brussels sprouts and would never have helped herself to them. "You put them there!" she accused softly.

Colt gazed at her with wide-eyed innocence. "Never!" He speared a sprout with his fork and held it up to her mouth. "Here you go. Yummy!"

"Yuck!" She pushed his hand away.

He laughed and tried again. Noticing her distinct lack of interest in Brussels sprouts, he had served her some while she wasn't looking, figuring that her reaction to the stunt would be a good way of testing her mettle. He was attracted to her, but considering his grandparent's track record at meddling, he knew he had to be careful. If Amelia didn't have a mind of her own, she would be easy prey for Helen and Michael's schemes, and therefore more trouble than she was worth.

With a look of vengeance Amelia batted his hand away again, stood up calmly, and poured the Brussels sprouts onto his plate. "So there!" she said spitefully before gathering the other empty dishes from the table and walking into the kitchen. "Here are the dishes, Helen, except for Colt's. He hasn't finished his Brussels sprouts."

"Thank you, dear. Finish your sprouts, Colt," Helen admonished. "Or no dessert."

Leaning against the doorjamb, Amelia folded her arms over her breasts and stuck her tongue out at Colt, chuckling at his stunned reaction. He sat there, looking first at her and then at the faded green marblelike vegetables rolling around on his plate.

"I'll get you for this," he promised in a whisper.

It probably wasn't wise, but Amelia couldn't resist taunting him. "You can try," she whispered back, then turned on her heel and strolled triumphantly into the kitchen.

Colt scowled after her, but secretly he was very pleased. No one would have an easy time bending this woman to their will, including his grandparents. Now to put the next step of his plan into action.

Unaware of the plot being hatched in the dining room, Amelia joined Helen at the kitchen counter. "Can I help with anything?"

"No, let's just sit down and relax with our tea, shall we? Or did you want coffee? At Michael's and my age the doctors only allow us coffee in the morning, and only one cup." She rolled her soft brown eyes dramatically. "But what do they know? You can't let all the little pleasures in life pass you by."

"Tea will be fine."

There was something about Helen that made you want to reach out and hug the daylights out of her. She was such a sweet, lovable person. But she also had a devious mind, Amelia reminded herself, and right now that mind was working on pairing her up with Colt. Her methods were indeed different from Michael's, easier to deal with, but their goals were the same and she'd better not forget that.

Amelia didn't look at Colt as she followed Helen

73

into the sitting room with the silver tea service. He held out his arm after Helen passed by, effectively blocking her way. She couldn't miss the husky sound of his voice directly behind her as he stood up.

"I told you I'd get you back," he whispered close to her ear, letting his hand glide slowly down her spine, touching each vertebra before coming to rest on the womanly swell of her buttocks. He squeezed her gently. "Touché."

Amelia jumped away from his intimate caress, making the teapot slide precariously on the tray. Obviously, Colt wasn't as cool and aloof toward her as she'd thought. Nor was she nearly as calm and in control of herself as she wanted to be. A fire had smoldered to life between her thighs at his fondling touch, the tingling sensations leaping straight into the pit of her stomach.

"Who do you think you are?" she managed to ask.

He grinned. "Your intended, by the look of things."

"What do you mean?" Surely Michael hadn't told him?

"Relax. They're always trying to match people up." He leaned close and nibbled on her ear. "But that doesn't mean we can't have some fun when they're not looking."

She glared at him briefly, then strode past him into the next room, trying to ignore both him and her singing nerve endings. This threw an entirely different light on things. Now she had to be on guard against his rapacious advances as well as her own desires. How dare her body react so strongly to his provocative stroking?

He was right behind her again, not touching her, but she could feel his breath on her cheek, the spicy scent of his skin unmistakable.

"Here, let me help," he said, taking the tray and setting it down on a low table in front of Helen.

What was he up to? Amelia was baffled by his behavior and she was still tingling from his sizzling caress. This whole situation was getting crazier by the moment. He was every bit as tricky as his grandfather, only much younger, and that made him a dangerous man in more ways than one. Just who was going to end up doing the seducing here?

Keeping a wary eye on him, Amelia took her cup of tea and went to sit in a comfortable, plush armchair off to one side, as far away from Colt as possible.

The sitting room was small and cozy, with a television and stereo in one corner. It bore absolutely no resemblance to the very formal living room she had seen earlier, which Helen said they rarely used. It was as if they were doing their best to show her what it was like to be one of the family, and that, too, was a part of the plan, judging by the huge smile Michael gave her when he joined them.

When his grandfather entered the room, Colt rose from the love seat and casually plopped down on the low matching footstool of Amelia's chair. The move was innocent enough, since the only other seat was occupied by three sleeping balls of fluff, but it was obvious to her what he was up to.

"You can move the cats," Michael offered as he sat down on the love seat beside his wife.

"Thanks, but no thanks," Colt replied, leaning back to use the arm of Amelia's chair for a backseat, stretching his long legs out in front of him. "I remember the last time you tried to move them off their throne, Pop."

"Nasty little beasts. Scratched me up good." He glanced fondly at the three cats curled up together on the large golden recliner, snoozing away. "Not very ladylike, are you, girls?"

They all looked alike, multicolored cats, a little of every feline shade Amelia had ever seen. "Are they related?"

"Sisters. They have a brother, too, but he's always outside catting around," Michael replied. "Goes off for days at a time, then comes home looking like he found a bowl of heavy cream."

Amelia was far too aware of Colt sitting so close to her. She could feel the heat of his skin through the thin white shirt as his shoulder pressed against her leg, warming the places it touched. She deliberately moved away from him.

It didn't seem to be a conscious gesture on his part, but he had managed to sit with his facial scar hidden from her view, and it made her wonder even more how he had come by the thin red line. Probably a simple accident, though she rather liked the romantic notion that it was a badge of courage, a dueling scar received in a fight over a fair maiden.

Amelia chastised herself for being silly, but her mind wasn't paying attention to her this evening.

Colt's thick black hair was easily within her grasp and she was seized by the desire to reach out and run her fingers through it, feel its silky texture.

Then she felt his hand moving down the length of her thigh on the side his grandparent's couldn't see, so she did touch his hair, not to feel its softness but to give the ends a warning yank.

"Youch!" he yelled, making Amelia jump and almost spill her tea all over him.

Maybe he wasn't as tough as he looked. She hadn't pulled his hair that hard. "What's wrong?" she asked sweetly.

"All right, you little beast," he muttered, bending over and coming up with a cat from under the footstool. "This is Tom, the meanest of the lot and appropriately named."

He was bigger than his sisters and looked tougher. Colt stood up and dropped him in her lap, then took her cup from her. "Get her, Tom. She deserves it," he muttered, rubbing the back of his head.

Smiling innocently, Amelia stroked Tom's furry head between his pointed ears and talked to him quietly. "You shouldn't poke people, Thomas. Not even if they're mean and nasty." He curled up on her lap and started purring.

Colt glared at her. Michael howled with laughter. "Colt, that cat just doesn't like men, that's all there is to it."

"He's probably hungry," Helen said, standing up and walking toward the kitchen. The sound of the can opener sent all four cats flying out of the room at once.

Amelia got up, poured herself another cup of tea, then returned to her seat without so much as looking at Colt. First he behaves as if she's not there, then he teases her at the dinner table, and then practically pounces on her. And that outrageous statement about having fun while the old folks aren't looking! She wasn't sure what Colt was playing at, but if he thought she was going to fall willingly into his open arms for a quickie, he was nuts.

"Now, where was I?" Helen asked when she rejoined them. "Oh, yes, I was going to tell you how Michael and I ended up together."

"She means how she chased me shamelessly," Michael interjected.

"Oh, shush, I'm telling this story. When I first met him he was still grieving over his first wife, Mary. She had been gone not quite a year, I believe."

Michael leaned forward in his chair and told Amelia in a sage tone, "I didn't have a chance. She caught me in a weak moment and seduced my socks off."

"I see," Amelia said. Did she ever. That was how he had come up with his brilliant idea. Evidently he figured that if it had worked on him it would work on his grandson.

"Michael! Are you going to let me tell this story?"

"Yes, my love. Please go on."

"I knew after I'd met him a couple of times that he was the man I wanted for my husband," Helen continued, obviously seeing nothing unusual in

78

such a decision. "But there was a problem. He was still grieving for his first wife, and that's hard competition, believe me. He was determined never to get married again, never to expose himself to any more pain and heartache."

Amelia watched as Michael reached over and intertwined his fingers with Helen's, absently rubbing her hand. "I hadn't yet learned that to win big, one must take big risks."

"Well, I certainly took risks. I tried everything to get him to notice me, even tried raising my skirts when we were sitting together at a church meeting," she said with a chuckle.

"I must have been blind," Michael commented with a roguish glance at her calves.

Helen tilted her head and looked down her nose at him. "You certainly were. I had very nice legs back then."

"Still do."

"Hush! Anyway, he never noticed. I went to a lot of trouble to find out his routine, what sort of functions he would be attending and so on, then arranged to sit beside him whenever I could."

Michael chuckled, shaking his head at how foggy his mind had been at the time. "It wasn't until later that I realized Helen had been around all those months, trying to comfort me and cheer me up, help me."

"It was a serious chase, dear, and it went on for over three months before I decided that drastic action was required."

"I'll say," Colt added dryly from somewhere behind Amelia's chair.

She didn't like having him where she couldn't see him, but was so enthralled by Helen's story, she managed to ignore the way the hair stood up on the back of her neck. Fifty years ago a woman rarely stalked a man.

"What did you do?" Amelia asked.

"Appealed to his baser instincts. The next night I told my parents I was going to spend the night with my girlfriend. Instead, I went over to Michael's apartment house, slipped up the fire escape and in through his open window," she confided, her eyes twinkling merrily. "He didn't get off work until eleven that night and I fell asleep waiting for him to come home."

Michael was looking at his wife, the depth of his affection for her apparent to all. "I'll never forget the sight of you half naked in that bed, bold as brass."

"You mean you . . ." Amelia trailed off, eyes wide.

Helen nodded, then reached out and cupped Michael's cheek. "You know, until the moment we came face to face in that room, I'd never once thought of failure. But at that instant I was scared to death you'd refuse me, or ask me to leave."

"But I didn't," he said softly.

"No. I love you, Michael."

They kissed tenderly. Amelia wriggled in her chair, feeling unneeded and wanting to leave them to their private moment. She started to get up, but Colt stopped her.

"Stay," his hushed voice commanded as he placed a warm hand on each side of her neck. "It's

80

like this every time they tell it together, and they're not embarrassed. They're happy and proud that they overcame such odds to make it work."

The hands on her shoulders were kneading the muscles of her neck, taut from tension Amelia dared not think about. He worked deftly, gently, trying to loosen the knotted mass. Instead of relaxing, however, her tension increased, and she could feel herself tightening up even more as his fingers strayed from her shoulders to glide down her arms. Sensitive nerve endings cried out for his touch, making a mockery of her attempts to pull away from him. His knuckles brushed against the sides of her breasts, bringing both nipples to tautness.

"Are you frustrated?" he whispered.

Amelia jerked away from his touch, glaring up at him over the back of her chair. "How dare you?"

Colt shrugged indifferently, then gestured toward his grandparents. "If you haven't noticed, this is a family of daring individualists."

She had noticed, all right, and the thought didn't comfort her. No wonder Michael saw nothing wrong with what he was asking her to do. His own wife had done it to him, and in a much less enlightened age at that.

"I want you to know, Amelia," Helen said, drawing her attention back to the loving couple, "that what they say about good girls getting into trouble from one time isn't always true. It took me five months to get pregnant. And back then we had to sneak around; we weren't allowed the freedom you young people have today."

"Made it much more exciting, though," Michael added.

"My heavens, yes! Planning rendezvous, times to be alone, that little extra thrill at the thought of getting caught."

Amelia could feel Colt tangling his fingers in her hair, his thumb glancing back and forth across the nape of her neck, trying to distract her—and succeeding.

"I'll never forget the look on your face when I told you I was pregnant, Michael. You were so stunned."

He grinned. "I remember. I asked you how it happened."

"And I offered to show you, again and again." They laughed together, caught up in their memories. "It certainly put a stop to your aversion to wedding bells. I've never seen a man so quick to marry."

Amelia sat there, Colt secretly stroking the back of her neck, Michael and Helen looking at her expectantly, a feeling of total unreality fogging her brain. What the heck had she gotten herself into?

"That's quite a story," she said at last, leaning forward to get away from Colt's tantalizing caress. "But I'm curious, Helen. Didn't you feel as if you had trapped Michael into marrying you?"

"Well, of course I trapped him!"

"But—"

Helen laughed, rocking back and forth in her seat. "My dear, sweet child, that was the whole idea," she informed her. "All's fair in love and war, you know."

"And you, Michael," Amelia persisted, staring at him intently. "Didn't you feel . . . used?"

Michael didn't bat an eye at her veiled accusation. "That's me. Used and abused," he said with a contented sigh. "No, Amelia, I didn't feel used. I felt in love. And man wasn't meant to live alone, I'm firmly convinced of that now." He turned his gaze to his grandson, who was suddenly looking rather uncomfortable. "What do you think, Colt?"

Amelia looked at him, too, waiting expectantly for his answer. He scowled, opened his mouth, then stopped and put a hand to his ear. "Is that the phone?"

"Saved by the bell," Amelia muttered under her breath.

"It's the private line in my study," Michael said, starting to get up.

Colt was already moving toward the door. "Sit still, Pop. I'll get it."

She watched him stride swiftly out of the room, a man in a hurry. The glimpse she'd had of his face, suddenly cold and harsh, had her wondering what kind of calls came through on Michael's private line.

"Pop!" The urgency of Colt's tone carried across the intervening rooms.

Michael struggled out of his seat. "Coming," he called back, and went to join his grandson.

Amelia could barely contain her curiosity. She wanted to know what was going on and if it in-

volved her brother. Fat chance they'd tell her anything, though. She'd just have to wait it out.

Needing something to keep her hands busy and
her mind off her brother, she started collecting
teacups and loading the tray. "I'll help you clean
up the kitchen, Helen."

"Thank you, dear, together it'll take us no time
at all."

The job went quickly, and they were having a
lively discussion about Helen's many plants when
Michael came back, looking particularly pleased
with himself.

"Colt has to leave," he announced.

"Oh, my," Helen fretted. "And I promised him
dessert." Smiling indulgently, she cut a thick slice
of chocolate cake and put it in a plastic container.
"There. Would you give this to him, Amelia? I've
just realized I'm missing my favorite nighttime
soap opera. It's silly, I know, but I'm absolutely
addicted to the dumb thing."

She hurried off, and shortly the wheedling voice
of the woman America loved to hate drifted out of
the sitting room, accompanied by a scathing commentary from Helen. Michael smiled, then, his expression growing serious, he turned his attention
to Amelia.

"That was Jerry Enger on the phone," he informed her. "The doctors have given the go-ahead
and we're all set. We move him tonight."

Amelia felt an odd mixture of relief and sheer
terror at the news. Nathan had to get out of that
hospital, but the move would be dangerous. His
doctors were good and if they said he could go,

84

that was one worry off her mind. On the other hand there was no telling what the people who were after him might do if they caught wind of the ploy.

"Can I see him?"

Michael shook his head. "No. It isn't safe. After we get him settled at his final destination, we'll see. Until then it would be best if you and John Smith have no contact whatsoever."

"I understand," she said, though she sighed dejectedly. Then a frown wrinkled her forehead. "What do you mean his final destination? And now that I'm on the subject, just where are you taking him?"

"A safe place," Michael replied cryptically. "Once again, I think it would be best if you don't know, for the time being anyway."

Amelia stiffened. "What's the matter?" she asked through clenched teeth. "Don't you trust me?"

"Amelia, one of the few things we know about the people who are after your brother is that they are a tricky bunch," he replied calmly. "I wouldn't put it past them to somehow find out about you and attempt to kidnap you. I have no intention of letting that happen, but if it did, surely you can see the advantage of not knowing where he is."

Yes, she could. She couldn't tell them what she didn't know. It wasn't a pleasant prospect, but she supposed the old man was right. Again. It set her teeth on edge.

She looked down at the container she held in her hand. "I'd better give this to Colt. Helen would never forgive me if I sent him off without his cake. Is he in the study?" she asked, turning in that direction.

"I'm not sure. He was still talking to Jerry when I left him." Michael reached out and grabbed her by the arm. "Just a minute, Amelia. I told you the time would come when we had business to discuss. The time is now."

Amelia turned back to face him. Gone was the sweet old man who had so openly displayed his love for his wife. Now he was the hard businessman who had shrewdly gained the wealth that surrounded them, the tough, experienced investor manipulating everything and everyone to suit his purposes.

"I've met him. I've told you I can't promise any more than that for now."

His eyes bored into hers. "You can and will, my dear."

"I thought you said you wouldn't threaten me."

"Perhaps I've changed my mind."

Michael turned and went to the kitchen window, peering out into the darkness for a moment, seemingly fighting some inner battle. When he faced her again, his decision was made. There was an edge to his voice sharp enough to cut paper.

"You're not fooling anyone, you know," he said. "I have sharp eyes and ears for a man my age. I may have seemed distracted, but I noticed the way my grandson looks at you, and the way you look at him."

Amelia glared at him indignantly. "What's that supposed to mean?" she asked, though she knew very well what he meant. The kind of attraction she had for Colt—and he for her, evidently—was nearly impossible to hide. "I don't have any idea what—"

"Come, now, Amelia," Michael interrupted. "I could feel it in the air like an electrical charge. So could Helen. What's more, we're enough in tune with that sort of thing and our own grandson to know you're not going to have to do much pursuing to nab him."

"Mr. Colt." She was seething, angry at him and the whole world. "I am not going to nab anybody. Just because your grandson and I find each other reasonably attractive is no sign that we should marry and have children!"

"Bah! Life is too short to quibble over such nonsense."

"Nonsense? Michael . . ." She was so mad she couldn't go on.

He grinned. "I can certainly understand why Colt is suddenly so full of vim and vigor. You are a pretty little thing, even when you're furious." He stepped over to her, his face suddenly serious again, that artic edge back in his voice. "Do we have a deal?" he asked, very softly.

Amelia leaned back against the wall. For some reason, evidently because he had caught the scent of success, the old coot had suddenly become very volatile. She wasn't certain if he was threatening her or not, or whether he would carry out such a threat. He was, however, capable of anything. It was quite possible he was acting, heaven knew he was good enough at it, but she couldn't afford to take the chance.

She was trapped. She could guarantee her brother's safety or let him take his chances. Of course, that still didn't mean she would actually have to go through with the deal, just put up a convincing show. It would be hard, but she could do it, and would keep her eyes and ears open along the way for an opportunity to get out of this insane asylum.

Amelia held out her hand. "All right. Yes. You've got a deal."

They shook hands. Michael was grinning from ear to ear. "Excellent. Now go take Colt his cake and wish him a safe journey." Before she had taken two steps, he added, "And I'm well aware, Amelia, that you're planning to fudge on our bargain. Just remember how observant I am. I know Colt, and I'm getting to know you better than you think too. I want you for a granddaughter-in-law, my dear, and I have decided I'll go to almost any lengths to get you."

She spun on her heel and marched off, his warnings and final promise ringing in her ears. "We'll see about that, you old geezer," she muttered.

Michael watched her go, then sagged against the counter with a heavy sigh. "I'm getting too old for this stuff."

But it had worked. He hadn't been a top-notch poker-player all these years for nothing. If Amelia decided to call his bluff—and she was just fiery enough to do so—he would have to come up with some other method of getting her and Colt together. He was determined to do so, however.

Helen and he had agreed; they were perfect for each other. This time, he wouldn't give up until that boy was hitched.

Down the hall he could hear Amelia's tentative footsteps as she went looking for his grandson. He chuckled mischievously and went after her on tiptoe.

"Colt?" Amelia called again, stepping into the dimly lighted study. "Are you in here?"

The door closed behind her. A strong arm curled around her stomach from behind and pulled her tight against a rock-hard body. Amelia opened her mouth to scream but a hand clamped tightly over her lips. Then she could smell Colt's spicy cologne and relaxed a bit. At least she wasn't being kidnapped. However, her body was suddenly alive with a delicious, tingling fire from head to toe.

"Don't get any ideas while I'm gone."

Amelia started to bite his hand, but he was too quick. "Damn you, Colt," she said, trying to pull away from him, "you scared me half to death."

"Good," he murmured. His arms held her tightly. "It serves you right, you little witch. Making me eat Brussels sprouts and pulling my hair. Promising, though," he added, his lips brushing her ear. "I like my women fiery."

"Why, you—"

"But I repeat, don't get any ideas. Those two mean well, you just have to play the game without taking their plans to heart."

Amelia's heart was racing and she was sure he could see guilt written all over her face in the shadowy light. Still, she asked, "What plans?"

"Knowing them as I do, I'd say a stroll down the aisle, followed closely by the patter of little feet," he whispered, turning her around in his embrace, her womanly curves pressing tightly into him. "Same old story. At least they've finally figured out what I like. I'm not ready for marriage, but I'll definitely make a pass at this lady in glasses."

She could feel the powerful beat of his heart beneath her fingers as she tried to push against his chest. He seemed to swoop down out of the darkness to cover her mouth, devouring her, his tongue delicately probing.

Though Amelia tried to fight the sensations flooding through her, it was a losing battle. Colt coaxed her mouth into willingness, nibbling on her lower lip, tracing its shape again and again as he drank deeply of her honeyed nectar. She moaned as his tongue filled her mouth, and leaned against him for support.

Colt felt a bit dizzy himself. Why did this woman get to him so? He hadn't meant to kiss her and now he didn't want to stop. At last he managed to pull back, looking at her mouth, swollen and wine-red. She was lovely, tender and petal soft. He wanted her with a desperation that disturbed him, rattled him to his very core.

"That was nice," he said, his voice hoarse and with an unusual note of roughness. "Very nice. We'll be good together, Amelia. You know it and I know it. As long as you remember that an affair is all I'll go for, we'll get along just fine." Then he turned abruptly, opened the door, and left her standing alone in the study.

Her mind reeling from Colt's unexpected onslaught and her sensual reaction to it, Amelia slumped into one of the leather chairs by the desk. She certainly knew the score now, didn't she? He wanted her, was infuriatingly capable of making her body react to his need with a burning desire of her own. And that passion was all he wanted.

An affair. She felt frightened and excited at the same time, a curious mix that left her lightheaded. Most of all, however, she felt as if Colt had just thrown down the gauntlet, challenged not only her ability to carry out his grandfather's plans, but her very womanhood.

A roll in the hay and farewell, my dear? "That's what you think, wise guy," she said to herself in a vindictive tone that surprised her. If she rolled the dice, it was going to be all or nothing. "Either I find a way out of this predicament, or you are going to marry me, buster."

CHAPTER SIX

Colt stood like a silent sentinel in the near darkness at the edge of the clearing, his broad back pressed up against the rough bark of a tree. Completely hidden from view, he waited, tense and alert for any unusual sounds. It was very quiet. The driver was late, and it worried him, but when he thought about who the driver was he grinned and chuckled to himself. It was true. There was never a cop around when you needed one.

Then he heard the low mutter of a well-tuned car exhaust and the crunch of tires on the broken rock path off to his left. Colt straightened, staying hidden from view until he was certain of the identity of his visitor. Satisfied, he breathed a sigh of relief and stepped out of the shadows toward the vehicle.

"Everything go according to plan?" Colt asked, opening the door of the unmarked station wagon.

Sergeant Jerry Enger stepped out of the car. "Smooth as glass. It just took longer than we thought," he replied, then answered the next question before it was asked. "It was maybe a little too smooth."

"What didn't you like?" Colt asked, leaning up against the side of the car. He could see the shrug of Jerry's big shoulders in the filtered moonlight.

"Nothing I can put a finger on, just a feeling of apprehension." He grinned at the other man. Although they were of about equal height, Jerry was definitely bigger, built like a solid oak barrel. "Good to meet you, by the way," he said, extending his hand. Colt's grasp was good and solid. "Don't mind me. I'm a cop, you know. We're all a little paranoid."

"I doubt it. You kept the number of people involved to a minimum?"

"Four. All policemen I trust. We entered the empty warehouse as planned, switched John over to one of the ambulances we parked there earlier, and then had them all leave a minute apart heading in different directions. As best we could tell, not one of them was followed."

Colt nodded, the lines around his eyes pinched in a frown. "I see what you mean. Too smooth." He shrugged. Nothing to do but forge onward. "How's the patient?"

"Great. Sleeping like a baby the last time I saw him," Jerry replied. "According to the nurse he'll do just fine. My man delivered them to this mysterious landing site of yours and reported in, said your two passengers will be ready and waiting in the helicopter by the time you arrive."

The plan was convoluted, but the false trails were necessary, as was this separate rendezvous with Jerry. They were using radios and telephones as little as possible, just in case. And Colt was the only one who knew all the details of the scheme, to reduce further the number of weak links. Besides, part of the plan wasn't strictly legal, and Colt didn't want to get Jerry or the other policemen in trouble.

It would be nice to know what this John Smith had been involved in to warrant all this attention, but Colt accepted the fact that he'd probably never know. "Okay. We'll be airborne inside of half an hour. You won't hear from me unless something goes wrong."

"Fine."

While Jerry was leaving the area in one direction, Colt left in another, zipping west on the Capital of Texas Highway in a dark sedan. He'd decided the best time to land at his friend's place was before dawn, and if he didn't hurry it would be daylight before they arrived.

His mind was on the task before him. He hadn't flown a military helicopter since his National Guard days, but it would come back to him. Technically he was borrowing the machine, although some would probably consider it stealing. If anybody found out, his grandfather and he would have to do some fast talking and pull in a lot of favors. But on such short notice it was the only medically equipped aircraft he could get without arousing suspicion.

The all-night grocery store on the outskirts of town was a popular place, its parking lot so busy that nobody would notice a man dropping off one vehicle and leaving in another. Colt spotted the one he was looking for, pulled in behind it, then locked up his car and slid into the passenger seat of the other.

"Hey, Pete," Colt said, giving the driver a hearty slap on the back. "Good to see you."

Peter Sloan and he had trained together in the army, their mutual, burning desire to fly big machines a common ground. Colt had chosen to serve his tour and get out, with an additional stint in the Guard, but his friend found he liked the army and made it his career. They'd managed to stay in touch over the years.

Pete was a slim, dark-haired, somewhat nondescript man with a noticeable military bearing and a quick smile. "Good to see you, too, Colt," he said, then started the car and pulled out of the parking lot, heading away from the city into darkness. "How's it going?"

"Can't complain."

"Same here, or if I do nobody listens."

Colt chuckled. "Everything ready?"

"With one slight problem," Pete replied. "You'll have to have the bird back by midnight tomorrow. It's listed as being out for repairs."

"Does it need any?" Colt asked, arching his eyebrows.

Pete glanced at him, a big grin on his thin face. "Now, would I do that to you?"

"Probably."

"Relax, it's fine. How's Pop?"

"He doesn't change, as wily as ever."

They drove on, his friend's grin growing wider as he said, "I'll have to bring the kids by for a visit."

"Don't do me any favors," Colt grumbled. Wild, full laughter rang loudly in his ears. "Your visits are always followed by one of his lectures on the joys of matrimony."

"He's still harping at you?"

"Hell hasn't frozen over yet, has it? Seriously, Pete, I love your kids, but I would appreciate it if you wouldn't bring them by for the next two weeks or so. I'll have to be in Austin at least that long, and the situation at the house is, um, a bit confused at the moment."

Pete absorbed that information thoughtfully. "She must be something special."

"Who?"

"The lady they're trying to fix you up with this time."

Amelia was indeed something special, Colt couldn't deny it, not with the way his pulse quickened just thinking about her. But there was something disquieting about the way he felt when he was around her as well, a feeling of losing control. He wasn't used to that feeling and wasn't sure he liked it at all.

"Who said anything about a lady?" he asked irritably.

"Just a guess," Pete replied. "Right on the mark, too, judging by that look on your face. You can't hide stuff like that from your old buddy."

Colt scowled. "She's nothing more than a pleasant diversion. Now, mind your business and drive, will you?"

"Sure." He shrugged, still grinning from ear to ear. "Your problem, my friend, is that you just don't want to settle down. Happens to the best of us, you know."

"I will when I'm ready."

"The older you get the harder it is."

"How would you know?" Colt asked. "You've been married for eleven years and have five kids."

"Simple fact of life, Colt. You get old and it takes you longer to do everything."

"Oh, yeah?" he remarked slyly.

Pete shook his head in disgust. "Get your mind out of the gutter. I don't know why I waste my breath trying to give you the benefit of my experience." He slowed the car and pulled off the road, turning into an area shielded from the highway by trees. "We're here. You shouldn't have any problems with the noise. Night maneuvers have been going on all week, so the sounds that beast makes won't alarm anyone."

Colt got out of the car and peered through the trees into the clearing beyond, just able to make out the shape of the big, camouflage-painted helicopter that sat there like some modern-day dinosaur.

"Thanks, Pete."

"Sure. See you tomorrow. And don't put a scratch on her," he added as Colt disappeared into the trees.

Once across the deserted clearing, Colt gave the helicopter a quick once-over out of habit, though he knew Pete would have already checked it out thoroughly. Then he opened the door and slid into the pilot's seat. At that instant something cold and metallic pressed hard against the side of his neck, just beneath his ear.

"Don't move," a very feminine voice ordered. "Now, very slowly, spread your fingers wide and hold your hands in front of you."

For a moment panic gripped him and he had to fight the stupid urge that told him to grab or avoid the object at his throat. But the chilling reality of the gun barrel jarred him back to his senses and he did exactly as he was told.

"Now turn your face back toward me, slowly."

Very slowly Colt turned his head to look at her. He couldn't see much, crouched as she was in the shadows behind his seat. She was of medium height, with a pale face and jet-black hair, completely dressed in dark clothes. It wasn't the usual attire of a nurse, but then, this nurse was anything but usual.

"Hello, Teri," he said softly, his voice filled with relief. "Would you mind taking your gun out of my ear? It tickles something awful."

She chuckled, equally relieved. "It's about time you got here, Colt. Sorry about the theatrics. It's spooky out here in the dark." The gun was lowered as she straightened and backed away from him. "I thought you might be one of Mr. Smith's friends come to pay him a nocturnal visit."

"No harm done. That's what you're here for, or half of what you're here for," he told her with a good-natured grin. "I don't imagine you took more than one or two good years off my life."

He didn't know all of Teri's background—nor did anyone he was aware of—but he knew he

98

didn't have to ask if she would have used that gun had he been one of the bad guys. She had been in the service, too, which was where she had learned both her nursing and firearm-handling skills. But from there on her past got a bit hazy.

Right now she was a combination private duty nurse and bodyguard, under contract to his grandfather, and he was glad she was there. "How's our patient?" he asked.

"Stable." She put her weapon away and moved back into the belly of the helicopter, turning on a small light that cast strange shadows in the cavernous hull. Now that the danger had passed, she was a health-care professional again, as she knelt down beside Amelia's brother. "His pulse is good and he's tough. He'll make the trip just fine."

Colt nodded, then turned around and familiarized himself with the aircraft. "Since you seem to have everything else under control, I guess it's time I got busy and did my part."

"All buckled in and ready to fly, Captain," Teri said.

"Captain Colt. Hmm. Has a nice ring to it," he said.

Talk became impossible as the noise of the engine built up to a high, thumping whine and they became airborne, leaving first the clearing and then the twinkling lights of Austin far behind.

Amelia squinted at the clock near her head, gasped, and sprang out of bed, heading for the connecting bathroom off her room. Michael had co-

99

erced her into having lunch with him this afternoon and she was going to be late.

Last night, or very early this morning, to be precise, Colt had called from somewhere to assure Michael that everything had gone well and was proceeding ahead of schedule. Michael hadn't told her anything else, such as where Colt had taken her brother, but between the good news that he was safe and two snifters of Cognac she'd had no trouble falling into a deep and restful sleep. The last few days had taken their toll on her and she'd slept fourteen hours straight.

The weather appeared to be warm and sunny, making for a mild fall day. She thumbed through her clothes in the closet, frowning, not knowing what to wear. Her choices were limited; she hadn't brought that much with her to Austin in the first place. Some washing would have to be done soon, and if she could convince Michael to allow it, a trip to her San Antonio apartment to pick up some more of her things would be nice.

The doorbell pealed through the house, but she ignored it. Michael and Helen would be home by now, the former most likely waiting impatiently for her downstairs. Amelia pulled a colorful cotton sweater and skirt from the closet, put them on the bed, then with a careful hand finished applying her makeup. The incessant ringing continued.

"Michael? Helen?" she called. No answer except the steady ding-dong of the bell. "How rude!" she exclaimed, referring to whatever unmannerly caller was at the door.

Someone would have to be literally leaning on

the bell to cause such an obnoxious clamor. It echoed in her ears, driving her to distraction. Amelia pulled the towel off her dry hair, threw it on the bed, and pushed her glasses back up on her nose. Whoever was at the door wasn't going to leave.

With her knee-length royal-blue robe belted tightly around her waist, she made her way downstairs. She couldn't believe anyone had so few manners. Without a thought to her safety Amelia flipped the dead bolt and wrenched open the front door.

"Stop that!"

"About time someone answered." Colt was leaning against the white-painted jamb, looking as if he had all the time in the world.

"I should have known," she retorted sarcastically, stepping back from the entrance. "What's the matter? Don't you have a key?"

He followed close behind her, slamming the door shut behind him. "Not to the new dead bolts. Pop misplaced the set of keys he had made for me."

"Why doesn't he just get you another set?"

"Because he refuses to admit he lost them, that's why."

It sounded just like Michael, but Amelia fought the urge to smile. "He probably just doesn't want a vandal like you loose in his home."

"My, aren't we sassy today?"

Silence surrounded them as they stood at the foot of the stairs, surveying each other, both remembering their last meeting. His dark gray corduroy jeans hugged his thighs, the lighter gray shirt making him seem even bigger and taller. Amelia felt practically naked in her robe.

"I like your outfit. New style?" he asked, his thumb rubbing the nubbly weave of the fabric against her sensitive collarbone.

Her blue robe didn't reveal nearly enough, but he approved of what he could see. She had slender knees and calves, pale, smooth, tapering to strong yet dainty feet, the toenails painted a burnished shade of copper. Colt held his breath, afraid any sound would send her scampering up the stairs. The rapid beat of her pulse beneath his touch confirmed her nervousness.

"I, um, was just getting dressed," she explained.

Colt's eyebrows arched. "And hadn't finished? That's an interesting bit of information."

He hadn't been able to get her out of his mind, from her curving womanly body pressing into his to the honeyed sweetness of her mouth. He wanted to taste her again and again, to strip away every barrier between them, to have her feminine scent intertwine with his in passion. He could feel his body responding to his thoughts. It was that disturbing lack of control again, making him give in to temptation.

Amelia couldn't seem to move away from him. The long, lean fingers of his right hand were inside the edge of her robe, just barely touching the delicate bone. Then his hand was slipping at a snail's pace down toward her quivering breasts.

Her breath caught in her throat, stifled, her body unwilling to move away from his touch. She could feel the few dark hairs on the backs of his fingers as they seemed to float across her skin, leaving a trail of smoldering fire behind them. Betraying her excitement, her nipples hardened and grew to rigid peaks of attention as his wandering hand slid closer and closer.

His fingers paused at the point where the fabric crossed over, but only for a moment, then began their teasing assent up the other side. Her breasts seemed to cry out as if in protest, straining against their covering. Colt felt her shiver as he rubbed his thumb across the soft, nearly translucent skin of her throat, the racing pulse beneath his touch matching his own.

"Amelia." The name was magic. His hand slid beneath the shining, tangled mass of her hair and drew her closer.

"No, I . . ." Amelia backed onto the first step of the staircase. He seemed to be drawing her closer even as she tried to slip away. She was almost on eye level with him.

"Better," he whispered, his hands cradling her face.

His mouth sought hers, gently, with infinite care, nibbling the soft surface of her lips into submission. In her mind Amelia saw herself slapping him, pushing him away, but she found she couldn't even move. Her fingers clutched his shoulders, her mouth opening, welcoming him, giving in. The texture of his lips was like velvet, the smoothness of his tongue like silk as it dipped inside her lower lip, an erotic thrusting motion sending waves of desire through her.

She moaned softly, raspy little sounds coming

from deep inside her throat. Of their own volition her hands slid up and around his neck, pulling him closer as she wrapped her fingers in his dark, thick hair. Over and over their lips met, giving and taking, discovering more with each passing caress.

It wasn't enough for Colt. He slipped his hands down between them, struggling with the tightly knotted sash of her robe. He ached to see her, to let his hands and mouth careen across her body at will. Impatient, he dropped the knot and slid his hands up under the robe to feel her creamy smoothness, cupping her buttocks with eager fingers. His hands fondled the silky skin of her thighs, brushing against her femininity.

Startled by his intimate touch, Amelia drew back away from him, returning to reality with a jarring jolt. "No!" she exclaimed, her voice little more than a whisper.

With great effort she managed to step up two more stairs and out of his reach. Her limbs were trembling; she was eager to return to his arms, but she had to think. It wasn't supposed to happen this way. Her agreement with Michael had been a ruse, a ploy to gain time. But this wasn't an act, not at all. She wanted Colt.

"No? Are you sure?" he coaxed, grabbing hold of the hem of her robe and tugging it downward.

"Y-yes," she stammered, refusing to look at him.

Amelia took another step up but he followed her, his other hand grasping the robe higher right above her waist. She started to turn away from him, expecting him to release her. He didn't.

"I suppose you're right," Colt murmured, eyes gleaming as he drank in the sight of her. "We should leave something for the next time."

One milky-white, rose-tipped breast peeked out at him. He couldn't resist, even if it did send her dashing to her room. One lone finger brushed across the pink tip and he felt her quiver at his touch, watching as the plump orb puckered into a tight little mound.

"Next time?" she mumbled as if in a trance. She was struggling with herself, her body more than willing to betray her mind. Was she actually swaying toward him?

Then the sensual trance was broken by the sound of car doors slamming, jolting her into action. She pulled away from him, grasping the edges of her robe and pulling them tightly closed as she ran up the stairs two at a time.

"Saved," he taunted when he caught up with her at the bedroom door. "For now."

"Would you go away?" Her voice was throaty, breathless. "I can find my way into my room by myself."

"I'm sure you can, but at the moment I'm not in any shape to meet anyone either," he informed her with a sly smile. "Anyone but you, that is."

Involuntarily, her eyes dropped to his jeans, widened, then flew right back up to his face. There was no mistaking his problem. Erotic thoughts flowed into her mind, making her grip the doorknob tightly to keep from being swept away.

Colt's emerald-green eyes seemed to laugh at her as he watched a hot pink blush envelop her in a rosy glow. "What's the matter? Cat got your tongue?"

"You . . . I . . ." she spluttered, then found her tongue at last. "Oh, stuff it!"

"I'd love to," he taunted, laughing out loud at her look of pure outrage. "Next time."

Amelia practically fell into the room, flinging the door shut behind her and collapsing against it. She could still hear his hearty masculine laugh as he moved down the hall. Damn that man anyway!

A moment later a soft knock sounded on the door. She jumped away from it as if burned. "Go away!"

"Amelia?" a confused feminine voice inquired. "Are you all right, dear?"

She closed her eyes tightly and stifled a groan of embarrassment. "Yes, Helen."

"We're running a little behind and I still have to change my clothes," she said through the closed door. "I'm sorry. I'm sure you're starving by now."

"No, not at all." At least someone was on her side today. "As you can see," Amelia told her, opening the door, "I'm not ready, either, so your timing is perfect," she assured her.

"Lovely. Just give me fifteen minutes."

Amelia fell on the bed in a wilting heap. What was she going to do about him? She knew what she'd like to do to him, perhaps something along the lines of strangulation.

Then she sighed in guilty resignation. In all honesty, murder was the farthest thing from her mind. What she'd really like to do with Colt was engage in some more of his brand of mouth-to-mouth resuscitation. Her body tingled at the vivid memory her mind called up. She could still feel the heat of his hands caressing her hips, strong, slightly callused fingers kneading her flesh.

It was a good thing she didn't have more time to think, she decided, rolling off the bed and untying the knot of her belt with a hard jerk, because her thoughts were going to get her in trouble. Her filmy lingerie only added to her already heightened senses, knowing as she did how the wisps of lace looked on her, knowing how much Colt would enjoy seeing her in them.

Stop it! Forcing herself to concentrate on the task at hand, she slipped on her pantyhose with care, then slid into her shoes. The taupe-and-red-printed challis skirt fit well, falling into graceful folds to just below her knees. Amelia was picking up her red silk sweater when she heard a noise behind her.

"Very nice."

She whirled around, holding the sweater up in front of her as a barrier. "What do you think you're doing?"

"Admiring the view," Colt replied from his position in the doorway of her bathroom. One of his muscular arms was casually braced against the wall. "And a lovely view it is, I might add."

"Out!" she ordered, pointing at the opening. "Get out of here right now." He was devouring her with his eyes, and heaven help her but a very large part of her was enjoying his desirous gaze.

Her chest was heaving, probably in anger,

though he couldn't really tell. The fire in her eyes was appealing, and he knew anger could easily be turned into raging passion given time. "It's my bathroom, too, Amelia. Are you done?" he inquired mildly.

"Yes. No!" She needed her hairbrush, and the rest of her things were still spread out all over the counter. "Use another bathroom."

"But this one connects to my room." His low, sexy tone implied many things, played hovoc with her already overwrought senses. "Convenient, don't you think?"

"Great," she muttered bitterly. "Just peachy." She should have known the room next to hers belonged to Colt. Michael was going to throw them together constantly to try and get his wish fulfilled. "Give me five minutes."

He nodded his head and slipped out of her sight. But Amelia didn't trust him. She pulled the sweater over her head, almost mangling her glasses with her haste. "Damn," she muttered, straightening first her glasses and then her twisted sweater.

She stood in front of the huge mirror and saw a well-dressed woman looking back at her, perfect except for her hair. It looked as if she'd been standing in front of a wind machine. Or tumbling in bed all morning. *Wishful thinking?* The little voice inside her head wouldn't leave her alone.

She swept the brush through her tawny hair, pleased with the way the simple straight cut fell into a silky line around her shoulders, the wispy bangs perfect. Her hairdresser had done a good job last time.

"Definitely an improvement," she told herself.

"I'll say." Colt was back, laughing at the nasty look Amelia threw him. "Your five minutes are up," he said, holding out his beeping watch for her to hear. "Don't bother to move anything, I'll manage." His eyes lingered on her red-and-taupe sweater, liking the way it defined her feminine curves.

Amelia froze in place. Colt was unbuttoning his shirt. "Want to wash my back?" he asked, pulling the shirt free of his pants.

His voice again suggested many things, conjuring up all sorts of erotic visions in her mind. "No, thank you," she shot back, although her reply had an uncertain tone that even she could hear.

With a knowing smile he leaned over the tub and turned the water on full blast, adjusting the temperature to his liking. A hot, steamy fog began to fill the room. She tried to move and couldn't, tried not to look but found her eyes straying to his reflection in the mirror anyway. He dropped his shirt to the floor.

He looked tan and fit, his broad chest sprinkled with dark hairs. He must have spent a lot of time outdoors. Her eyes slid lower, noticing that his flat stomach didn't have a trace of fat. A dark, narrow column of hair ran down his belly and disappeared into his pants.

"What big eyes you have. Want to see more?" he murmured, following the direction of her gaze, his hands unzipping his jeans to reveal dark briefs.

"Stop right there." Amelia gulped silently and met his eyes in the mirror, the hunger and intense desire she felt almost palpable. She had to get out of here fast. "I—I have to go," she whispered, fleeing the room in a hurry.

Amelia couldn't believe she'd acted like such a voyeur. Her eyes had been glued to his every movement, every nuance of his voice causing a reaction in her. It was no use kidding herself now, she was in big trouble; the act she had planned to put on for Michael's benefit was within inches of becoming a real, live seduction. She'd barely been able to drag herself from his tempting masculine presence. As Colt had promised, there would definitely be a next time.

Then she smiled. In a strange, dangerous way she was only living up to the woman she had always known she could be when the right man came along. Colt had issued a challenge of sorts, and she was rising to the occasion. If she actually went ahead and seduced him, the poor man might never recover from her attack.

The little voice in her head was screaming at her, but she didn't have time to listen right now. If she didn't hurry up and get downstairs, Helen or Michael would begin to lend their own interpretation to her absence.

Back in their shared bathroom Colt was chuckling as he stripped off the rest of his clothes and eased his sore body into the tub of hot water. It had been a rough night and an even rougher morning. The endless drone of the big military helicopter still sounded in his ears, his neck was stiff, and his mind numb from the hours of intense concentration.

Most of his pains would benefit from a long, soothing soak, but there was only one thing that could ease the other, more intimate ache in his loins. Closing his eyes and slipping beneath the steaming surface of his bath, he sighed, hoping he could bring the delectable Amelia around quickly. The torment was sweet, but he didn't think he could stand it for very long.

CHAPTER SEVEN

Amelia's first week in the Colt household took her on a roller coaster ride of emotion. Helen and Michael were doing their utmost to make her welcome in their home, treating her more as if she were a close relative than a guest. It felt good, was in fact a much-needed vacation. With a brother who worked undercover and seemed to get shot on a regular basis, she couldn't resist the opportunity to share the burden of watching and worrying about him for a while.

Then there was the down side. Every day, she had to wonder about what her kind, congenial host and hostess would try next. Combined with her own confused feelings about Colt, the endless and highly imaginative schemes they came up with to thrust their grandson and her together were tying her emotions up in knots.

What was making the situation unbearable, however, was Colt's sudden decision to play some sort of strange game of his own. His disdain for his grandparent's matchmaking plans was evident, so it didn't surprise Amelia when he managed deftly to sidestep every one of them, claiming business problems on several occasions and even taking an unexplained trip or two out of town.

But he had taken his evasive tactics too far, in her opinion. Not once had they been alone, and not once had he touched her again, even casually. It irked her. If she couldn't get close to him, how was she going to find out if the shock waves between them were just chemistry or something more? Had Colt decided she wasn't worth pursuing after all?

Amelia couldn't believe that, not after their wanton behavior on the stairs a week ago. Her memory of the incident was still so clear she could almost feel his touch upon her skin, see his hard, tanned body reflected in the mirror of the steamy bathroom. She hadn't imagined the flying sparks, had she?

Colt was due back today, and his business-trip excuse was wearing thin. He couldn't avoid her forever. At the first opportunity she was going to kiss him and satisfy her curiosity. If her body came alive like last time, if the sparks were real, she was going to give some serious thought to an all-out pursuit of Colt.

After all, she wasn't getting any younger. In his own infuriating way Michael was right; it was perhaps about time she considered settling down and raising a family.

But not this morning. As she perused the contents of her closet for the umpteenth time, she was reminded once again of how erratic her packing had been the day Jerry had called about Nathan. She had one pair of blue jeans, two shirts, and a few tailored suits that she usually wore to work. The jeans were all right, she supposed, but she had worn this black-and-red plaid blouse one time too many, and the other combinations were almost as overused.

It hadn't been easy, but Amelia had finally convinced Michael that her clothing situation was desperate. How could he expect her to be seductive if she looked like a ragamuffin? Today she intended to drive to San Antonio and check on her apartment, pick up her mail, pay a few bills, and of course add to her wardrobe.

"I'll have to make a detailed list on my drive home," she muttered to herself, her mind clicking away as she made her way to the kitchen. Helen was already there, as usual.

"Good morning," Amelia told her cheerfully.

"Morning, dear. Help yourself, there's coffee and tea ready." Helen was standing on a stepladder with a pair of small scissors, snipping leaves off one of the green plants. "I'm not sure what's wrong with this poor thing, but I don't want it to spread. I'll be done in a few minutes. Oh, the orange juice is in the fridge, dear."

Amelia smiled, amused at Helen's energetic cheerfulness. The way she ran on sometimes it was a surprise she didn't monopolize every conversation. Actually, the opposite was true. Helen would often sit quietly and listen, ask very probing questions, and then wait patiently for the answers. She was a remarkable woman. A very busy woman too. Her different meetings and clubs were a secretary's nightmare. But Helen kept them all straight somehow and enjoyed every moment.

Amelia went about getting her breakfast, so absorbed in planning her day that she failed to notice a third presence in the room. From his position in the corner Colt observed her silently. Though he had gotten back earlier than he had expected, he was so tired he could barely keep his eyes open. The sight of Amelia, however, sent new life surging through his veins.

The shirt she wore was tight across her chest, and when her hands slid into her back pockets as she looked up at Helen, her breasts jutted out, mocking him. Then she turned and reached for something on the counter, giving him an excellent view of her shapely rear end encased in tight jeans. Colt liked her full curves. So many women these days were reed thin.

After pouring herself a glass of juice, Amelia grabbed a pear from the fruit bowl and turned around. She almost dropped both when she saw Colt sitting at the far end of the table. How could she have missed seeing him? He looked tired, his black hair thrown across his brow in rumpled disarray. The striped shirt he wore was wrinkled and had a distinctly slept-in look. But his sharp eyes were wide open and full of life.

He was tilting back in his chair, staring at her with a thoughtful expression, a large glass full of orange juice in one hand. His eyes seemed to see right through her clothes and she felt her skin begin to tingle as his gaze roved over her with blatant interest.

Then she realized Colt wasn't merely taking her clothes off with his eyes, he was already beneath them—and letting her know it. The man had a colossal nerve after ignoring her all week long!

Amelia felt something snap in her mind, a little switch being thrown from the side which warned "caution," to the "who-cares" position. One minute the pear she had planned to eat for breakfast was in her hand, the next it was hurtling through the air toward his arrogant, smug face.

Colt blinked and managed to jump up in the nick of time, his chair crashing to the ground as he dodged the flying missile. It hit the wall with a resounding thud, bounced off, and landed on his foot. He looked at it for a moment, then up at her.

She stared back at him, her mouth hanging open in stunned disbelief at her own actions. What had she done? There was orange juice dripping down the front of his striped blue-and-white shirt and wet splotches on his blue jeans. Her pear sat like a juicy ornament on the toe of his shoe.

"Are you all right, dear?" Helen asked from her perch behind a big hanging plant, her voice perplexed. "How could you have fallen? You've been leaning back in my chairs that way for years, despite my scoldings."

Amelia gulped and set her glass of juice down on the counter. He had been leering at her and she had retaliated, but she didn't much care for the look in his eyes right now either. "Now, Colt," she began in a coaxing tone, "there's no harm done. Here's a dish towel." She picked it up and threw it to him—very softly—but he didn't even try to grab it and it fell to the floor.

"Come here," he ordered, his teeth clenched.

"No way."

Revenge was probably the uppermost thought on his mind. And he seemed much too physically able for her. She studied the distance between him and the exit, deciding that her chances of making it through that door to safety didn't look too good.

"Right now, Amelia."

"Bye!"

Without a second thought Amelia took off at a dead run for the opposite door, out onto the patio, and across the backyard lawn, heading for the trees at the rear of the huge lot. She ran as if the devil himself was after her, which in a way he was. Colt had looked mad enough to spit fire and brimstone.

When she had sprinted far enough into the trees to make her movements hard to see, she turned and twisted and then doubled back a short distance until she could run no farther. She stopped with her back pressed against a huge tree and peered around the thick trunk toward the house. Not a soul in sight. With a relieved sigh she sank to the ground, taking deep, ragged breaths.

Maybe he hadn't followed her. He had looked pretty tired, after all. Anyway, it didn't matter now, because she had gotten the jump on him and would be able to hear him coming long before he reached her out here. Dry, crackling leaves blanketed the ground like heavy snow, silent now and lying in golden piles after yesterday's wild winds.

117

What had come over her? She didn't possess a temper to speak of, yet Colt seemed to bring out the worst in her. Never in her adult life had she thrown anything at anyone, not even her ex-fiancé, Richard, and he had deserved her anger and then some.

They had known each other for a year and been engaged for two months when he had announced his preference for casual sex. It wasn't that she didn't satisfy him, he had hastened to reassure her, but the last few months with her had proven to him he couldn't live without having more than one woman.

He had planned on marrying her anyway, certain that she wouldn't object to his other interests. His enormous ego had actually led him to believe that she would marry him and accept him as he was. Amelia had wasted no time in setting him straight on what marriage vows meant to her. She had calmly removed her engagement ring, set it on the low coffee table, and left him for good.

Months later, after her requested transfer to San Antonio was complete, she came to realize the full extent of her good fortune. At least Richard had been honest with her, had given her the opportunity to see what kind of man he was before she consented to spend the rest of her life with him. She'd even sent him a thank-you card, not so much for what he had given her, as for what he hadn't, considering his promiscuity.

Shortly after that she began to date again, liking men too much to let one bad experience get her down. But she had become much more selective.

There would be no playboys for Amelia. Her dreams for the future included a husband who loved her alone, and children. She was back in the chase.

Now here she was two years later, hiding behind a tree from a man far more devastating than any she'd ever encountered before. He brought out facets of her personality she had never known existed, from the raging temper she had just displayed to an almost irrepressible, burning desire for him.

The trouble was, he might be a playboy, too, and she knew what they were like. You couldn't change them. Or could you? That was the real challenge, the one she suddenly realized she had decided to accept.

Assuming he didn't murder her for having thrown a pear at him.

With a shrug of her shoulders she leaned back against the damp earth and crackling leaves. It felt so good to be outside, the warm sun dappling through the trees, throwing shadows and patterns across her body. Amelia closed her eyes and stretched her limbs out, letting herself feel the soft blades of grass, listening to the busy sounds of nature. Nothing interfered with those sounds out here, not traffic or people or phones. Just a few more minutes alone, then she'd go back and face the music.

But she wasn't nearly as safe as she imagined. Colt had spent a fair amount of his boyhood playing among these trees. He knew the woods well, and had plenty of training at moving with stealth.

As Amelia was sprawling out with innocent abandon, he was creeping silently toward her.

She didn't appear too worried about his possible wrath, he noticed. It was going to be a lot of fun teaching her the error of her ways. Granted he had undressed her with his eyes and had been well on the way to doing more in his mind, but so what? So what if she had been provoked? Did that give her the right to throw fruit at him? It most certainly did not.

He stood over her and released the somewhat battered pear. It hit right on target, rolling off her flat stomach to the ground and back toward him. Colt picked it up and thought seriously about dropping it on her again.

"What the . . ."

Amelia struggled to sit up, but found she had to settle for propping herself up on her elbows. Colt was standing between her legs, his boots planted firmly on the hem of her jeans near each of her feet.

"Remember me?" Colt asked softly.

"I'd rather not," she muttered, plopping back to the ground, one arm covering her face. Why did she feel like she was in big trouble? "I'd apologize, but I'm not a bit sorry."

Colt let the comment pass. She would pay for it soon enough. "What have you got against pears? I've always liked their shape myself."

Amelia dropped her arm above her head and stared up at him. He was holding the pear in the palm of his hand and smoothing his thumb over the yellow, softly rounded bottom.

120

"And how long have you had this thing for fruit?"

The hint of a smile appeared on his face, one of his coal-black eyebrows rising queruously. The expression stretched his scar into a long, thin line, giving him a roguish appearance that Amelia found unbelievably exciting. He was planning something. Her heart thumped in her chest.

"Aren't you in a rather precarious position to be making wisecracks?" he asked, moving her legs a bit farther apart with his feet. Her eyes went wide and Colt chuckled, then dropped the pear again.

This time she caught it gracefully, but her triumph turned into distaste. "Yuck! It's all soft on the bottom."

"So are you, if I remember correctly."

Did she dare? He made such a perfect target. She hefted the fruit in her hand, the temptation to throw it at him dangerously overwhelming in spite of the consequences.

"Go ahead," he taunted, kneeling between her legs and placing his hands to each side of her head. With a subtle, sensuous motion, he rubbed one of his knees along the inside of her thigh. "In the immortal words of Dirty Harry, 'make my day.'"

"You wouldn't!"

"Try me. We can't be seen or heard from the house out here," he informed her. His voice was soft, but there was an evil gleam in his eyes.

Amelia's body seemed poured into her skintight jeans. Colt didn't know how she managed to zip them up, but he was going to find out how to unzip them, sooner or later. The middle button on her plaid blouse was straining to remain closed under her rapid breathing, making him want to help it along, pop it open to reveal the rest of her lacy brassiere and the soft flesh beneath.

She blushed a fetching pale pink that cascaded down her face to disappear into the open collar of her shirt. Colt was doing it to her again, mentally stripping her of every last piece of clothing. Amelia wiggled under him, feeling vulnerable and aroused at the same time, his body now scant inches from hers. The heat of his legs seemed to sear right through the fabric of their jeans and scorch the sensitive skin of her thighs. His fingers were tangling in her hair as his lips teased her mouth into opening up for him.

She struggled for a moment, then realized she wanted this kiss as much as he did. She gave in to the pleasure, her lips hungry against his. He sucked gently on her tongue, drawing it deeper into his mouth.

Her whole body seemed to tighten in a passionate reflex that was almost frustration, as a part of her fought the desire welling up within her. Her hands clenched, especially the one which held the pear.

"Oh, gross!" she shrieked, throwing the offending stuff aside in a spray of juice.

Colt roared with laughter. "Justice!"

"I'll get you for this," she vowed, bringing her arm around to wipe her hand on his clean jeans.

He rolled out of her range and stood up, brushing himself off. "You already did," he reminded her.

"You asked for it." She stood up, too, glaring at him.

"You mean the way I looked at you in the kitchen?" Colt asked, laughing at her outrage. "If you get this mad when I just envision you with your clothes off, I can hardly wait to see what happens when I take them off for real."

"Fat chance!"

He picked a leaf from her hair and ran his fingers through the silky brown tresses. "Here, let me help you."

Amelia backed away from him. "No. I think you've helped quite enough already, thank you!"

She only had a certain amount of control and he was testing it to the limit. The outline of his masculine form was still imprinted clearly on her tingling body, making her want his touch. The fact that she needed his touch so much told her that she couldn't allow it, not right now anyway. She needed time to think rationally about her actions.

"Afraid?"

As a matter of fact she was. But she wasn't going to let him know that. "I can remove a few leaves, I'm not helpless," she retorted, then turned and started walking swiftly toward the house.

Colt easily kept pace with her, enjoying the way she bounced along. Her hands were rhythmically clenching into tight little fists. He grinned broadly, delighted to know he was getting to her. Before she could go through the glass patio doors, he put a hand on her shoulder and stopped her.

"Just answer me one thing."

"And that is?" Amelia looked at him warily,

trying to ignore the heat of his fingers as he held her still.

He leaned close to her ear and whispered softly, "What color are your panties?"

She jerked away from him, struggling not to sock him in the nose, knowing how he would retaliate this time. His eyes were dancing merrily, mischief evident as he raised his brows. It wasn't all that shocking a question, but the intimacy it implied sent a liquid fire boiling into her lower abdomen.

"You'll never find out," she replied, then strolled into the house with as much dignity as her shaking limbs would allow.

Colt leaned against the doorjamb, silently accepting the challenge she had thrown at him. Amelia was slowly permeating his life, even his dreams. He hadn't been able to get her out of his mind for the last two days, and it had been a rough struggle not to touch her in the last week.

There were a lot of reasons he had been so evasive, not the least of which were his grandparents' devious plans. He had lived through so many of their attempts to find him a wife that he made it a point to outwit them simply on principle. Some very real business concerns had also served to help him stay away from Amelia, in particular a stock deal that was driving him crazy and the woman who owned that stock. She seemed bent on hanging him as a trophy on her bedroom wall in return for the controlling shares Colt so badly wanted.

And then there was Amelia herself, a woman he sensed was looking for a lasting relationship—she wasn't the type to have casual affairs. At first he had been bound and determined to steer a wide path around her.

Colt still didn't know why he'd reacted so strongly to her a week ago. But seeing her clad in that skimpy blue robe, knowing she was stark naked beneath, had driven him wild with desire. For the first time he was actually interested in the woman being thrown at him. And he was worried. He had been running so long from her type he wasn't sure how to proceed—or if he really wanted to. Only time would tell.

He entered the kitchen to find his grandparents seated at the table drinking coffee. Amelia wasn't present, thank heavens. He didn't know how much longer he could keep up the charade of not being interested in her.

"Colt, I was going to come looking for you, boy."

The look in Michael's eyes immediately put him on guard. He helped himself to a cup of coffee and leaned against the counter with studied nonchalance. Distance sometimes helped when dealing with these two consummate manipulators.

"What's up?"

"Amelia's driving down to San Antonio today."

"So?"

"What do you mean, so? We don't want her driving all that way alone, do we? Anything could go wrong."

Colt was well aware of that fact. The people after her brother could easily switch targets. Now that he knew her plans, he was going to accompany Amelia whether she liked it or not. He was not, however, going to make it easy for his grandfather. Michael had more meddling in mind.

"I don't know, Pop. I'm pretty tired."

"You can nap on the way. She is our guest, after all."

Colt almost smiled at how easily he had changed tactics, going from an appeal to his protective nature to prodding his sense of hospitality in the space of a breath. "I—"

"I know you're free today," Helen interrupted. Then she brought in the big guns, giving him a look he knew only too well. *Do this or suffer the consequences.* When he was little it had been a spanking; now she withheld desserts.

He couldn't stop the smile this time. "Yes, ma'am. When does she want to leave?"

Pop consulted his watch. "In ten minutes. Get moving."

"Can I finish my coffee first?" he asked, gesturing with his mug as he struggled not to laugh at their antics.

"Oh, Michael, where did his parents go wrong?" Helen asked, shaking her head in despair. "All we ask is one little favor and look how he treats us."

"Have you two ever considered going onto the stage together?" he asked, then went and gave Helen a kiss on the cheek. "Don't worry. I'll see to it that our guest doesn't meet her demise." He set his cup in the sink and turned to his grandfather. "I need to talk to you about a call that might come in, Pop."

"Let's go into my study, then. At my age I have to take notes."

Colt followed him out of the kitchen, enjoying the way his grandfather was playing the game. No matter what Michael implied, Colt knew his mind was still as sharp and clear as it ever had been. He used his age entirely to his favor, and those who didn't know him well got sucked in every time.

Michael seated himself in the big leather chair behind his antique desk. Before Colt could say anything he went right for the jugular. "Any luck with the Clarkson deal?"

"Not yet," Colt replied with a grimace, taking a seat.

A smug smile flitted across the old man's mouth. "I won't say I told you so. Yet."

"Thanks," Colt returned dryly. If this stock deal didn't work out, his father and grandfather would never let him live it down. Both had advised him to steer clear of the mess, but the challenge had been too great for him and the profit potential enormous. "Gloria Clarkson will come around, I know it. At the moment, however, her asking price is a bit steep."

Michael chuckled. "Meaning she's asking for a lot of money as well as trying to get her teeth into you."

"It's not her teeth I'm worried about. It's her hands."

"That woman's a maneating tiger shark, boy. I told you that. Why, even I was lucky to get away from her with my skin intact."

Colt looked at him in surprise. "The vamp of Austin made a play for you too?"

Michael nodded in disgust. "With Helen close by at that. But it wasn't Gloria I was worried about at the time, it was Helen. If I had looked twice at that sultry, curvaceous blonde, Helen would have skinned me alive."

"Don't worry, Pop, I'm watching my backside."

"I'll bet she is too," Michael said, chortling with great amusement. "And every other part of your anatomy."

"Are we going to get down to business, or are you planning on teasing me to death?"

His grandfather shrugged. "Ready when you are," he replied, a sly grin spreading across his time-weathered face. "I wouldn't want to make you late for your date with Amelia."

CHAPTER EIGHT

"What are you doing in my car?"

Colt leaned back more comfortably in the reclining bucket seat and kept his eyes closed. "Trying to take a well-deserved nap."

"Get out," Amelia ordered, wrenching open the door on the passenger side. "Right now."

"Can't."

She glared at him. He looked quite at home, snoozing away in her car, his black hair brushing down across his forehead with boyish appeal. "Why not?"

"Orders."

"From whom?"

"I'll give you two guesses," he replied lazily. "Now, quit fooling around and let's go. I sleep better in a moving car."

This was not a part of her plans for the day. She had been looking forward to a nice, quiet drive alone. "Your presence is not wanted or appreciated," she told him. "Are you listening to me? Colt?" She leaned over and yelled right in his ear. "Look at me when I'm talking to you! You are not going to San Antonio with me and that's final."

One lazy, tanned eye lid, richly edged with dark lashes, lifted slightly. He peered through the narrow slit at her and asked, very softly, "What did you say?"

His tone was deadly and Amelia took a step away from the car. "I—I know Helen and Michael mean well, but I really need some time alone, Colt. Just make up some excuse, like you've been doing all week. Tell them you can't go."

"I tried."

"Try harder."

Colt's other eye opened a tiny crack. "It was pointed out to me that it isn't wise for you to go anywhere alone, and I'm afraid I agree. The people after your mysterious John Smith are still at large, you know." A tiny smile lifted the corners of his mouth at the way Amelia's face went suddenly pale. "Besides," he returned, closing his eyes again. "I've decided I want to go. I need the rest, and I won't get it if I'm here worrying about you."

Her heart gave a little jump at the thought. Was he actually worried about her safety? Probably not. She decided he was more likely worried about what Helen and Michael would do to him if he didn't go and something happened to her. And he undoubtedly had something else in mind as well, like pouncing on her the moment they were alone in her apartment.

With a sigh of frustrated resignation Amelia realized that the discussion was over. Colt was going and that was that. He was right, of course; the killers after Nathan might find out about her and try to kidnap her. At the moment, however, that seemed almost preferable to being trapped in the close confines of her car with Colt for a few hours.

The thought made her nerve endings twitch. With an angry snap of her wrist she slammed the car door shut and walked stiffly around to the driver's side, grousing all the way. "Lovely. So much for my peaceful, relaxing trip. I'm a big girl. I can take care of myself. Men!" she exclaimed, slamming her own door and turning the key with a vicious twist. The engine roared to life.

"Don't run over your suitcase."

"What?" Amelia glanced in the rearview mirror and saw the offending piece of luggage sitting exactly where she'd dropped it upon discovering Colt in her car. "Oh," she mumbled sheepishly.

"You weren't planning on going home and staying there, were you? That would be even more dangerous than taking a trip alone."

That plan had indeed crossed her mind. She was getting tired of Michael's meddling, had almost decided to push him to the limit and see what happened. It was possible his threat to abandon her brother was a bluff, and she didn't think he would bring her kicking and screaming back to Austin in any case.

But to Colt she said, "I, um, thought it would be handy to bring back my clothes in."

Colt's sleepy laugh told her he knew that wasn't the whole story. "Sure you did. It won't be good for anything if you squash it flat, though. Would you like me to get it for you?" he offered, his voice mild and clear of any emotion.

Amelia looked at him, but his face was turned

131

away from her, pressed against the plush gray velour seat, his eyes still closed. "Yes."

"Yes what?" he asked, not moving.

"Yes, please," she snapped through clenched teeth.

"Anything for you, honey," he said with an exaggerated southern twang. Easing his length out of the car, he retrieved her suitcase and stowed it in the trunk, then got back into the car and made himself comfortable again. "Ready when you are. Or should I say I'm ready for you anytime?"

His voice was pure velvet, full of unmistakable sexual innuendo. Amelia's hands trembled as she yanked her seat belt across her lap and fumbled with the closure. "B-buckle up," she stammered nervously.

"Allow me."

Nimble fingers closed over hers and eased the latch into place. She pulled her hands away as if stung by a bee. His scent was a spicy lemon aftershave, tart and bracing. Ignoring her glare, he adjusted her shoulder strap, following the four inch width down across her body.

Amelia sucked in her breath and pressed herself back into the bucket seat away from his touch. The back of his head was practically in her throat and effectively hid her view of his actions. Deliberately, his fingers flicked her puckered nipples, their taut forms clearly visible through her thin shirt and sheer bra.

"Excuse me. Terribly sorry," he murmured.

"Sure." Amelia shot him a venomous glare and

put the car into gear, easing down the driveway and onto the road.

"Aren't you going to wait for me to buckle in too?"

"How careless of me," she replied with an evil smile. "We wouldn't want you falling out, would we?"

Colt laughed, buckled his belt, and settled back into his seat. "You wouldn't want to lose me, Amelia."

"No?"

"No. I've got your brother hidden away, remember? And you don't know where he is. You'd better be nice to me or I'll forget where I put him."

"That's blackmail!"

"Sure is," he agreed. Then he yawned and turned his head toward the window, ignoring her outrage. "Wake me when we get to town."

Fuming, Amelia gritted her teeth and negotiated the car into the flow of traffic on the interstate. Colt and his grandfather were very much alike. Blackmailing, manipulating, creepy crawling rodents! This was going to be a long day.

As the miles droned on, Amelia almost managed to forget about her silent, unwanted passenger. Then a guttural noise joined the whine of the tires on asphalt and the rush of wind slipping by outside. She glanced at him out of the corner of her eye.

Colt was sleeping peacefully beside her. His face was turned away from her, and all she could see was a strong jaw and the back of a tanned neck, brushed by black hair. He'd gotten a haircut in the

133

last few days and it looked good, no longer shaggy and out of place. Amelia turned both eyes back to the long, flat road stretching out before her.

What was she going to do? This trip was supposed to be her stand of defiance, her opportunity to call Michael's bluff. According to the reports she was getting on him via Helen, her brother was doing better. He was awake and able to sit up now, even complaining about his confinement. His need of Michael's help and protection would soon be over.

As usual, the old man had thrown a monkey wrench in the works. Colt was along to keep her safe from the killers, but he was also an unwitting pawn in his grandfather's game, there to make sure she returned to Austin. Not that he didn't have his own reasons for making the trip with her, she was sure. She would have to be on guard against his seductive attentions every moment.

Amelia sighed, knowing in her heart it was probably just as well her plans to stand up to Michael had been thwarted. The need for his help might be nearing an end, but there were other things he could do. She didn't want to believe he was so desperate to have a great-grandchild and see Colt married that he would threaten to expose Nathan's true identity, but it was possible.

Defying him was a dead end, for now. Since she couldn't be sure just what he was capable of, what he might do if she openly refused to comply with his wishes, she had to approach the problem differently. Back to the other possibilities.

Actually, there was only one. Deal with Colt.

He was more than a little appealing to her. Just the thought of going to bed with Colt had her senses churning. She wanted him with a burning desire that was completely foreign to her, an all-consuming passion she had never felt before. With him all coherent thoughts went flying out the window, leaving her struggling and defenseless. So far she had managed to return to her senses in the nick of time, but how long could she hold out?

She hadn't forgotten her own private vow to meet his challenge to her womanhood, bend him to her will instead of submitting to his. It was so wonderfully tempting. And it might solve all her problems. Seduce Colt, or allow herself to be seduced by him, and follow Michael's nefarious scheme to its eventual conclusion. But that brought up another problem, one that seemed impossible to get around.

Could a marriage survive on sizzling sex? Maybe, but that part of a relationship might fizzle out as quickly as it began, and it didn't seem like a good basis for a marriage. The last thing she wanted was an unwilling husband or one who wouldn't be faithful to his wife. On that point she was positive of her feelings. When she married, she wanted it to last the rest of her life. Love was the basis she wanted, and she had found herself wondering lately if Colt knew the meaning of the word.

As if to mock her inner turmoil, Colt moved in his sleep and his hand slipped between her jean-clad thighs, snuggling in comfortably. She almost lost control of the car for a moment, then managed to calm down, gripping the steering wheel tightly and glancing over at him.

He appeared to be sound asleep but it was hard to tell with the rest of his body turned away from her gaze. Amelia could feel the warming heat of his hand on her tingling skin through the thick denim material, and felt the nipples of her breasts changing into small, firm rosette buds. His fingers moved slightly and she suppressed a gasp of surprised pleasure.

This had to stop. With a calm she did not feel, Amelia picked his hand up by the wrist and placed it carefully on his waist. He didn't even twitch. Was he acting? She'd long ago decided that he had inherited more than a smidgen of his grandfather's acting abilities.

What a crazy situation her sisterly love for Nathan had gotten her into! She had promised to seduce this tantalizing man. Her every cell cried out for her to go ahead and do so. Even her own logical mind told her that trapping Colt into matrimony and fatherhood was the best way to deal with her predicament—maybe the only way, whether she liked it or not.

Amelia shook her head in disgust. There weren't going to be any easy solutions, and until she got to know Colt much better—mentally, not physically —she wasn't going to make any more rash decisions. It was enough to make a girl want to run away and hide.

"Colt, we're in San Antonio."
Amelia felt the muscles of his arm stiffen be-

neath her touch as he woke up. She removed her hand and grabbed her purse, then got out of the car. "I'll be in my apartment," she told him.

He watched her walk up the cement apron skirting her place and enter an apartment, leaving the door partially open. With a groan he hauled his long body out of the vehicle and stretched his arms wide, then followed her inside, shutting the door behind him.

It was a typical rental, small, every room and door visible from his vantage point in the entryway. He made a thorough perusal of the place, noting its warm, cozy, lived-in feeling. Nothing matched, the furniture from different periods and styles. Small potted plants dotted the windowsill and covered an old carved hope-chest in the living room.

Entering the kitchen, he opened the refrigerator and removed a can of diet pop. That was all there was to drink besides some thick, pink, frothy-looking stuff in a jar, and he wasn't going to take his chances. It might be anything. There also didn't seem to be anything sweet hidden in there waiting for him.

"Make yourself at home," Amelia commented dryly when she found him with his arm hung over the door of her refrigerator, studying its contents.

"I am," he returned, opening a can of soda. "Want one?" he offered, holding the drink out toward her.

Amelia managed to take the can without touching his fingers. "Thank you." He still looked tired, his face drawn as if his nap had hindered rather than helped him. "What are you looking for?"

"Don't you keep anything sweet in here?" he asked.

Amelia smiled at the question. "Look in the freezer."

Colt opened the tiny compartment and glanced inside. He pulled out some frozen miniature candy bars. "I was really hoping for something I could eat right away, not next Wednesday," he said, hitting a chocolate bar on the counter.

"Here." She took the candy away from him, unwrapped it, and started to eat the fragments that had broken off when he'd hit it on the hard surface. "See? These are great frozen. You just have to know how to eat them."

Colt raised his eyebrows, skeptical of her claim. But he tried it her way, found that he liked it, and finished off five of the rock-hard confections one after the other, while Amelia watched and laughed. He ignored her. The chocolate was starting to make him feel like a human being again. He just might make it till lunch.

"What's on the agenda today?"

"I," she stressed, "meaning I, and I alone, am going to pick up my mail from a neighbor, run a few errands, and check in at work."

"Fine with me. You know the town, it should be safe enough," he said with a thoughtful nod. "I've had about four hours sleep in the last forty-eight and I'm out on my feet. Just point me toward your bed and go on without me."

Amelia didn't know whether to be pleased or

disturbed. She didn't want him along when she ran her errands, but she didn't particularly relish the thought of him in her bed either. Her mind was already conjuring up erotic pictures of him tangled in her sheets.

"It's easy to find," she said, pleased with the solid, even level of her voice. "I need to change my clothes first, then the bedroom is all yours."

"All right." Colt scrutinized her firm derrière as she turned around and left the room. "If you're sure you don't need any help."

"I'll manage," she called back.

"I knew you were going to say that," he muttered, then sighed and grabbed another candy bar, settling down on the brown corduroy sofa to await her return.

Amelia closed the bedroom door, wishing she had a lock on it. But it wouldn't keep him out anyway, she supposed, so she shrugged and hastily stripped off her clothes. She had already decided on what to wear and was dressed in minutes. A quick perusal of the room satisfied her. The bed was made and she hadn't left anything feminine out to give him ideas. He had enough of his own.

Colt opened his eyes a crack when she emerged from the bedroom. Then he promptly opened them wider. "Very nice," he commented.

A long-sleeved, high-necked blouse the color of cocoa was teamed with a matching skirt that had a cocoa-and-jungle-leaves print. Sensible low-heeled walking sandals completed the outfit. He could see red-and-gold earrings peeking out from beneath the swirl of her hair as she picked up her purse and walked to the front door.

"I'll be gone a couple of hours. If you decide to leave, there's a spare key in the silverware drawer." She couldn't miss his appreciative gaze. It felt nice, made her feel quite feminine, she realized.

Colt stood up and stretched. "I'm not going anywhere except into that bed," he murmured. "Care to join me?"

She opened the door and stepped outside, not bothering to answer him. It was good to be back on her home turf again. Austin was beautiful, with its rolling, tree-covered hills and inviting lakes, but San Antonio had been her home for some time now. Although the area was somewhat more barren and hot, she liked it just as well. There was a sense of history here, Texas history. Downtown was the Alamo, where a group of brave men had taken a stand against Santa Anna, fighting to their deaths.

Then there was the River Walk, where you could stroll along the banks, feeling almost lost in time, yet all the while enjoy wonderful food or listen to a jazz trio playing at a sidewalk café. It was a pleasant town, big and growing. The Tower of the Americas was a soaring reminder that it had been the location of the Hemisfair.

Amelia finished up her errands quickly, but it still took her longer than she'd planned. And yet, when she returned, she sat out in front of her apartment for a bit longer, steeling her nerves to go inside.

As tired as he had looked, Colt was probably still asleep in her bed, tangled up in her pale gray sheets. They were her favorites, with bold lemon stripes running horizontally and diagonally. His dark tan would stand out even better against those colors. She could almost see his muscular thighs and broad back against that background now, and realized she was picturing him in the nude. Her curiosity was killing her.

"Why are you torturing yourself this way?" she asked, chiding her reflection in the mirror. She didn't have an answer for herself, so she collected her suitcase and the large stack of mail she'd received in her absence and made her way into the apartment.

At first, silence greeted her. Maybe he had decided to go somewhere after all, probably a bakery. She smiled, surprised by the affection she felt when she thought about his sweet tooth. Then she heard the shower running. The door to her bedroom stood wide open, and she viewed the empty bed, the rumpled sheets thrown helter skelter. If she had gotten here sooner, perhaps she would have caught him by surprise, stumbling to the bathroom sleepy eyed and undressed.

She gave herself a mental slap, then walked over to the breakfast bar separating the kitchen from the living room and sat down with a resolute sigh. Time to pay the bills.

After carefully reading each piece of mail and making sure of the proper amounts, she started writing checks, trying to ignore everything but the task before her. When the bathroom door opened she kept her back to him, pretending he wasn't even there. She could tell by the sounds he was making that he was getting dressed.

"I'm starved," Colt announced as he entered the room.

Amelia turned in her chair and was greeted by a new man, refreshed, eyes sparkling with life. "What did you want to eat?"

"Hmm?" Colt hummed, mesmerized as he watched her lick a stamp for her phone bill and press it in the corner of the blue envelope. He wished her tongue would caress him that way. "Oh. Why don't we go down to the River Walk and decide from there?"

"Sounds good," she responded, and gathered up her bills. "I need to mail these along the way."

"Can it wait until after we eat? My stomach is getting ready to file a petition to divorce me for cruelty." He patted his taut belly ruefully.

Amelia laughed. "Sure. Mine's a bit restless too."

After savoring a hearty meal of the spicy cuisine known as Tex-Mex, the pair walked along the river, enjoying the festive mood of the tourists and the cooler temperature near the water. They were also enjoying each other's company, much to their mutual surprise. It seemed they got along quite well when the getting together was their idea and not Helen's or Michael's.

Finally, Colt broke down and looked at his watch. "We need to get going," he said with obvious reluctance. He'd slept part of the day away and now wasn't going to have time for his seduction plans. "We left the car over this way, I think."

"One street over," Amelia agreed. "But what's the hurry?"

Colt looked at her in surprise. "The party, remember?"

"Party?" It was her turn to look baffled. "I don't know anything about a party."

"The one by the state capitol building," he prompted.

She was still confused, so confused she let him drive, a mistake she had vowed not to make again after the ride to the restaurant. Colt may have been a fine helicopter pilot, but he had to be the world's worst driver, perhaps because there wasn't an air traffic controller telling him where to go. They hadn't hit anybody, but it wasn't for lack of trying on his part.

Amelia took hold of the dashboard and gritted her teeth. "No one told me about a party, near the capitol building or anywhere else. And what does it have to do with me, anyway?"

"We're attending a formal function tonight with Helen and Michael, no excuses accepted."

He had to go, and Amelia was going with him whether she liked it or not. She would be a perfect buffer between him and Gloria Clarkson. It might not throw the maneating blonde off her stride by much, but it was worth a try.

Amelia was staring at him. *"We're* attending?"

He nodded, concentrating on the increasing flow of traffic. "I'm going for very important business reasons, and you're going because I need an es-

143

cort." What he needed was a shield to keep Gloria's claws off him, but Amelia didn't need to know that. "Besides, my grandparents are going, and you know as well as I do they won't let you stay home alone."

She grimaced in distaste. "I hate big parties."

"I usually avoid social functions like the plague too," Colt told her, giving her a sympathetic smile. "But this one is a must."

"I won't go."

A smile tugged at his lips, his eyes crinkling at the corners. "Tell that to Helen and Michael."

She fell back in her seat, frustrated beyond belief. No one had tried to direct her life this much since she'd left home at eighteen, and that was seven years ago. Maybe the party was a must, but she knew what Michael was really up to; he wanted to show off his grandson and the newest mate he'd found for him.

"Well?" Colt prompted. "Are you going to tell them you won't go?"

"Stuff it."

Colt had to laugh at her peeved expression. He'd been on the receiving end of his grandparents' good intentions too many times not to feel sorry for her. But it just so happened that this time their plans meshed with his own. And who knows, he thought, his smile one of wicked, sensuous anticipation. Maybe he could get Amelia tipsy and convince her to drop this charade of keeping her distance from him.

They drove on in silence for a moment, Colt whistling merrily and Amelia fuming.

"How formal?" she asked at last.

"Tuxedos for the men. The ladies usually deck out in long gowns and jewels."

She breathed a sigh of relief. "That lets me out. I don't own either of those things."

"Don't count on it. I'm sure your fairy godmother, Helen, intends to provide for you."

The conviction in his voice only reinforced her own disheartening belief that he was right. There wasn't any chance they were going to let her get out of this party tonight. She hated big, formal affairs, had never felt at ease in such situations. Her mother was a gifted social butterfly, able to talk to anyone about anything, but she hadn't passed that particular trait along to her daughter.

They arrived at her apartment, and Colt came around to open her door for her. "Are you going to sulk all night?" he asked.

"I'm not sulking," she snapped, following him up the concrete walk.

"Fooled me." He unlocked the door and allowed her to enter first. "You've got ten minutes to pack," he said, consulting his watch.

She entered the bedroom without a reply. Her fate was sealed and she might as well accept it gracefully for the time being. While she packed, Colt went to use her phone, making no effort to hide the conversation from her. She kept an ear cocked in the direction of the bedroom door, hoping to pick up some useful information. Knowing where her brother was might not help much at this point, but it couldn't hurt.

"Hey, Pete. Did you get the bird back all right?"

There was a moment of silence, then Colt's laughter. "No, no problems. Except for a wild woman with a gun, things went according to my plans."

What was he talking about? The bird was probably a helicopter, but what was that about a wild woman with a gun? Had there been another attempt on Nathan's life and no one was telling her? The thought infuriated her.

"I'll give you every juicy detail the next time we meet," Colt was saying. Amelia's frown deepened. What juicy details? "I'll keep you posted, Pete. Thanks again."

He hung up the phone and Amelia doubled her packing efforts, her allotted time almost gone. A woman with a gun, a wild one who no doubt accounted for the juicy details Colt spoke of, and a man named Pete who evidently figured in her brother's late-night escape from Austin. Amelia wanted to know what was going on, and before this day was over, she intended to do just that. Maybe this party would come in handy after all. It wouldn't be easy, considering his size, but she could try to get him tipsy and see what sort of secrets she could get him to inadvertently spill.

"Ready?"

His presence startled her but she didn't look at him, worried that her dismay would show through. "Almost," she replied, folding a pair of jeans and adding them to the bag.

"Bring the ones you wore today." His words came across as a direct order. The man was definitely used to being obeyed when he issued a command. "I like the way they fit you. Nice and tight." He grinned.

Choosing to ignore him, Amelia closed the suitcase and clicked the locks shut. Colt moved forward and lifted it off the bed. For a moment their eyes met, then he looked longingly at the tangled sheets.

"Thanks for the use of the bed," he murmured close to her ear. His free hand was resting on the small of her back. "Nice firm mattress. Just right for two."

Amelia stepped away from his touch, her spine warm and tingling. "Give me a minute and I'll be ready," she said, entering the bathroom and shutting the door firmly.

With practiced ease she removed her contacts, cleaned them, and slipped on her new half-rimmed glasses. It was a good thing she had a lot of frames she looked nice in, since on doctor's orders she couldn't wear her contacts as much as she used to. It was a shame she couldn't find a doctor who could order her to stay away from Colt; the man was definitely hazardous to her nervous system.

With a few strokes of the brush her hair fell obediently into place, and she felt as prepared as she ever would be to make it through the rest of the day with him. He wasn't anywhere to be seen when she emerged from the bathroom, however, so she made the bed, closed the blinds, and turned off the lights. It might be some time before she got back.

She strode to the front door, hurrying, not wanting him to be angry with her for taking so much time. The better Colt's mood, the more she might be able to get out of him on the drive back to Austin. In her haste to leave, she flung open the door and barged right into him.

"Did you miss me?" he murmured, holding her in the circle of his arms.

"W-where were you?"

"Talking to your neighbor."

More than likely he'd been trapped by her. LeaAnn was the most proficient gossip in the complex. If Amelia saw her coming, she went the other way. "Interesting, I'm sure."

"Mmm, I'll say. Do you really date a different guy every night? Seven days a week?"

"Wouldn't you like to know?"

"I certainly would."

Amelia struggled and he allowed her to escape his inviting grasp. The question had sounded like jealousy, but she knew that couldn't be. They scarcely knew each other. Ignoring his intent gaze, she went back inside to get her purse, then shut and locked the door behind her on her way out. He was still standing there, his expression speculative.

"I'll drive," she said, knowing that would get his mind off whatever her nosy neighbor had told him.

"You wouldn't get us to Austin on time."

"But we'll get there alive and in one piece," she returned, holding her hand out for the keys.

He shook his head, turned, and got into the car, starting the engine as she joined him. "We can't be late. Relax. I've never had a ticket or a wreck in my life."

"Dumb luck," Amelia muttered, buckling her seat belt firmly before he could do it for her.

"And just what is wrong with my driving, may I ask?"

"For one thing, you go too fast for my taste."

Amelia fixed him with a glare that told him she wasn't just talking about his driving. Colt's laughter rang in her ears. He put one strong hand on her leg, gently caressing the sensitive skin on the inside of her thigh with his fingertips.

"Lady," he said softly, his voice full of an infinite, sensual promise, "you haven't even had a taste of how fast I can move yet."

CHAPTER NINE

Given the choice, Amelia would have preferred to walk back to Austin. For one thing, compared to her sedate style, Colt drove like a maniac. Then there was the way he would occasionally glance at her or place his hand intimately on her thigh, his eyes gleaming mischievously, as if he had some private party of his own in mind for her this evening. All in all, she decided she had liked it better when she was at the wheel and he was fast asleep.

Then again, she couldn't ask questions with him napping, so she tried to ignore the uneasy feeling of impending doom and concentrated on getting him to talk. She had already wasted enough time sulking; the blazing sun was setting in the west and a purplish dusk was beginning to descend upon them.

"I'm curious, Colt," she said at last.

"She speaks!"

Amelia ignored his theatrics. "Do you work for your grandfather, or is it a partnership?"

"Not really a partnership. More of a family business. . . . All the Colts are involved," he explained, somewhat surprised by the question. "Michael and Helen, me, my father and mother. I suppose Pop is the executive officer—in his mind he certainly is—but we all have equal say."

"I thought your father was a lawyer."

"He is."

It occurred to her she knew more about the family in general than she did about Colt. "Are you one also?"

He chuckled quietly. "Hardly. My father would have liked that, I suppose, but he didn't push. As it was I barely survived college to get my degree—a degree Michael insisted I had to get even though he didn't make it through high school himself."

"What do you mean you barely survived? College isn't all that bad."

"It was for me," he replied with a sour grimace. "My father was a good student, but I'd already had a taste of making my own money and living alone. Those business classes never made sense to me and still don't. I learned more from Dad and Pop in a couple of months than I did in three years of college."

Amelia laughed. "That reminds me. Three Michaels. People must have a heck of a time when they have to deal with all of you at once." Her smile faltered. What a horrible concept! If Colt's father was anything like his grandfather . . . She forced the thought out of her mind and continued. "I mean, what does everyone call your father?"

"Mr. Colt," he answered in a somber voice, his expression ominous. "You'll see. Along with about six hundred of the social élite, you'll be meeting

151

my parents tonight as well. This party is for charity, one of my mother's pet projects."

Meet his parents! No wonder Michael wanted her at this party; she was being led like a sacrificial lamb to the altar. "Oh, brother," she muttered under her breath. "There has to be some way out of this."

Colt took one look at her face and started laughing so hard he had to slow the car down for a moment. "You really don't like socializing, do you?" he managed at last, interpreting her horrified expression as stage fright. "Relax. I was just kidding. There will be some snobs there to be sure, but I'll be right by your side and I know the people to avoid. And my folks are really nice. You'll love them."

"Peachy," Amelia grumbled. It wasn't the crowd she was worried about. It was the whole idea of meeting his parents. That was, after all, one of the steps along the path to marriage. Would there be no end to the torture this evening? "Just peachy."

She didn't notice, but Colt was frowning now as well. Amelia would like his parents. They'd like her too. And they weren't above doing a bit of matchmaking themselves, though they weren't in his grandparents' league by a long shot. There wasn't any help for it, though. If he wanted to get through the night without Gloria Clarkson's fingerprints all over him, he would have to keep Amelia at his side no matter what his family made of the situation.

"They'll be pretty busy, though," Colt said, as

much to reassure himself as Amelia. He forced his mind back to the conversation and smiled at her. "And most people call my father Mike."

Amelia was quite willing to forget about the evening to come as well. "Michael, Mike, and Colt," she said, looking at him thoughtfully. "I guess you lucked out, didn't you?"

"Why do you say that?"

"Because," she replied, trying not to laugh but giggling helplessly anyway, "the most logical progression would have been Michael, Mike, and little Mikey."

She didn't know how close that had come to being a reality. He glared at her, but she was still laughing and didn't notice. "It took a lot of temper tantrums to keep that from happening," he informed her. "And it's not funny."

"I think Mikey is cute." The name didn't suit him at all, but she couldn't resist teasing him.

He slid his sunglasses down his nose, peering over the rims and shooting her a sharp, steely glance. "Forget it!"

"Yes, sir!" Amelia returned, giving him a mock salute.

She watched him as he removed his sunglasses completely and put them on the dashboard. Then, one finger smoothed its way down the scar on his cheek, almost as if he was easing the tightness there. She really wanted to ask him how he'd gotten that scar. But the few times she'd seen him touch it his face had become shuttered and his demeanor unapproachable, as he was now. Her curiosity would have to wait till she knew him better.

153

And there was only one way to do that. After a while his frown went away and he started smiling again, a rather evil smile, she noted, but a smile nonetheless.

"What exactly is it that you do for a living?" she asked, deciding to venture another question.

Colt glanced at her, wondering what her interest was in knowing all this. Was she taking his grandparents' cloaked invitation to wed him seriously? "We buy stock in companies, usually small ones that are undervalued and have good growth potential."

"That's it?" She didn't understand his explanation, or how they made money, but then she'd never understood how the stock market worked either. "Seems awfully simple."

He chuckled, feeling his bad mood slip away. There were a lot of things bothering him. The Clarkson deal was going to drive him insane, and then there was his undeniable need for Amelia and his doubts about where that might lead. As far as Amelia went, however, the problem was the cure. There was something about her that made him feel carefree and young, able to forget his business problems for a while.

"It is pretty simple in theory, the old Wall Street standby. Buy low, then sell the stock when it appreciates to an acceptable level."

Now, that part made sense to her. "Sounds like a precarious way to make a living." She had always held a job that handed her a steady paycheck, and usually it included lots of overtime.

"It has it moments. Generally we don't go after

154

the huge profits; we're content with a good return, and that makes the transactions less risky for us."

"What happens if the stock goes way down?"

Colt shot her an amused look. She really didn't know anything about stock. "We buy a controlling interest in companies and make sure management is doing its job. If they are, then a company will prosper; if they aren't, then we see to it that management is replaced."

"Pretty cold blooded," Amelia said, shivering at the underlying cold steel in his voice.

He shrugged. "Business usually is. But think about it," he added, wanting her to understand. If he had trouble with the Clarkson woman tonight, Amelia might serve not only as a shield but as a referee. "If a company is mismanaged and goes under, the employees of that company are left out in the freezing cold, without jobs."

"I guess I never looked at it that way before," she admitted thoughtfully.

"A lot of people don't. As a matter of fact, I've been dealing all week with a person who doesn't, and it has me so mad I can barely see straight," he said bitterly. "My family likes to make money, no question of that, but at least we look at the larger picture. When you take control of a company, you have to take the responsibilities that go with it."

Colt breathed deeply, struggling to control the almost murderous emotions he felt when he thought about Gloria Clarkson and her stupidity. She didn't have the vaguest idea of how to run the small company her husband had left her. If vital decisions weren't made in the near future, she was going to drive the firm right into bankruptcy.

That would be more than a shame, it would be a crime, considering the company's potential. Colt held a significant number of shares in it, but not enough, and she was playing cat-and-mouse games with him as he tried to outmaneuver her for the controlling interest. There was a lot of money to be made, but the firm would have to be put back on its feet first. All Gloria could think about was getting Colt into her bed and if at all possible a ring on her finger.

Amelia studied the troubled, preoccupied expression on his face, wondering what had him so riled up. His hands were clenching the steering wheel and his knuckles were chalk-white. Fascinated, she observed him as he seemed to unwind, like a spinning top letting go of the thread. His shoulders relaxed and his breathing deepened until he had himself under control again.

"What was that all about?" she asked him.

"Excuse me?" He looked at her, then smiled and shrugged self-consciously. "Oh. Sorry. I tend to get wrapped up in my work sometimes."

Amelia nodded. "I know what you mean. You should learn to relax."

"I have a few ideas on that subject," he said, placing his hand suggestively on her thigh and moving it slowly upward. "Care to hear them?"

She picked his hand up and placed it back in his lap. "That won't be necessary. I have the feeling I know exactly what you have in mind."

"Good." Colt gave her a winning smile, then let

his gaze linger for a moment on her legs as she shifted in the bucket seat, her nylon-clad calves shapely and appealing. "Then it won't come as a surprise."

"Very little you do surprises me anymore," she informed him with a haughty air. Suddenly, he hit the brakes. Amelia lunged for the dashboard. "Except that."

"Sorry." He pointed up ahead at the police cruiser that sat behind a car at the side of the road, its lights flashing in the gathering darkness. "Poor guy. But better him than me."

"Real compassionate, Colt."

"You have to look for the positive side in everything," he informed her. "That's my mother's philosophy."

Amelia was still looking for the positive side to the mess she'd gotten herself involved in, but she wasn't sure there was one. At least this trip had been good for one thing: she had gotten Colt talking, and quite candidly at that. Maybe she wouldn't have to get him drunk after all.

"Where do you live?" she asked abruptly.

His eyebrows shot up. "Now, there's an opening line if I ever heard one."

"Seriously."

Michael had ordered him not to tell Amelia about the ranch, something about it being safer for her and her brother if she didn't know where he would end up. Colt didn't really see the logic in that. If someone kidnapped her, they'd be more likely to hold her for ransom to get at the mysterious John Smith than to waste time questioning her.

Besides, he wanted Amelia willingly by his side tonight, and if that meant answering her questions, he would. He just wouldn't let her know her brother would be going there.

"I have a ranch between Austin and Dallas," he replied.

What Amelia knew about ranches you could write on a one-by-two-inch piece of paper. "You own livestock?"

"Horses, and a few head of cattle. Hold on."

Amelia grabbed for the dashboard again as he suddenly swerved from the far left side of the road across three lanes of sparse traffic to make their exit. "We could have circled back," she said, her heart pounding furiously.

"It would have taken us too long, and we're already late. Besides, there wasn't a car within hitting distance."

"Sure. They just honked at you to say hello."

Colt did a lot of twisting and turning, and though she had to hold on for dear life, she also had to admit that he was actually a pretty capable driver. A lunatic, perhaps, but capable. The road they ended up on was evidently a shortcut; it didn't seem like any time at all before they were pulling down his grandparents' driveway.

"Here we are," Colt announced, parking her car off to one side of the three-car garage. "All safe and sound."

"Like I said before. Dumb luck," she muttered, getting out of the car.

Helen was standing in the open garage, hands on her hips, glaring at them as they walked down the brightly lighted driveway. "And just where have you two been? It's after seven!"

Colt grinned lazily at his grandmother. "Amelia didn't want to come back."

"You're such a terrible tease. And an even worse liar," Helen returned, shaking a finger at him. Then she turned toward Amelia and took hold of her arm, guiding her into the house. "We have to hurry, dear. Kathleen—that's Colt's mother, I'm sure he forgot to tell you—doesn't want us to be late." Her eyes sparkled. "Just wait till you see the dress I found for you!"

Fortunately, it was easy to get lost in a room with six hundred or so people. Amelia simply skirted around the outside of the circles formed by the different conversation groups, pretending she knew where she was going and keeping an eye out for Colt. He had lived up to his promise to stay by her side for the most part, but when he had gotten trapped into a business discussion with a cigar smoking gentleman, Amelia saw her chance and excused herself to look for the ladies' room. Then she set off to look for a means of covert escape.

Not that the party was all that bad, really. Dinner had been served at eight, for the smaller gathering of people who had made quite substantial contributions to Kathleen Colt's charity. Amelia and Colt shared a table with his grandparents and four other people, Helen easily keeping the conversational ball bouncing.

After dinner everyone had drifted into the cavernous reception room, where they joined the rest of the invited guests. In the name of charity they had all proceeded to delve into the supplies of the well-stocked cash bars situated at either end of the vast hall.

The cocktail party was a huge success, but Amelia, not much of a drinker and even less of an idle chatterer, had stood about all the socializing she could for one evening. She worked her way toward an exit, smiling at people as if she knew them, deliverance almost within her grasp.

Then someone grabbed her arm. "Coward," Colt whispered in her ear, slipping his arm around her waist.

"Oh! I was, um, still looking for the powder room."

"You'll have plenty to powder. Lying makes your nose grow longer, you know," he told her sagely. "Allow me to escort you."

They stepped through the door together, Colt right beside her as they strolled down a hallway with deep-red carpeting. Amelia looked longingly at the exit at the end of the corridor. So near and yet so far.

"This way," he murmured, steering her by the arm around a corner and indicating the door with a nod of his head.

"Thank you."

Her innocent smile gave way to a defeated pout as she went into the lounge. At least it was quiet and peaceful in there, the hustle and bustle of the party far away. Amelia sat down on one of the

160

cushiony sofas scattered around the room and slipped off her delicate high heels.

Mirrors ran from one end of the wall to the other, soft lights spaced at intervals over a long mauve counter with matching chairs. It felt so good to sit down and rest her feet, but she knew she couldn't hide forever. She could even hear her mother's voice, reminding her to be a good guest, stand up straight, and not look like she was being tortured.

Her moment of blissful peace was shattered by a large group of women entering the powder room. With a resigned sigh she slid her shoes on and left the once quiet sanctuary. Her escort was waiting patiently for her, much to her dismay.

Colt eyed the vision floating down the hall toward him. Amelia's silky brown hair was twisted into an elegant knot. Her shimmering silk dress of burnt orange silhouetted her curves to perfection. It was long sleeved and had a pleated high neck in front, but plunged low in the back, draping in billowy folds from her shoulders almost to her waist. A slit on the left side opened up past her knee as she walked, revealing her legs, sleek in sheer nylons.

Amelia's heart took a little jump when she looked at Colt, seeing the fire in his eyes. He was so very suave and distinguished, dressed in his evening clothes, leaning against the fabric-covered wall with a drink in his hand.

"Waiting for me?" she asked as he moved away from the wall and fell in step beside her. "How kind."

"Helen would never forgive me if I abandoned her little lamb," he quipped, leading her back to the party. "Besides, if I'd turned my back for a minute, you would have been gone like a shot."

"Me?"

Colt chuckled. "Keep practicing. You'll learn to act as well as the rest of the family in no time."

Just like one of the family. He hadn't meant it that way, Amelia knew, but to her heightened senses that was the way the remark sounded. All evening people had been looking at them slyly— some of the women a bit green around the eyes, she had noticed—and making comments about what a lovely couple they were.

To protest would be to give validity to their suspicions, so she had simply smiled and said nothing. Michael, however, had been grinning from ear to ear since they arrived. She half expected him to jump up and offer to give the bride away at any moment.

They joined the crowd and circulated. Colt was doing his best to avoid Gloria Clarkson, and so far had succeeded, but he knew his good fortune couldn't last forever. Sure enough, she approached them now, and he realized she had probably been stalking them for some time, sizing up the competition.

"Hello, Colt," a very feminine voice purred.

Amelia took an instant dislike to the woman. She was perfect, from the top of her carefully coiffed head right down to the tip of her toes. Her blond hair looked natural, but who could tell these days? And if there were any lines on that perfectly made up china-doll face, they didn't show.

Her thoughts were so catty and out of character that Amelia frowned, trying to put a finger on her feelings. Surely it couldn't be jealousy. Granted, the blond bombshell was looking at Colt as if they had already been intimate or soon would be, but that didn't matter to her. Did it? It was just a healthy case of envy, that's all.

She was beautiful. She fairly reeked of money and careful care, her age indeterminate, maybe in her early forties. And she was overly endowed, too, Amelia decided rather viciously as the woman standing before them moved her shoulders together, her ample bosom threatening to spill out of her strapless, ice-blue gossamer dress.

"Gloria," Colt said. "Enjoying the party?"

"How could I be?" Her lower lip protruded in a theatrical pout. "You've been ignoring me, you terrible man."

Colt didn't seem overly perturbed by her accusation. In fact, he was smiling. "This is Amelia," he said introducing them, his hand sliding up possessively to caress the bare skin of Amelia's back.

The woman completely ignored her, turning instead to place one small, well-manicured hand intimately on the lapel of his tuxedo. "I do believe we have some business to discuss, Colt. Will you see me home?" She was practically purring.

"Oh, I'm sorry, Gloria," he said, his tone of voice revealing anything but regret. "Amelia is here as my date for this evening. I'll be taking her home later." Colt moved closer to Amelia, his

163

hand slipping inside the low-cut back of her dress to stroke her waist and side.

Amelia managed not to gasp and kept a placid smile on her face, but the rest of her was on fire. She had had one glass of champagne, just enough to loosen the careful control she had been exercising over her emotions all day. His tantalizing touch felt so good, she almost had to lean against him for support.

Then she realized what he was doing. It was obvious to anyone and everyone that Gloria was after Colt, and he was using Amelia as a shield! She straightened, trying to ignore his caresses, tempted to walk away and leave Colt on his own to handle this vamp. There was, however, one slight problem. She couldn't get away.

Colt had her effectively trapped, his fingers gripping her waist firmly. He evidently knew what she was planning and was preventing her from leaving him stranded there with this walking barracuda. But why? He was polite, to be sure, but if something bothered him he didn't hesitate to act upon it. Why didn't he simply tell Gloria to get lost?

She looked at his face, and a glimmer of an explanation came to her. In his eyes was the same barely contained rage she had glimpsed on the trip back to Austin this afternoon. At the time he had been talking about someone who didn't understand that controlling a company meant taking responsibility for the people who depended on that company for their livelihoods. Someone he had been dealing with who had him so mad he could barely see straight.

Gloria? Amelia's smile got a bit larger. If he was going to use her as a shield, she might as well have a bit of fun. "Tell me, Gloria," she said. "Are you in the cosmetics industry?"

"Excuse me?" The woman seemed surprised that Amelia had the power of speech. "What did you say?"

"I thought you might be in cosmetics," she repeated. Colt gave her a warning pinch but she ignored him. "You seem to have an endless supply of them."

Gloria glared at her, ice crystals in her eyes. "For your information, I *own* a small manufacturing firm," she said through white, perfectly spaced teeth, then turned her attention back to Colt. Her voice became dulcet toned, dripping with sensuality. "We really should talk, Colt. I've been thinking about your offer, and have decided we need to burn some midnight oil hammering out the details."

Amelia grinned, unable to hide her triumph. Colt was being as cordial as he could to this woman because she had something he wanted, probably stock in her company. And he was using her as a shield because Gloria wanted to hammer out more than details while that midnight oil burned.

It was too good to be true. Colt was being held for ransom, with the price set at seduction, so much like her own situation she had to bite her tongue not to laugh out loud. "Gosh!" Amelia exclaimed, feigning wide-eyed innocence. "Maybe

165

you'd better talk to her, Colt. She seems quite desperate."

Colt wasted perhaps half a second standing there with a stunned expression on his face, then managed to open his mouth. "If you'll excuse us, Gloria," he blurted, "I see my grandmother trying to get our attention." With amazing speed he maneuvered them deep into the crowd.

Amelia glanced over her shoulder in time to see Gloria turn on her heel and stalk off, her plans for the evening derailed. She doubted, however, that Colt had seen the last of her. It was really hilarious, until she reminded herself that Colt had been using her.

"You're safe now. Kindly remove your hand before I . . ." Before she what? It was tempting to kick him in the shins in front of all these people, but that was hardly proper behavior for a guest at a charity function. "Let go of me, or the next time you need my help you can go fish!"

Colt looked at her, enjoying the healthy glow of anger coloring her skin. "Thanks, Amelia. You did me a big favor back there, and I won't forget it." He dipped his head and kissed her on the cheek. "You're really something. And the way you sassed Gloria! I didn't think you were that tough."

A kiss with everyone watching, not to mention his appreciation and praise! His behavior was so unexpected Amelia felt her anger drain away, to be replaced by a warm, rather disarming sensation, as if every square inch of her skin had suddenly come alive. She smiled at him, discovering she really didn't mind having his arm around her after all.

When they reached him, Michael was smiling, too, his eyes gleaming with amusement. "Good move, boy," he said, clapping his grandson on the back and chuckling softly. "Saw the whole thing." He winked at Amelia. "It was sweet of you to play along, my dear. That woman is a shark."

"I thought she resembled a piranha myself," Amelia commented. "Did you see those teeth?"

Michael cackled gleefully, enjoying the comparison. Colt, however, looked decidedly uncomfortable. He didn't find Gloria's attentions the least bit funny. All he wanted was her stock, and as much as he had enjoyed Amelia's adept performance, he knew he would probably live to regret his part in it. Gloria Clarkson was a vindictive woman; dealing with her would be even harder after tonight.

"Have you seen Helen? I'm more than ready to get out of here," Colt said, tugging on his bow tie.

"She's over with your mother and father. I believe she's ready to leave too." He flanked Amelia on the other side as they moved through the crowds. "Kathleen is thrilled with how well things went for the handicapped children's fund. They far exceeded their goals for this evening."

Helen was standing near the entrance, elegant in a long, pale blue sheath. Her hair was a riot of bouncy silver-gray curls. Next to her were Colt's mother and father, playing the host and hostess, thanking their guests as they left.

"Congratulations, Mom," Colt said, leaning down a bit to kiss her cheek.

Kathleen was a beautiful woman, tall, though not quite as tall as her husband or son, her light

brown hair swept up into a swirl like a sophisticated crown. She was absolutely stunning in a
black jersey gown beaded with tiny seed pearls.

"Thank you, dear," Kathleen said, her hand caressing her son's cheek for a moment. "Thank you
for coming, and for bringing such a charming
young lady," she added, smiling at Amelia.

"My pleasure," Colt said, his arm securely
wrapped around Amelia, not allowing her to escape. He continued to stroke her back, his hip
pressed firmly against hers.

"How is the Clarkson deal progressing, Colt?"
his father asked. "Ready to admit defeat and take
the loss yet?"

Colt pursed his lips in dismay. "Not just yet."

As Amelia looked first at him, then at his father,
and finally at Michael, she had the feeling she was
looking at a progression, something like a stages-
of-man exhibit. There was Colt as he looked now,
then how he would look at his father's and his
grandfather's ages. It was startling yet pleasant.
Colt would age well, she realized, and found herself wondering why the thought pleased her so.

Colt was a handsome man, in that rough sort of
way she preferred, and his father was an older,
gray-haired version cut from the same cloth. Even
Michael, for all his scheming ways, was undeni-
ably attractive. Not in the heart-stopping, nerve-
tingling way Colt was, of course; the difference in
their ages was too great for him to have that effect
on her. But she had been inexplicably taken with
the old man the first time they had met in the
hospital corridor.

168

The direction her thoughts were taking her was frightening, yet at the same time almost reassuring. If she did seduce Colt—or, as seemed more likely at the moment, he seduced her—if Michael's plan reached the conclusion he sought, she would go through these stages with him. They'd grow older together, enjoying life side by side. Perhaps they'd keep the same excitement she knew Helen and her husband shared, and could tell Kathleen and Colt's father shared, too, if the way they touched and looked at each other was any indication.

Good Lord! What on earth was she thinking? Had she actually convinced herself to go through with all this? Was there, somewhere deep down in the tangle of her emotions, the first glimmer of more than simple attraction for Colt? Could she be falling in love with him?

"Amelia?" Helen's voice jerked her attention back from her private thoughts. She suddenly felt as if she had had considerably more to drink than a single glass of wine. "Amelia, dear, are you feeling all right? You look as if you've just seen a ghost!"

In fact she had; the ghost of her future, or what her future could be like. "I—I'm fine," she murmured, managing a smile that seemed to reassure the five curious people who were looking at her with obvious concern. "I guess it's just been a long day, that's all. I'm tired."

"Well, of course you are, you poor dear," Helen said, taking her by the hand and giving it a comforting pat. "Come on, Michael. Colt, you drive, your grandfather had one too many glasses of champagne for me to allow him behind the wheel. You'd have thought he was celebrating or something."

Amelia thanked Colt's mother and father, then allowed herself to be led to the car, just as she had allowed herself to be led to this party in the first place. Somehow, she had to get control of things again, take hold of her confused emotions and mixed-up feelings before they led her into a decision she wasn't ready to make.

Helen kept up a steady buzz of conversation on the ride home, lulling Amelia into that now familiar feeling of being safe and secure, of belonging. Colt was driving the bronze Lincoln and Amelia sat beside him, Helen, Michael, and even Colt himself, seeming to consider that her place, at his side. Amelia sighed and tried to relax, afraid even to think about it anymore. For the second time that day all she wanted to do was run away and hide.

CHAPTER TEN

"Amelia. We're home, dear," Helen said softly.

"What? Oh. I must have fallen asleep."

Helen laughed. "I know how you feel. I was ready to leave at midnight, but it's so hard to get away from those charity functions," she said, yawning delicately.

Colt smiled at Amelia, but she turned away, stepping out of the car without accepting the help he offered. His smile disappeared. Now what? Everything had been going so well there for a while, then all of a sudden she was back on the defensive. It was enough to drive a man crazy.

"I need a drink," he announced, and stalked off.

"A quick nightcap will help us all sleep better," Helen agreed amiably, though she frowned after her grandson. He had seemed so happy on the ride home, with Amelia's head nestled against his shoulder.

Michael ushered them inside impatiently. "A nightcap is an excellent idea. Warm us up from the chilly night air."

They all joined Colt, who was already in the study with a brandy snifter in his hand. Helen poured a golden dollop of the liquor into three remaining glasses that were sitting out on a tray. She handed them around.

"To another of Kathleen's successful fund raisers," she toasted, holding her glass up to clink with the others.

Amelia sipped at the liquid fire. It warmed her entire body, singing through her veins with amazing speed. She risked a glance at Colt, who was now studiously ignoring her. Perhaps she wasn't being fair, with this on-again, off-again behavior, but she simply couldn't help it. If only she could see Nathan, talk to him. He would know what to do, or could at the very least offer his advice.

But was that such a good idea? If she told him the whole story, he would let her off the hook, tell her to do what she wanted and forget about him. Her sense of duty was too strong to do that; it was what had gotten her into this mess in the first place. Great, she thought, just what she needed. Another quandary.

"I believe I'll take my nightcap to bed. And my man," Helen said, waiting for Michael to join her. He did so promptly with a broad smile. "See you in the morning children."

"I have a few calls to make, then I'll lock up," Colt informed them, his eyes on the blinking red light of the answering machine. "Good night." He turned his back on them and picked up the phone.

Amelia walked over to the door, clearly dismissed. It was fine with her. She had a lot of thinking to do. "Good night, Colt. Thanks for an interesting evening."

172

Colt nodded at her. "Close the door on your way out."

She was tempted to slam the thing in his face. Instead she gently shut the door, leaving it barely cracked. After a momentary hesitation she pressed her ear to the slit.

"What's wrong?" Colt was asking whoever was on the other end of the line. "What sort of strangers? Damn! Can John be moved?"

He was talking about Nathan! Amelia strained to hear every nuance of his voice. Whether she could tell him what was going on or not, she was suddenly overcome by the urge to see her brother. They had kept her away from him for too long, and she would put a stop to it no matter what she had to do, including eavesdropping.

"Good," Colt was saying. "Sounds like he's making a remarkable recovery." Outside the study door Amelia practically jumped for joy. "Well, when does your sale begin?" he asked. "Are you sure there'll be enough aircraft coming and going to confuse the issue? All right, then, we'll have to try it. There'll be too many unknown people floating around every stretch of your place to keep him safely hidden anyway."

Amelia wished she could hear the entire conversation. She wanted to know what they were planning, and if it was really safe for Nathan to be moved again so soon. Then again, it sounded as if he was no longer safe where he was right now. But he was making a remarkable recovery!

Colt's deep, rich voice had taken on that hard, decisive quality. "Do me a favor and call Sergeant

Jerry Enger for me. He'll need to know and may have some ideas on the subject. Right, the secure line. Thanks, I'll see you at sunup."

Amelia heard him hang up the phone and she took a step backward, at war with herself. Should she stay and listen, taking the chance of getting caught? The decision was made for her when she heard Colt's voice again.

"Randy, this is Colt. Can you have my helicopter ready to fly in one hour? Great. Thanks."

She heard him hang up again, but this time the desk chair creaked and she could hear him coming toward the door. Her heart in her throat, Amelia scampered up the carpeted stairs and flew into her room, easing the door shut behind her. She collapsed against it, breathing heavily.

Colt was going to move her brother again! Maybe she couldn't talk to him about the deal Michael had coerced her into, but it was high time she took control of some part of his recuperation. She had to take control of something, for heaven's sake! This could be it, her chance to escape, and Amelia planned to grab it with both hands.

No one was going to move her brother again without her being there. As a matter of fact, she had finally made a decision; from now on she wasn't going to allow anyone to dangle her brother's life over her head. Nathan had an incredibly devious mind. He would know what to do about Michael.

She hadn't had time to unpack the suitcase she'd brought back from San Antonio yet, so the items she needed were still in there. Hands shaking with excitement and just a little bit of fear, she opened up the bag and rifled through the contents. Dark clothing. Black leather high-top tennis shoes. Amelia the midnight skulker.

She changed quickly, then removed her contacts and slipped on her glasses. After taking a moment to hang up the elegant evening dress Helen had bought her, she stuffed a few necessities into her oversize purse. Grabbing the brandy snifter, she downed the contents in one swallow to give her added courage, and turned off the bedroom lights.

At the door Amelia paused, listening for any unusual sounds. There were none, so she carefully turned the knob and stepped into the empty hallway, closing the door silently behind her. Relief washed over her when she saw a crack of light coming from beneath Colt's bedroom door and heard him moving around inside. He hadn't left yet.

The rest of the house was dark and quiet as she made her way down to the garage. There were three cars parked there. Only Michael and Helen used the Lincoln, so that was out. Of the two remaining she decided on the one she'd seen Colt driving the most this past week.

It was a compact sedan, with a typically cramped backseat, but the front seat was a long, solid bench that would hide her from the driver. Amelia crawled in back and spread herself on the floor face down, the drive-shaft hump in the middle pressing uncomfortably into her stomach. She waited.

Inside the house Colt stood in the darkened upstairs hall, his duffel bag of hurriedly packed necessities in one hand, his other on the doorknob of Amelia's room. He was tempted to look in on her, maybe even tell her where he was going and why. But he changed his mind. It was very possible he would see her attired in a sexy nightgown and not be able to tear himself away. His desire for her was very close to the edge; he would undoubtedly strip off all his clothes and slip into bed beside her.

There wasn't time for that now. But the hour of her reckoning was fast approaching. He turned and went down the stairs, then into the garage, trying to keep his mind on the task at hand. It wasn't easy in spite of all he had to do.

That woman was getting to him, and this interruption was going to serve a dual purpose. He needed some time away from Amelia, to think about his feelings toward her. Tonight, when he'd put his arm around her and held her close, his body had gone haywire. He could still feel the softness of her skin beneath his fingers, feel the warmth and texture of it as she responded to his caress. Colt wanted her. And he was going to have her.

But at what price?

That was the problem. In the past if he desired a certain woman he had simply set his mind toward having her, and nine times out of ten accomplished his goal. This time, though, he was dealing with a completely different kind of female. That nosy neighbor of hers had suggested otherwise, but Colt knew better. Amelia wasn't the kind to sleep around. She was, in fact, one of those women his grandfather referred to as the marrying kind. One who expected and wanted a husband and probably children.

Colt had been doing a fair amount of soul searching lately. Though he didn't want to admit it even to himself, he was well aware that he was getting older, was starting to feel the urge to settle down. Still, a part of him, a very large part actually, just couldn't come to grips with that kind of permanency. And he didn't know why.

It wasn't as if he'd come from a broken home; exactly the opposite was true. He knew deep down he wanted the same kind of lasting, loving marriage his parents and grandparents had achieved. But that could only happen if he chose the right woman to love, and if she loved him in return. And to be perfectly honest, in spite of the examples his own family gave him, Colt wasn't sure true love really existed.

At least it didn't seem to exist for him. A long time ago, he had imagined himself deeply in love with his high-school sweetheart. They had been happily planning their life together when, without warning, she broke off their engagement. Yet, after this happened, he only felt a brief sense of loss, followed quickly by relief. Furthermore, his experience taught him a lesson, and left him unwilling to share anything deeper than passion with the stream of women who came afterward.

He had decided simply to have fun, and he went out with all different kinds of women, some adventurous, some serious, too many of them turning out to be social climbers attracted by his family

177

name. His caution grew with each betrayal, as did the strength of the shield around his heart. Love had become an elusive emotion, reserved only for his family and old, trusted friends. Colt was beginning to think there wasn't a woman out there for him.

He opened the car door, threw his bag carelessly into the backseat, then got in and started the engine, totally absorbed in his thoughts. Absence was supposed to make the heart grow fonder, right? This time apart would either increase his desire for Amelia, perhaps pointing the way toward the future, or else it would extinguish the flame he felt simmering inside him. At the moment, however, as he pulled away from the house where Amelia slept peacefully unaware of his departure, all Colt knew was that he already missed her.

If Amelia had stopped to think twice, she never would have hidden on the floorboard of a car with Colt at the wheel. She felt like one big sore spot, was quite certain she would be sporting numerous bruises tomorrow. Evidently, Colt had taken another of his so-called shortcuts, so the trip to wherever he kept his helicopter hadn't been all that long. What the ride lacked in length, however, it more than made up for in sheer bumpiness. She had bounced around the rear of the compact like a Ping-Pong ball.

But they had finally, thankfully come to a screeching, shuddering stop, and she was once again alone. She counted to ten, slowly, listening to the sound of his footsteps as he walked away from the car. Then she raised her head and peeked over the edge of the front seat, ready to dive for cover. If Colt discovered her now, her search for her brother would end immediately.

Colt was entering a small building marked OFFICE, on the other side of the sparsely lighted parking lot. As she scanned the surrounding darkness, Amelia realized she was in trouble. Small planes and helicopters dotted the area for as far as she could see, one looking pretty much like another to her untrained eye. Which one was his? And how was she going to get to it without his seeing her even if she figured it out?

One thing was certain. He had left his duffel bag —the one that had hit her on top of the head when he'd gotten in the car—and would be coming back to collect it soon. Colt was sure to see her.

How did her brother do things like this for a living all the time without developing an ulcer? She was flat scared out of her wits and beginning to panic. *Think,* she told herself desperately, *think rationally and use your brain.*

The first thing she had to do was get out of this car. Holding her breath, Amelia opened the door, grabbed her purse, then closed the door as quietly as possible behind her. Staying in the shadows, she scrambled across the parking lot and hid behind a metal structure near the neat rows of parked aircraft, adrenaline pumping wildly through her veins. She almost fainted at how close she'd come to getting caught when she peered around the edge of the building and saw Colt step out of the office.

He retrieved his bag, then crossed the lot to a

shiny helicopter off to her left. Just as she started to panic again, thinking that the ride here had been in vain, Colt tossed the duffel bag into the back of the aircraft and went back into the office. Amelia ran to the open door and crawled inside. Pitch blackness surrounded the inner cabin and she banged her elbows and shins as she quickly crawled to the rear of the vehicle to hide.

A moment later Colt climbed into the pilot's seat. A few more moments passed and the beast beneath her awoke with a shivering whine. That was when Amelia realized she'd forgotten one very important aspect of this spur-of-the-moment plan. She had never flown in a helicopter before.

The whole world seemed to rise up beneath her and she stifled a scream of terror, her stomach feeling as if it were floating in midair. *Please,* Amelia begged silently, *please, please don't let me get sick. I'll never do anything like this again, I swear.*

Then she heard Colt mutter a curse, and something came hurtling across the slanting floor of the craft to land near her knees. She grinned affectionately and picked up the half-eaten candy bar, knowing she was going to be just fine.

Amelia had heard the term *deafening silence,* but had never really known what it meant until now. Her ears still buzzed from the chopping noise the helicopter made, even though the blades had stopped slicing through the air some time ago. Wherever they were, it was very, very quiet, as if they were miles from nowhere. She crawled to the front of the aircraft, staying on her hands and knees just in case Colt returned unexpectedly.

The view from the cockpit confirmed her feeling of isolation. All she could see was dry, rough prairie, without a building in sight. Dawn was beginning to break, the brilliant orange sun barely peeking over the flat, endless horizon.

The sunrise would be beautiful. It would be nice to sit back and enjoy the early dawn, and Amelia's nerves were so jangled that she was sorely tempted to do so. However, she had to decide what to do next. She was beginning to realize that bravery wasn't one of her strong points, but if she wanted to find her brother she was going to have to venture farther afield than the seat of this helicopter.

She took a tight hold on her purse, eased the door open, and stepped out. It was chilly out here on the lone prairie! Hugging herself, Amelia bumped the door shut with her shoulder, then turned around. Her mouth dropped open.

"Enjoy the ride?"

Leaning against the side of the helicopter, his arms crossed over his chest, stood Colt. His glittering green eyes seemed to pin her back against the side of the machine, making her shiver from more than just the cool dawn.

Amelia blinked, once, just to make sure he was really there. He was. "I—I didn't hear you come back," she blurted out foolishly.

"I came to see what was taking you so long."

Amelia stared at him blankly for a moment before she understood what he was saying. "You knew I was in there?" she asked incredulously. He nodded. "How?"

The tiny beginning of a smile played at the corners of his mouth. "I scented you."

"You what?"

"I didn't see you, I smelled you," Colt explained. "You forgot about your fragrance, dear heart."

He wasn't about to tell her that he hadn't seen her because he was so preoccupied with thinking about her, or that at first he'd believed her perfume was just a teasing memory that wouldn't go away.

"My perfume!"

"For future reference," he added dryly, "don't wear perfume of any kind unless you wish to be found."

"Thanks for the tip," she retorted. Swinging away from his piercing, know-it-all gaze, she began to walk toward the open prairie.

"Where are you going?"

"To find my brother."

"He's in the exact opposite of the direction you're heading."

Amelia stopped and swung back to face him. He hadn't moved an inch. "Why, pray tell, should I believe you?" she asked sarcastically, the bright sun behind his back making her squint.

"Do you have a choice?" he returned, and walked off at a brisk pace in the other direction.

Amelia looked around. All of the land seemed the same to her, dry, barren, and with no distinguishing landmarks. Maybe she'd better follow him.

"Colt, wait up," she yelled.

"Run, it won't hurt you," he shouted back, not slowing down any. "Isn't that why you're wearing sneaky black tennis shoes?"

Grumbling, wanting childishly to kick his helicopter as she passed it, she broke into a trot and went after him. He disappeared from view for a moment, as if the landscape had simply swallowed him up. She started to run, heading for the spot where she'd seen him last.

Amelia nearly tumbled head over heels into the valley that had been hidden from view by the gentle rise of the plateau they had landed on. Colt was leaning casually against a fence post. Behind him stood a vast, rustic array of buildings, and her eyes widened with the knowledge that her brother was in one of those white houses with their red tile roofs.

He was gazing at her, enjoying the gentle rise and fall of her breasts as she breathed deeply from her exertions. She refused to cross her arms over her chest, not about to give him the satisfaction of knowing he was getting to her. Instead, she pushed her glasses back up on her nose and glared at him.

"Well?" she asked impatiently. "Lead on!"

"No hurry, the others won't be here for a while."

"What others?"

Maybe he would explain the plan to her later. He hadn't decided yet. Right now explanations were the last thing on his mind. This excursion was supposed to have given him time away from her, to think and explore his feelings. But the only thoughts and feelings he was having at the moment were decidedly erotic, and instead of wanting to be away from her, he wanted to be as close to her as he could get. Very close. If she wanted to be a part of this plan, so be it.

"You have other things to worry about."

Amelia stared at him, not giving an inch. "I want to see my brother and I want to see him now!"

He quirked an eyebrow high, causing the long scar to stretch out into a thin line. "You're not in any position to be giving orders, Miss Stowaway. And you'll do exactly as you're told."

"Who's going to make me?" she shot back defiantly.

He suddenly pushed away from the post and advanced toward her. "Is that a challenge?" he asked, his deep voice full of sensual threat. "Or an invitation?"

"Now, Colt," she cautioned, not liking the gleam in his eyes one bit.

The girl had guts, he had to give her that. She was holding her ground, not swaying an inch as he approached her. "Maybe not right now," he informed her, his low, velvety tone of voice practically reaching out to caress her. "But soon. Very soon." The heat of his words sizzled across her frazzled senses, seducing her on yet another level. "I had in mind a soft, downy bed, a very leisurely and thorough exploration, just the way it should be for our first time."

"No," she whispered, shaking her head. He stood with just inches between their bodies and gazed down at her. She could feel his warmth, as if his entire body were touching hers. And the heat low in her belly boiled ever hotter as he touched her.

His gentle hands cupped her face, tilting her head back, soft yet demanding. "Yes," he murmured, his callused thumbs slipping along the soft curves of her jawline. She drew back slightly, but her warm, sherry-brown eyes were inviting him closer.

His thumb skimmed across the slightly parted petals of her mouth and then went back to slowly trace the delicate curve of her full bottom lip. The tip of her pink tongue darted out to flick wetly across his finger, then quickly escaped his touch. A smothered moan escaped him at her caress and all common sense fled his mind.

As his mouth covered hers, Amelia gave in to the emotions coursing through her, reaching up and sliding her hands up his neck and into the thick, coal-black hair. Opening her mouth, she met his tongue with hers eagerly, the hot cavern welcoming him. Again and again they kissed, trying to quench an intolerable thirst.

Her body was awash with sensations as his hands pulled her unbuttoned shirt free and pushed the cotton material to each side, revealing her lacy navy-blue brassiere. She felt one hand slip around under her shirt to grasp her waist and hold her close, kneading the soft skin of her side. The other sought the clasp, unhooking it deftly, and he brushed the filmy blue cloth aside.

185

"Lovely," he murmured, gazing at the beauty before him, his senses slowly taking in the sight.

"Colt, someone will—"

"Not out here," he assured her.

Amelia leaned closer to him, using his body to support her quivering form. His hand skimmed across the soft skin of her ribs before enclosing one breast in the gentle cup of his palm, then moving on to the other, cherishing their sweet weight. Colt dipped his head, unable to resist, hearing her soft gasp as he flicked the taut rosebud tips with his tongue, bringing them both to a new pebbled hardness.

With trembling fingers Amelia freed two buttons and slid her hand inside his shirt, across the hardness of his abdomen and up toward his broadening chest. Her hand slid upward, feeling his strength, then moved down slowly to the taut muscles of his stomach again, felt them grow tense at her feathery touch.

Lost in passion, neither Colt nor Amelia noticed when behind them, first the crown, then the brim of a weathered white hat poked above the edge of the ridge. Its equally weathered owner uttered a surprised exclamation and sank back down out of sight. He cleared his throat. Then he cleared it louder, modestly looking the other way even though he couldn't see a thing from where he stood behind the grassy knoll.

"Go away, William," Colt ordered, enclosing Amelia tightly in his embrace as she tried to pull away.

"The others should be here within five minutes,"

the intruder drawled sorrowfully. "We've got John ready to be moved. Time to pull your beast down into the compound."

Colt calmly turned Amelia around in his arms, her back to his stomach now as he rehooked her open brassiere. He then made quick work of the buttons on her dark plaid flannel shirt, enjoying the way she struggled against him.

"I can do that," Amelia objected angrily as his nimble fingers began slipping her shirt back inside the waistband of her jeans.

His fingers seemed to be straying from the task at hand and refueling her desire for him. The sound of William's voice had been like a bucket of cold water poured on her heated skin, yet all it took was a few teasing caresses for her to forget what she was doing, even why she was here in the first place.

"But I'm enjoying it so much more than you would," he murmured, not ceasing with his help till he was satisfied with her appearance. "You look good in pink," he teased, fixing the collar of her shirt.

Amelia squirmed free of his hold. The hot, pink tone of her skin turned even redder as the full implications of being caught like this hit her. So much for his assurance that they wouldn't be seen! Colt didn't even appear to be fazed. Maybe he got caught a lot, she thought waspishly, and was used to it. Well she wasn't!

Yes, Colt had successfully managed to distract her again. But she wasn't going to be sidetracked from her task now. "I want to see my brother!" she

187

demanded, addressing William. He had sauntered over the hill and was now standing on the other side of the fence with his back to them.

William turned to look questioningly at Colt. "Go ahead and take her down," Colt directed, then strode back up the hill toward the helicopter at a brisk pace.

Amelia sized up the man facing her. He looked like a rancher, jeans and blue chambray work shirt, his hat pulled low over his brow, almost hiding the carved teaklike features of his face. His age was impossible to determine—anywhere from forty on up, she supposed.

"Do you want to go over or under the fence?" William asked, pointing to the barbed wire between them, his face expressionless.

"Under." At least that way she wouldn't fall on top of those sharp little spears. William held up the bottom wire to give her more clearance. "Don't you believe in gates?" she asked, brushing the dust from her jeans.

A smile cracked the carved teak, revealing white, even teeth. "Sure do, up the way about a mile. Want to crawl back under and take a little hike? Be happy to oblige you, ma'am."

Amelia smiled at his friendly teasing. "No, thanks." Knowing Colt, he had probably chosen this spot on purpose. Keeping pace with his long stride, she added, "And please don't call me ma'am. Makes me feel like my mother. My name is Amelia."

He nodded his head at her, grabbing hold of her

elbow to keep her from falling on the uneven ground. "Okay. Mine's William."

"How's my brother doing?" she asked, stepping more carefully around the gaping holes some animals had burrowed; passageways to underground homes.

"Remarkably well, considering his injuries. You can see him, but I'll warn you ahead of time, he's been sedated for the move."

"Why?"

William shrugged. "He's a tough one, but the boy's still in pain. His nurse sees no reason to have him feel more hurt than he needs to."

Amelia couldn't argue with his logic. They were nearing the first of the white buildings, with additional structures on each side of them. "What and where is this place?"

He cackled. "Oh, this is just my little old ranch," he informed her. "The closest real town to us is San Angelo, and that's quite a ways away."

Amelia glanced at the man beside her. He owned all of this, and had agreed to keep a man he didn't know who had killers after him whom nobody seemed able to catch. "Thank you for letting my brother stay."

"No problem, barely notice a few extras on a place this size anyway." They stopped in front of a huge white home. "Your brother is on the first floor, right down the left corridor to the third door. You'd better hurry."

"Why—" The unmistakable sound of a helicopter pierced the still morning air, then another and another, a thundering barrage of them landing in some kind of pattern around the place. "Who are these people?"

"Friends, helping other friends. You'd better hurry if you want to see your brother before they all take off again."

Amelia ran up the stairs and in the open front door, her mind not even registering the sumptuous decor. She went down a wide hallway to the third room, opened the door, and came to a very sudden halt. A shiny black gun was pointing straight at her, held by a very determined, dark-haired woman.

"I—I'm—" She didn't know what to do or say with that gun pointing right at her nose. It was a situation totally alien to her.

"Amelia," the woman said lowering the gun. "I was informed of your possible arrival."

Colt second-guessing her again, she thought irritably. The man was becoming a real pain. "Who are you?"

"His nurse."

His nurse! Amelia took a closer look at the woman. So this was the mysterious, quick-thinking stranger who had saved her brother's life at the hospital. She was dressed in casual clothes, but all the same you could tell she was a complete professional. A professional at what, however, Amelia was almost afraid to guess. Nursing and gun-slinging seemed to be at opposite ends of the spectrum, but she had proven herself to be on Nathan's side, and Amelia was glad to have her.

"Thank you for all you've done," Amelia said, then knelt down beside her brother and gently touched his curled hand. He was deeply asleep. "How's he doing?"

"Good. Very good. He's tough and he has a great desire to live. Keeps talking about something he has to finish." She closed the hall door. "Give him another week and I'll have to forcibly tie him to the bed to keep him there long enough to completely recover."

"He's lost weight," Amelia murmured, her eyes skimming over his blanket-covered form. To a stranger there was nothing memorable about his face. It looked like so many others, with his medium skin-tone, brownish-black hair, and average nose. He had said his nondescript features were part of what made him so good at his job. However to Amelia, it was the face she had wanted most in the world to see, and she couldn't tear her eyes away from him.

"It'll come back. He's on solid food again and eating like a . . ." She trailed off and put a finger to her lips, her eyes glued to the bedroom door. "Ssh!" Amelia froze as the woman raised the gun again and waited, tense.

"Teri, darling, don't do anything foolish. I'm rather fond of my nose," intoned a familiar voice.

"Come on in, Colt." He entered the room and she hugged him briefly. "It's good to see you."

"We've got to stop meeting like this."

Teri crinkled her nose at him. "Let's not. Any other way would be so boring."

Colt chuckled. "You, dear, are addicted to adrenaline." He looked at the sleeping man tucked securely into a roll-away stretcher. "Is he ready?"

"Of course."

Amelia felt like a nonentity, completely useless and in the way. Worse, neither Colt nor the woman called Teri were even bothering to acknowledge her presence in the room. Just how well did he know her? It was obvious that these two people thought of each other with a great deal of affection. How far did it go?

For a second she tried to deny her feelings, willing to call them anything but jealousy. After all, she had a vested interest in Colt; she was expected to seduce him. Then she realized that her self-denials were useless. She was jealous, all right, there was no longer any doubt about it.

Amelia stood quietly out of the way as her brother was taken carefully outside, loaded into another helicopter, and readied for his journey. When it looked as if they had all forgotten about her, however, she decided to speak up.

"What about me?" she asked, trying not to sound petulant.

"You and I," Colt announced, taking hold of her arm and leading her toward his machine, "have some unfinished business to attend to."

"What are you talking about?"

Amelia let him strap her firmly into the passenger seat, though she wasn't at all sure she wanted such a clear view. It had been bad enough in the back where she couldn't see where they were going.

"What else? Our nice leisurely seduction of each other, without any interruptions this time."

"Don't I have any say in this matter?"

"You don't have to say a thing," he assured her. "I'm sure your actions will speak much louder than words."

She crossed her arms over her breasts and glared at him. "But I don't even know what's going on! What's happening to my brother? Where—"

"I'll explain on the way," Colt interrupted. "You wanted in on this deal, and now you're in. When we get to our destination," he added, his eyes on fire with a passion held just barely in check, "you won't have any trouble at all figuring out what's going on."

CHAPTER ELEVEN

Being a passenger was better than being a stowaway, Amelia supposed, but the reasons why eluded her at the moment. As a stowaway you didn't know what was going on; as a front-seat guest you got to see it all, whether you wanted to or not. She wasn't sure if the flip-flops her stomach was doing were from the ride, or from the curious combination of anticipation and dread she felt.

"I thought you promised me an explanation," she said at last. She had been trying not to look at him, but the only alternative was looking out at the landscape far below them. Instead she glared in his general direction and did her best to ignore Colt's smug, wicked smile. "What are we doing? And why were all those other people hanging around back there?"

Colt chuckled. "They weren't hanging around, Amelia, they were helping. With the exception of the good and trusted friend who is presently en route to my ranch with your brother and Teri in the back of his helicopter, the rest of us are all part of a carefully timed diversion."

"What sort of diversion?" she asked, glad to have something to take her mind off the flight.

"When Pop asked me to move your brother someplace safe, I had initially thought of my ranch," he explained. "But I also figured it was a pretty good possibility the people who were after him might find out about the move and follow us. So I took him to William's place first, with the idea of transferring him later. As it turned out, they evidently didn't catch on to the plan in time to follow, so we decided to leave him there as long as it remained safe. Teri says the moves don't hurt him, but they don't help him either."

Amelia's eyes widened and her face grew pale. "But you're moving him now," she said, her voice a whisper. "That means . . ." She trailed off, her hand to her mouth.

Colt nodded. "We're pretty sure they tracked him down somehow. In these parts a stranger sticks out like a sore thumb. A pair of them pretty well constitutes an invasion, and two men showed up at the local feed and grain yesterday asking questions," he informed her.

"What kind of questions?"

"Who owns what, how many hands does so-and-so employ, that sort of thing," Colt replied. "They may just be land speculators, but we're not going to take any chances. If it is who we think, that means they're capable of finding him in the middle of Texas, which in turn means they're probably capable of following him in the air too."

"I see," Amelia said appreciatively. "That's why

195

you held a helicopter convention at William's place. The killers won't know who to follow."

"The old shell game," he agreed. "We did it when we moved him from the hospital, using ambulances instead of aircraft. We got the jump on them that time and the ruse turned out unnecessary. I'm hoping it will be this time too. William's having a big cattle sale, so maybe they won't be suspicious of all the air traffic until it's too late."

Amelia gazed at him with new respect. He was as good a tactician as he was a pilot. In spite of the ground whizzing by below them, she was almost starting to relax. It felt very good to know finally what was going on, and even better to be a part of it for a change.

"Thanks for letting me in on the secret, Colt," she told him, giving him a warm smile.

He shrugged. "Pop seems to think you should be kept in the dark about all this for some reason," he replied, a small frown puckering his brow, "but you're in it now whether he likes it or not. And he is your brother, after all."

"My sentiments exactly." She risked a look out the window. "Are we going to your ranch too?" she asked.

"Eventually."

"What—"

Colt interrupted her with a hearty laugh. "If they were watching, and they saw two helicopters head in the same direction, don't you think they'd catch on?"

"I suppose," she replied with chagrin. "But

where are we going? How long will it be before I can see my brother?"

"You're just full of questions, aren't you?" he asked, still laughing. "You'll see where we're going when we get there, and we'll be there for as long as it takes."

The wicked gleam was back in his eyes, and she stared at him suspiciously. "To do what?"

"You'll see."

"Secrets again?"

Colt glanced at her, his expression speculative. "I could also ask you a few questions I'll bet you won't answer either, you know. Why is it your brother rates all this cloak and dagger attention? Who are these people after him, and why do they want him out of the way?"

"I can't tell you," she replied, rather smugly.

"Hah! Can't, or won't?"

Amelia frowned, perturbed with herself. He was finally being honest with her—for the most part, anyway—and he was helping Nathan. She supposed she owed him some explanation.

"A little of both, Colt. I don't know the whole story, and the part I do know I can't tell, because of my brother's occupation," she said, being as honest as she could.

"Well, that's something, I guess." He was far from satisfied, however. "His occupation, you said?"

She laughed. "Don't be pushy. That's more than I should have told you as it is. If you want to know more, you'll have to ask Na—John Smith yourself."

197

"I intend to," Colt assured her.

They were silent and thoughtful for a while, both realizing they had gotten about as far as they were going to get on that particular subject. Amelia still wanted to know where they were going, and more importantly, what they were going to do when they arrived. But she would find that out soon enough, and certainly didn't see any point in starting an argument over it. She turned her mind to other questions.

"I'm curious, Colt—"

"You can say that again," he interjected.

She poked him in the ribs, gently, well aware that his skills and concentration were keeping them hovering a great distance above the earth. "Where do your parents live?"

"In Austin."

"And yet you stay with Michael and Helen when you're in town?" she asked, trying to find out if that was his habit or if this had been a special case.

Colt chuckled, his eyes sparkling. "Usually. What are you fishing for, Amelia? Do you want to know if I stayed with them this time because you were there? Are you hoping I'll tell you I was so taken with you that I just had to be close to you?"

She fought a blush. He was smart, all right, too smart for his own good. Crossing her arms over her breasts, Amelia told him in a cool voice, "I was just wondering, that's all. You seem to get along so well with your mother and father."

"You've almost got it," he said appreciatively. "A bit more work on your poker face and you'll be

198

able to hold your own against Pop any day." He reached a hand out and caressed her cheek, a brief touch that made her shiver. Colt grinned. "I do get along well with my parents. But their house is usually full of guests, visiting politicians, members of some charity drive or another, business associates of my father's. I don't enjoy the social patter they seem to thrive on, that's all."

"I see."

"But I must admit that I was even more anxious to stay with my grandparents than usual," Colt continued. "It must have been the thought of you blundering into the wrong room some night by accident and ending up in my bed." He looked at her, eyebrows arched rakishly. "Or would it have been an accident?"

Amelia turned away from him, his sensual teasing finally making her blush. Something was coming. She could feel it in the air, like the static charge of electricity before a rainstorm. Just when her stomach had at last calmed down and accepted the act of defying gravity, a new uneasiness gripped her.

This time, however, the feeling was almost pleasant, a tingling sensation that made her nipples harden and brought a molten flow of warmth to the center of her being. She closed her eyes, waiting for the feeling to pass. As she sat there listening to the throb of the helicopter motor and Colt's soft, masculine voice humming a happy tune, Amelia's sleepless night caught up with her.

When she awoke from her short, dreamless nap, they had landed. She rubbed her eyes, feeling curiously refreshed, and studied the area around them. They couldn't be too far from Austin, judging from the rolling hills and abundance of trees.

Colt reached across the cockpit and released her safety belt, his hand squeezing her thigh reassuringly. "All right?" he asked, his voice concerned and tender. It had never entered his mind that she wouldn't like flying, but it would be unfair if she was sick from the trip. Especially considering the day he had planned for them.

Amelia nodded. "Fine," she replied, not wanting to sound too frisky. He looked frisky enough for the both of them, and his simple caress, high up on her thigh, sent her pulse leaping into double time. "Where are we?"

"Roughly an hour's drive from downtown Austin."

He got out on his side, then crossed in front of the helicopter and helped her to the ground. It was remarkably quiet, the day full and ripe now, sunshine flowing over them as they walked away from the helicopter. They had landed in a clearing on top of a hill, the dense covering of trees hiding the house Amelia now saw off to one side. Her eyes widened. The feeling of anticipation that had gripped her before she had dozed off returned with dizzying force.

"Who owns this?" she asked, following him inside the large rustic dwelling.

One entire wall of the living room was constructed from blond Austin stone, with a large fireplace situated in the middle. The room felt cozy, very casually decorated in warm earth tones.

Amelia could feel a pulse beat in her throat, her blood racing through her veins.

"The family." Colt took her hand and led her swiftly up a flight of stairs, to a large loft bedroom. "As promised, a soft, downy bed," he murmured, drawing her into his arms, not giving her a chance to think. "No interruptions, and all the time in the world."

Her eyes widened. "Colt . . . I . . ."

"Don't think. Just feel," he coaxed, threading his hands into her rich brown hair as his mouth covered hers.

Amelia was lost the moment his lips touched hers. Now wasn't the time to worry about half-baked promises, not when every cell in her body was craving his intimacy. She kissed him hungrily, letting loose all the pent-up emotions she'd been struggling with for too long. No more denials. No more games. She wanted him, every bit as much as he wanted her. At the moment it didn't matter who had gotten her into this, what part Michael had played, or who was seducing whom. Her breath was coming out in husky little gasps as she leaned against his chest.

"You won't be needing these," Colt murmured, slipping her glasses off and putting them safely on a nearby dresser. "I'll be your guide to what you can't find."

Amelia blinked rapidly, pleased as Colt stepped closer and into better focus, his fuzzy outline taking on definite angles. "Don't worry. I'll feel my way."

Colt chuckled softly, his eyes on fire. "And I'm

sure you won't need this," he added, unbuttoning the plaid shirt, pausing to stroke her skin as it was revealed along the way.

Amelia returned his caresses, opening his black shirt and sliding it off his bronzed shoulders with eager hands. Now that she had made her decision, there was no stopping her. She knew what she wanted, and she wanted Colt. Busy fingers unsnapped his jeans, ready to unzip them, when he moved from her grasp.

"Hey," she protested softly when he stepped back from her. She watched his shirt fall to the ground and smiled in satisfaction. "That's better."

Her hands reached for his zipper again, impatient. Colt gently pushed them away, then slid her shirt off, which was quickly followed by her lacy brassiere. Amelia curled her arms around his waist, hugging him close, rubbing her breasts against his solid, warm chest. Short black hairs teased her already heightened senses, adding to her urgent need of him. The intense heat of his body intermingled with hers and ignited into full flame her simmering desire. Capriciously, of their own free will, her hands roamed over his smooth back as she sought to discover the muscular planes of his body, then urgently returned to his zipper.

"Easy," he murmured, stilling her hands. "We have lots of time. Slow and leisurely, remember?"

He was near to the breaking point himself, especially after the way she had rubbed her hands and body across his heated skin. But he needed to slow down for her pleasure. The first time he would take her gently, tenderly, hold the raging flood of his desire in check until he could be sure of her response.

"To hell with that," she muttered, boldly placing her hand flat across his lower abdomen and pressing with sensuous demand. "Now!"

Colt threw back his head and laughed openly. He couldn't have been more pleased or surprised. Here he had been worried about her, and she was the one ready to pounce on him. It thrilled him beyond reason. Had he perhaps found a perfect match, an equal after all?

"Well?" A very indignant, alluring Amelia stared at him. Her fingers were splayed along her naked waist, her jeans hanging open, tantalizing him with bits of navy-blue lace peeking out. "Are you all talk?"

His chest was still heaving with laughter, his green eyes sparkling as he surveyed her. "A tiny bit impatient, aren't we?"

"Not anymore." Amelia reached down for her shirt.

"Oh, no, you don't," Colt returned, whisking her up into his arms. He walked over to the bed and dropped her on it unceremoniously, watching as she sank into the downy softness before literally pouncing on her, pinning her down with his legs across hers. "Better?"

Had she teased him too much? He was a big man, strong, hard, and potent. "No, Colt," she moaned as he nuzzled the delicate skin on her neck, working his way down to plumper regions.

"Are you sure?" His tongue was tracing the pink rose bud of one milky white breast.

203

"I . . ." She trailed off with a deep, throaty groan of ecstasy as his hand gently but firmly clasped her femininity, the heat of his touch searing right through the thick denim.

"Do you want to stop now?" He was leaving the entire decision up to her, but using his own particular brand of persuasion to sway her toward him. "Well?" His voice mimicked hers, taunting her.

"No!" she gasped out as he gently suckled one taut nipple to pliant softness. Weaving her fingers in his coal-black hair, she pressed his face back between her quivering breasts as he raised his head.

Low laughter rumbled deep in his chest, communicating his feelings to her. "Don't worry, sweet Amelia. I'll stay right where you want me. Or will I?" he teased in a husky voice, nibbling his way down her ribcage, over the soft swell of her stomach to her open jeans.

Amelia could feel the heat coursing through her veins, pooling in a swirling mass low in her belly, aching for release. As he began easing her pants down her silky-smooth legs, she willingly lifted her hips to help him. When they dropped to the floor, she held Colt at bay with her toes.

"Take yours off," she ordered softly, then moved to help him strip off the last of his clothing.

Amelia stared wide eyed at his bronzed body, the strong legs, muscled thighs, taut buttocks curving into a lean waist before flaring out into a broad chest. Dark hair was sprinkled across his pectorals, culminating into a narrow line. She could feel the heat rising up her body, her face suffused in a warm shade of pink.

Colt was leaning over her now, coming closer and closer. Slipping her arms around his neck, she pulled him closer still, until he was on top of her. "I thought you'd never get here," she murmured huskily.

"But the invitation was so long in coming," he teased, cupping one ripe, succulent breast with his hand.

Her body was surging with need, begging for release, but he continued to torment her. "Colt, now!"

"Bossy little thing, aren't you?" he murmured in her ear, his tongue gliding along the curving edges.

"Yes!" she moaned, digging her fingernails into his hips as she guided him to her.

He filled her, her body awash with waves of desire as they came together, all pretense gone, no game in mind save that age-old rhythm of man and woman, taking and giving. The clashing of the waves soared higher and higher as they sought that elusive release, skimming along the edge until they surrendered to the passion that consumed them. And then they were falling, falling into a pool of warm emotion which lapped around them, rocking them gently into sleep.

Amelia awoke alone and disoriented. The sun was still shining brightly through the windows, but everything else was a blur. Struggling out of the tangled sheets, she found her glasses on top of the dresser. They didn't help much, her clothes still weren't readily visible. With a sigh she slipped on his black shirt and buttoned it. It covered her adequately, coming down almost to her knees.

Her stomach grumbled loudly, demanding to be fed. She went in search of the kitchen and found Colt looking out a wide bay window filled with plants. Faded blue jeans hugged his lean hips, his only piece of clothing.

She watched as he spooned up a huge bite of ice cream and carried it to his mouth. "Don't I get any?" Amelia asked, sauntering into the kitchen, suddenly feeling vulnerable and unsure of how to act after their morning together.

Colt held the spoon toward her and she accepted half the bite, the coffee ice cream soothing her parched throat. He ate the rest of her bite, licking the spoon clean before offering her another taste. She watched his tongue, feeling as if he'd touched her.

Eyes gleaming wickedly, she took another bite and teased him in return, the tip of her tongue darting out to catch an errant drop on her lips. His shirt completely enveloped her, yet made her look appealingly sexy at the same time. The sudden fire leaping in his loins surprised him. He wanted her again, and right now. Lowering his head, he flicked his tongue across the spot she'd just touched, then returned to her lower lip, probing gently. She jumped a little at his sudden caress, surprise showing in her sherry-brown eyes.

"I want to taste you," Colt murmured as his lips covered hers. Amelia opened her mouth, eager to

206

taste him too. "Mmm, you taste like coffee ice cream, my favorite."

"Your tongue is cold!"

"I'm sure you'll help me warm it up," he invited, leading her out of the kitchen.

A shaky little laugh escaped her. "How?"

"I'll show you," he promised, "it's much more fun."

They chased each other's passions again and again, quietly stunned by the depth of their mutual need. At last, the afternoon slipping away, they finally reached a temporary truce in their sensual battle. Amelia sat up in bed, the sheet wrapped demurely under her arms, watching as Colt slipped out of bed and went to the closet.

"I really am hungry. Two tiny bites of ice cream do not count as breakfast and lunch, and"—she glanced out at the slowly diminishing sun—"now it's time for an early dinner."

Colt glanced over his shoulder at her, his green eyes full of laughter. "Funny, I'm not that hungry."

Amelia threw a down pillow at him, missing by a long shot. "You ate that whole carton of ice cream—of course you're not hungry!"

He pulled a Burgundy-colored robe from the closet and put it on the bed at her feet. "Can you cook?"

Was this a test? "Can you?"

"Sometimes."

"Meaning?"

Colt shrugged his shoulders. "I cook. Sometimes it's edible and sometimes it's not."

Amelia rolled her eyes heavenward. "Is this going to be one of the edible times?"

"I don't know. We still haven't determined who's going to do the cooking," he said, giving her a playful smile.

She knew exactly what he was up to. The only problem with knowing what he was trying to do was that it didn't leave her any less susceptible to his innumerable charms. And she really was hungry.

"This time," she offered magnanimously, hugging her knees, "I'll do the cooking, but only because I'm famished."

"Sounds fair."

For some reason it pleased him that she wasn't falling all over herself to show him how good a cook she was. At the same time it bothered him, and he found himself wondering if he hadn't misjudged her. Maybe she wasn't as interested in the till-death-do-us-part routine as he'd thought. Why that should bother a confirmed bachelor like himself, he didn't know. In truth, he was almost afraid to think about it.

When she didn't make a move to leave the bed he turned toward the stairs. Shyness now? "I'll be downstairs," he said, pausing to watch her.

Amelia eyed suspiciously the robe at the foot of the bed. "Who does that belong to?"

She wasn't wearing any piece of clothing that belonged to one of his other women. Past women, she amended. She was going to be the only one in his future now, whether he knew it yet or not. But she was going to be very careful about leading him to that conclusion.

Colt kept a straight face as he picked up the robe. Her jealousy pleased him, and once again he was afraid to ask himself why. "From the length I'd say my mother. It'll be a bit long on you."

"Are you saying I'm short?"

"Never. You have everything you need where it counts."

Colt beat a hasty retreat while he was still ahead, and while she was still willing to cook. He was suddenly ravenous. Sparring with her seemed to have that effect on him. Enough soul searching, he decided. It was enough simply to enjoy the happy feeling inside him without delving too deeply to see where it came from. And he *was* happy. Happier than he'd ever been in his life.

Amelia combed her hair and then carefully descended the stairs with the robe held high. It was more than a little long for her. Colt was sitting at the kitchen table sipping a glass of orange juice. He held out a filled glass for her and grinned at her look of mock surprise.

"I can open cans and read simple directions."

"So I see." She smirked at his announcement, not fooled for a moment, but accepted his offering. "Is there any food to cook with?"

He pointed. "The freezer is to the left."

Amelia surveyed the contents, eyes widening. "What are you planning for, a month-long siege?" The huge freezer was filled with every conceivable item that could be frozen. "I'll cook," she informed him, completely befuddled by so many choices, "but you'll have to make suggestions."

"I can think of one or two," he returned slyly.

She glared at him. "Seriously."

"Seriously, anything is fine. There's a microwave if that helps any."

"A microwave? So much for roughing it in the wilds. Why don't you just jump in the helicopter and fly to the nearest hamburger stand?"

"They frown on people landing in their parking lots. Takes up too much space," he shot back. "And besides, we wouldn't fit in the drive-through."

Amelia rolled her eyes at his poor attempt at humor. "Enough! Do you have any cravings?"

"I'm sure I do."

His low, sexy drawl was unmistakable. He wasn't thinking of food. Amelia closed the freezer door and leaned back against it, her arms crossed over her chest. She fixed him with a baleful stare, although her body was responding to his remarks.

"Are you volunteering to cook?"

The sweetness of her tone didn't fool him. "No."

"Then I suggest you leave this kitchen until dinner is ready and you are called."

Colt drained his glass and put it by the sink. He wasn't foolish enough to upset an already temperamental cook by challenging her now. There were other ways and times to do that.

"Just a second. Is there anything you won't eat?" A broad grin split his face, an appealing crinkle around his eyes. She sighed. "Out! Right now. And put some clothes on."

He glanced at her over his shoulder as he beat a hasty retreat out the kitchen door. "Definitely too bossy."

Amelia ignored him and began planning dinner. The man appeared to have a one-track mind, and it wasn't on his stomach—it was on her! If she didn't keep her own mind off what had happened between them and concentrate on fixing their dinner, they would never eat tonight.

With the help of the microwave she managed to prepare a well-balanced meal. Chicken breasts, wild rice, and mixed vegetables. He'd already had his dessert. In more ways than one, she thought, surprised at her own wicked mind.

"Colt, dinner is served," she called from the kitchen.

He didn't reply. With a resigned sigh she searched the house for him, but he wasn't inside. She didn't intend to traipse all over the hills looking for him either. If he wasn't within earshot of her voice, she would eat without him. The way she felt at the moment, two dinners wouldn't begin to fill her up.

Walking out on the porch, she leaned against the railing and yelled, but he didn't answer. "Fine, I'll eat alone," she grumbled, disgruntled by his absence.

"You called?" Two hands slipped around her waist from behind and held her captive, easing her backward.

Amelia struggled to free herself from his embrace, but he wouldn't let go. "Blast you, Colt!"

"Are you that excited by my touch?" he murmured, sliding one hand up under her breasts.

"That pounding you feel is fear, you idiot, you just scared a few good years off my life."

"Then I'll have to make the remaining ones more enjoyable," he whispered before letting her go.

Amelia stiffened. "What did you say?"

Colt couldn't believe those words had come out of his own mouth. Was he serious? He didn't know himself just what he'd meant, so how could he possibly explain it to her?

"Is dinner ready?" he inquired innocently.

How could he possibly say something so provocative one minute, then turn around and ask something so mundane? Amelia whisked her robe up, stalked into the kitchen, and sat down. Was she actually going to marry this man? She'd better give this idea some serious thought. Sex wasn't everything. But that little voice inside her head cautioned her; it did count for an awful lot.

"This is wonderful, Amelia."

"Thank you."

With a few questions from her Colt began to tell her stories about the history and inhabitants of the surrounding area. She learned that his parents came up on a regular basis to get away from their hectic town life. They weren't at all far from Austin, and the place was easily accessible by car. Upon thinking about the way he drove, she much preferred his unusual but far more controlled mode of transportation. They finished dinner without once baiting each other and actually managed to load the dishwasher without a hitch.

Colt lighted the fire he'd set up earlier, and they relaxed on opposite ends of the sofa with brandy, Amelia curling her legs underneath her. She had vacillated over whether to bring up the subject of her brother and finally decided to bring it out in the open.

"What happens to my brother now?"

Her question had come out of nowhere, and he was hard pressed not to show his surprise. "We leave him at my ranch and hope they can't find him there."

"That's it?" Amelia sat up and glared at him. "We just leave him to be found?"

Colt rubbed a lone finger down the side of his face in silent worry. This woman was going to get herself into deep trouble someday if she kept taking her brother's problems on as her own. His occupation was still a mystery to Colt, but he sure as hell wasn't a door-to-door salesman. The men he seemed to deal with on a day-to-day basis were serious and deadly. They shot people.

"What would you like to do?" he asked, his tone very mild and noncommittal.

"Something, anything!" She stood up and started pacing back and forth in front of the fire. "There's got to be something we can do!"

"Such as?"

"Set up some kind of trap and nab these guys." She continued her pacing, tripping over the long robe in her fury and impatience.

Colt chuckled quietly to himself. "Good plan,"

213

he said. "I thought so, too, when I first came up with it."

Amelia stopped pacing. "Is that why you told William to call Jerry and . . ." She trailed off and clapped a hand over her mouth.

"Don't look so worried, sweetheart," he said, laughing heartily. "I know you listened in on my phone conversations last night. How else would you have known to hide in my car?"

"Oh."

"And yes, that's why Jerry was called. One of those helicopters that landed at William's place this morning contained Jerry and a few of his hand-picked men. Their job was to trail anyone who might follow us," Colt explained. "Catching the sort of people who are after your brother isn't the business of amateurs, Amelia."

Amelia had regained her equilibrium and was once again pacing excitedly. "Then we have to call them, find out what happened!"

"There's no phone here."

"There's a radio in the helicopter! We—"

"We," he interrupted seriously, "have instructions to keep our heads down and our mouths closed until Jerry contacts us." He stood up, facing her squarely. "And that's just what we're going to do. Every day at noon I'm supposed to listen to the radio on a prearranged frequency for Jerry's all-clear signal. This is a delicate operation, Amelia, and the folks who are trained for it have everything under control."

She glared at him, frustrated and incredulous.

"Maybe," she shot back. "Meanwhile, we just sit here twiddling our thumbs?"

With a quicksilver move Colt reached out and grabbed the sleeve of her robe as she began to turn away. He sat down on the plushly upholstered sofa, giving her sleeve a hard tug as he did so, and she fell into his lap.

"Colt! My brandy."

"Is gone," he said, setting the empty glass aside. Amelia glanced at it with surprise. In her agitated state she must have literally gulped it down. "We'll have a great many things to do beside twiddling our thumbs."

"But—"

"I'll see to it you don't get bored." Colt unzipped the Burgundy-colored robe and slid it off her shoulders. The warm, crackling fire shot shadows around the darkened room, a myriad of designs dancing on the walls. "You're even more beautiful by firelight, if that's possible," he murmured, his hands caressing the smooth white skin of her shoulders.

Amelia felt warm and fuzzy all at once. The brandy was playing with her senses, or perhaps it was just his sensuous, coaxing touch heightening them to a new pitch as his hands careened across her damp skin.

"What are you going to do?"

"I'm going to make love to you."

She melted into his arms. "I'd like that," she told him in a whisper, giving herself up to his overpowering touch. "I'd like that very much."

CHAPTER TWELVE

Colt stood silently at the foot of the bed, watching Amelia sleep. She was so lovely, to his eyes the most beautiful woman in the world as she lay dozing peacefully on her stomach. Only partially covered by the rumpled quilt, the creamy white skin of her legs and back tempted him, making him want to slip out of his clothes and awaken her by tenderly kissing every exposed inch of her.

She would turn willingly into his embrace that he knew, sleepy and warm, her eyes deep pools of emotion and desire. The thought intoxicated him. Amelia was his now, his and his alone. He sat down on the bed next to her and gently brushed the baby-soft wisps of hair away from the side of her face, dipping his head to kiss her cheek. Her eyelids fluttered and she moaned softly.

"What time is it?" she mumbled, still half in a dream.

Colt smiled at her, inhaling her fragrance. "A little after noon."

Amelia moaned again, stretching and yawning, then rolled to her hip and wrapped her arms

216

around his neck. "I am decadent, aren't I? Lolling in bed past twelve!"

"You deserve it." His eyes gleamed. "We didn't get to sleep until very late."

The memory of their lovemaking washed over her like a warm Caribbean tide. She tilted her head and kissed him, drawing him tighter into her embrace. "Now that I know the time, I have another question." Amelia gazed into his eyes, a wicked smile playing at the corners of her mouth. "What day is it?"

Colt laughed softly. "To tell you the truth, I'm not exactly sure. Does it matter?"

"No." She shook her head, her tousled hair swirling around her face. "Not really. Kiss me."

They sprawled together on the bed, sweet anticipation wrapping them in its gossamer web as they began to explore the vast ocean of their desire yet again. Both were more certain of those passionate waters now, and yet each new discovery still left them shaking and breathless. They were learning each other's needs, but there remained so much more to learn, a lifetime of tender research.

Amelia supposed she should care about how long they had been suspended here in time. But she truly didn't. She was vaguely aware that three days had passed since they had arrived at the cabin, days and nights of glorious freedom from the worries and doubts of the outside world.

Michael would be wondering where they were, would undoubtedly be drawing his own conclusions. She didn't care. Her brother was in safe hands, there was nothing she could do even if she was with him, and Amelia had discovered she enjoyed being relieved of the responsibility.

She had also discovered she was almost certainly falling in love with Colt. It wasn't anything like she'd expected it to be. There was no blinding flash of recognition, no sudden realization she was in love. Instead, it was building slowly, steadily, a tender flood of understanding as she found her every thought revolving around him. Her feelings for him grew stronger every day, every minute. She couldn't imagine life without him.

There was a shield around Colt's heart, she could feel it instinctively, but those same instincts told her it was weakening. Maybe he had made her his own, but she was making him hers as well. Step by step, they were moving toward the future Michael had envisioned for them. But it was no longer his plans she was interested in. It was her own. Amelia was meeting the challenge Colt had put to her; she was going to melt his heart.

As they lay side by side, basking in the glow of their desire, she stroked the taut muscles of his stomach with her hand and nibbled on his shoulder. He kissed her forehead and sighed.

"You're insatiable," he murmured, burying his face in the soft pillow of her hair. "I shouldn't have let you sleep so long."

Amelia propped herself up on one elbow and gazed into his eyes. "Is that a complaint I hear?"

"No." Colt laughed and pulled her on top of him. "While you were in here getting your beauty rest, I was doing my daily duty at the radio. I have good news."

"Good . . ." She trailed off and her eyes grew as wide as saucers. "Jerry caught them?"

"He did."

Amelia let out a whoop and started to get up, but Colt held her against his chest. "Aren't you excited?" she wanted to know.

"With you wriggling around on top of me, how could I be anything but excited?" He ran his hands down the length of her spine, then cupped her buttocks possessively. "Are you in that much of a hurry to leave here?" he asked.

She stopped struggling. He was right, of course. Now that the people who had been trying to kill Nathan had been apprehended, there was no longer any reason for them to stay here. It was time to return to the real world, a world full of distractions and interruptions.

"Not in a hurry, exactly," Amelia replied, feeling happy and sad at the same time. "But he is my brother, Colt. I need to go see him." Then her face brightened. "After I do, we can come back!"

Colt nodded and smiled, but his smile seemed forced all of a sudden. "We'll see," he said, then rolled her gently off of him and got up, searching for his clothes.

"What's wrong?"

"Nothing," he assured her, but his frown said otherwise. "It's just that I realized it's time we were getting back. I have business to attend to. And we're going to have to put up with a lot of ribbing from Pop and Helen about being up here alone together for so long as it is."

Amelia frowned too. It suddenly occurred to her

that once away from their little love nest, the spell might be broken. In fact, from the distant look in Colt's eyes as he dressed, she wondered if it wasn't already unraveling.

"Why should it bother you what they think?" she asked.

He glanced at her, then away. "Won't it bother you?"

She shrugged, confused by this change in his behavior. Then she realized what it was. Colt was behaving as if he had scented a trap, and in a way she supposed he had. Her trap was very tender, with only the best intentions—love, marriage, a life together—but to his bachelor mind a trap nonetheless. She was going to have to be very careful from now on. If she spooked him, he might literally fly off into the sunset.

"I don't particularly care what they think we've been doing up here," Amelia replied in a casual tone. "We're grown-ups. We can make our own decisions."

Colt looked at her intently for a moment. "My sentiments exactly," he said at last. "Go ahead and take a shower if you want. I'll load up the helicopter and we can leave as soon as you're dressed."

He left the room scowling, wondering what on earth had come over him. Something had simply snapped inside him when Amelia mentioned coming back to the cabin, like a switch being thrown in his brain. These past three and a half days had been the best in his life. But at the thought of leaving and then coming back, of the ongoing relationship that implied, Colt had suddenly awakened as if from a dream.

Was he falling in love with Amelia? Perhaps he was. The feelings of tenderness whenever he saw her, the dawning recognition that he couldn't imagine going forward from this point in his life without her. He wanted to come back here with her, didn't even want to leave now, and that was what had scared him.

A part of him didn't really believe that love could happen this easily. And yet, while he watched her sleep earlier, he'd been dreaming about making her his wife, coming to this cabin on their honeymoon. Was that what Amelia was thinking of too?

The idea panicked him, plain and simple. Everything was moving too fast. What he needed was some time to think his feelings through. Now that the people after the mysterious John Smith had been caught, he would have that opportunity. Colt would take Amelia to his ranch, and while she was visiting with her brother, he would slip quietly away to work things out. Lust was one thing, but falling in love was quite another. Before he even thought about the prospect of marriage he wanted to be certain he knew his own mind.

Nathan struggled to sit up in bed, leaning back with a sigh on the pillows Teri held in position for him. She called herself a nurse, and in fact was a very good one, but in spite of her secrecy he knew that there was more to her life story than the nursing academy. Her confident handling of the re-

221

volver at her hip suggested training not unlike his own.

The gun was not in evidence now, a sure sign that she knew quite well the visitor they were about to receive. He wasn't much comforted by that knowledge, however. Teri had been his main link to the outside world, but he knew so little about her or the situation he had found himself in once he'd been moved from the hospital in Austin.

Jerry had assured him that everything was all right, and he trusted Jerry, but that didn't mean he was going to get caught flat on his back in a weak, indefensible position. He reached beneath the covers and touched his own pistol, finding its presence —and the fact that Teri had let him keep it—very comforting.

"You won't be needing the gun," Teri assured him.

"I'll be the judge of that," he returned gruffly. "Who is this guy anyway?"

Teri adjusted the pillows behind him. "The man who is responsible for all this fine care you're receiving, that's who. Your benefactor, so to speak. I'd be nice to him if I were you."

"Why?"

"Because," she informed him, her eyes alive with quiet humor, "he might decide to take me off your case, and I've grown so fond of listening to you grumble and grouse."

Nathan grabbed her wrist and held it tightly. "I thought you were with the government!"

"Never! I work independently. Michael Colt hired me to take care of you." With a twist of her

222

wrist she was free. "You're not as well as you'd like to believe."

He grimaced in pain as he moved the injured part of his body in an effort to glare at her. "Who the hell is he?"

"You'll find out soon enough. I hear him on the stairs now." Teri smiled broadly at him, and he was struck by her dark good looks. "And I meant what I said. I really have grown fond of you, and it would be a shame if I had to leave before I got you up and around." She winked at him, then turned and walked out the door.

He watched her go, his questions about his visitor unanswered. Infuriating woman! "I'll get on my feet, all right," he muttered under his breath, "and when I do, I'm going to chase you all over this house!"

As Michael Colt entered the room, the phone on the bedside table began to ring. Nathan looked first at it, then at the white-haired old man standing at the foot of the bed.

"Go ahead and answer it," Michael told him.

"What?"

"Answer it. It's for you."

He picked up the receiver and pressed it to his ear, his eyes widening instantly. The conversation was brief, mainly one sided, the words he did say clipped, precise, and guarded. Through it all his hand never left the gun hidden beneath his blankets.

When he hung up, his eyes held a mixture of confusion and respect. However, the suspicion in his voice lingered. "Michael Colt?"

"At your service."

Michael seated himself in a chair close to the bed and studied the young man before him. He had familiar sherry-brown eyes, which were staring at him every bit as warily as his sister often did. His hair was a much less intriguing shade of brown, though. A strong chin, at this moment jutting out at a challenging angle. Yes, there was a family resemblance all right, that same stubbornness and guts.

"It seems," the younger man said, "that I am in your debt, Mr. Colt."

"Not at all, Mr. Nathan Drake." A very small smile cracked his weathered face. "Well, perhaps a little debt. We'll get around to that."

Hearing his full name spoken out loud startled him, and Nathan's hand tightened instinctively on the secret gun. He forced it to relax. Whoever this old codger was, he had clout.

He had been requested to extend to Michael Colt all his cooperation. Since it was a request, Nathan wasn't actually bound by regulations to comply, but his superiors had indicated it would probably be a good idea, and might even earn him a promotion.

The promotion would be to a supervisory position, a desk job, something Nathan had mixed feelings about. In view of the increasing number of holes in his body, though, he was giving it a lot of consideration.

"Just who are you, Mr. Colt?" Nathan asked.

"Please, call me Michael." He smiled and extended his hand. Nathan released his gun at last and shook hands with him. "I am a businessman. I am also a friend of Amelia's."

His sister? This was getting stranger by the minute. "I don't understand. How do you know Amelia?"

"I met her at the hospital. We struck up a friendship, and I discovered you were in need of assistance—"

"How?" Nathan demanded.

Michael shrugged. "How did I know whom to contact within your organization? How did I get them to call you here and verify my identity?"

"Good point," Nathan muttered. He had checked and rechecked his superior's identity over the phone, using code. He had been who he said he was, and that meant Michael Colt checked out too. That didn't mean he trusted him. "Go on."

"Where was I?" Michael asked, looking befuddled for a moment. "Oh, yes. Amelia. I offered my help, and she accepted. Along the way she became, shall we say, involved with my grandson," he added with a sly wink, "but that's another story."

Nathan blinked, not sure what to make of the wily old gentleman. "You offered your help? Just like that?"

"I do that from time to time," Michael replied with a modest shrug. "A hospital wing here, a donation to charity there, I sometimes—"

"Sometimes give aid to a man on the lam with killers on his tail?" Nathan offered.

Michael grinned. "Sometimes."

"Not to mention hiring a gun-slinging nurse to watch over him and save his hide. Who is she and

225

where did you find her?" Nathan asked suspiciously.

"I've known her for quite some time. You needed someone to keep you alive—in more ways than one—and she was the logical choice," he replied. "If she wants you to know anything else about her, she'll tell you herself."

The younger man grimaced. "What do you want?"

"I'm here to help you."

Nathan waved a hand at the room in general. "You're already helping me. As I said at the beginning of this odd conversation, I'm in your debt."

"Don't be obtuse, dear boy. You know what I mean."

The stock deal? Suddenly his suspicions doubled. "I don't need your help."

"Ah, but your superiors think you do." Michael leaned back in his chair, relaxing for the first time, and casually reeled off a few names.

One could have heard a pine needle drop in the ensuing silence. Nathan gazed at him, impressed by the old man's connections. The vision of that temptingly safe desk job danced in the back of his mind.

"What do you want from me?" he asked at last.

"I want you to agree to my plan for the apprehension of the men involved in this stock scam."

Nathan eyed him with an even higher degree of suspicion than before. "What exactly do you get out of this?"

"A feeling of a job well done for my government."

"Sure," Nathan returned derisively. "Try again."

"A feeling of accomplishment at helping my fellow man."

A small smile tugged at the corners of Nathan's mouth. The old man was good. It was extremely doubtful he was anywhere near as innocent or altruistic as he pretended, and yet Nathan was so intrigued by the whole situation, he was tempted to go along just to watch the old guy operate.

"Let's get something straight, Michael. My superiors have requested that I cooperate with you. In agency terms that means they're leaving it up to me, the man closest to the action, to decide whether I am willing to extend that cooperation," Nathan explained in a brusque, no-nonsense tone of voice. "Now, I want the truth from you, because until I know everything I'm not agreeing to give you the time of day."

Michael weighed the possibilities. Nathan Drake was a tough customer, mentally as well as physically. Wounded or not, he had already assessed the situation and come to the correct conclusion: Michael might be able to help him accomplish the job at hand more quickly and easily, but there was a price tag somewhere. He wanted to see it, right now, and if he didn't like the cost, that would be the end of the discussion.

"All right. Let me start off by assuring you that I do want to help. I am an investor myself, stocks and venture capital for the most part, as is my son, his son, and, well, the whole family really," Michael informed him. "It is to our advantage to clear the woodpile of people such as those you seek. Believe it or not, that is my primary reason for offering my assistance."

Nathan was watching him intently. "So far so good. But I had already assumed that much from what my superior told me about you. Get to the bottom line, Michael."

It was going to be a pleasure, Michael decided, to have a young man such as this as an in-law. His grin was wide as he announced calmly, "I want to have Amelia married to my grandson and producing babies."

"Excuse me?" Nathan asked, thinking he must have missed part of this conversation somewhere.

Michael laughed. "When I said earlier that she and my grandson had become involved, that's not strictly the truth. I have been working behind the scenes to bring that happy circumstance about, but those two youngsters are moving much too slowly for my taste. They need a little push, and I have devised a plan whereby I can give them that push and help you bring your stock hustlers to justice at the same time."

"Teri!" Nathan bellowed.

She appeared in the doorway. "Yes, John?"

"Call me Nathan," he muttered. "The whole world seems to know that's my real name anyway."

"Nathan. I like that." She smiled fetchingly. "Did you need something?"

"Have you been slipping me extra medication?"

"No. Why?"

"Just wondering." He waved her away. When

she disappeared again, he returned his gaze to Michael. "Are you telling me that you just decided that my sister and your grandson should get married and have your great-grandchildren?"

Michael nodded. "I am."

"And that helping me, hiring Teri, and now whatever plan it is you've cooked up to assist me in this phony stock operation, all of it has been a cover for your matchmaking scheme?"

"Not entirely," Michael replied. "I really am something of a philanthropist. And I do want to catch these men."

"But?"

"But Amelia and Colt are perfect for each other. That's what everyone calls my grandson, by the way, though his real name is Michael, like me," he added proudly. "When you see the two of them together, Nathan, I'm sure you'll agree they should be married. And I will see to it that they are, I assure you."

"I don't doubt it," he mumbled. Nathan still had the feeling he had been given too much painkiller. This was the craziest thing he'd ever heard.

Then again, the thought of his little sister married and with children of her own appealed to him somehow. He hadn't felt the need for that kind of permanency, at least not until just recently, but he knew Amelia had. Besides, as determined as the old man seemed, he didn't see how he could do much to stand in his way, especially not from a sickbed.

"All right," he said thoughtfully, "let's forget the wedding bells for a moment. I don't think in any case you can make my sister do anything she doesn't want to do."

Michael chuckled. "Oh, she wants to marry Colt. In fact, recent developments suggest she may be making great strides in that direction at this very moment," he assured him with a cryptic smile. "But you were saying?"

"You spoke of giving them some kind of push, one that coincided with exposing this stock fraud."

"I did indeed. Colt and Amelia figure prominently in my plan," Michael said. "They—"

Nathan interrupted him, his tone adamant. "No, I won't put Amelia or anyone else in the path of danger. Look what happened to me!"

Michael wasn't fooled. He'd done some careful checking of his own before he had planned this. He would never, even for a moment, consider putting his loved ones in danger either.

"You were shot because of something you got into on a previous case, one totally unrelated to this stock scam. The men who did this to you were caught earlier this morning, along with your fellow agent turned informer. None of them knew your real name." Pale blue eyes held him within their steel grip as he reemphasized his point. "Your condition has nothing to do with the case you're involved in now. The people we're dealing with have never shown any inclination toward violence. And both you and Teri will be close at hand the entire time."

"You've read the file," Nathan said, thinking aloud. "And you have all the inside information." He was in the hands of a master manipulator. No wonder his superior had strongly suggested he co-operate. "Who the hell are you, Michael Colt?"

Michael leaned closer. "I am the man who can help you pin these people to the wall, my boy. Do we have a deal?"

"Let's hear the plan," Nathan returned warily, although he was being sucked in and he knew it.

"You understand that this must appear to be your idea?" he asked. "That as far as Colt and Amelia are concerned, you are the one who formulated the plan and I merely helped you work out the business details?"

Nathan had to laugh. "You're a tricky old buzzard, Michael. All right, you've got a deal. Now tell me this scheme I'm supposed to have come up with."

CHAPTER THIRTEEN

"You want me to what?"

Michael smiled and repeated calmly, "I want you to pretend to marry Amelia."

Colt got to his feet, spilling his coffee on the floor as he did so. His housekeeper, Molita, threw her hands into the air and stalked out of the kitchen. Other areas of the ranch house needed her attention, and she could tell there was going to be quite a lot of yelling between Colt and his grandfather.

"No way, Pop," Colt told him loudly.

"Calm down, my boy. It's a vital part of Nathan's plan. I assured him that once I explained it to you—"

Colt cut him off with a wave of his hand. "That's another thing. Are you trying to tell me he just sprang this on you out of the blue?"

"Not immediately, no," Michael replied. "But once he realized who I was, the kind of business our family was in, you could practically hear the gears turning in his head. He's a smart boy, just like you." He smiled at his grandson. "His superiors must agree, because they're behind his plan one hundred percent."

"Well, I'm not," Colt said derisively. "I mean, it's great up to a point. I can understand the logic of us posing as potential investors for this sham company. We're well known around Austin, so our interest wouldn't spook the men behind it. And since Nathan was working undercover to gain their trust, he's the logical choice to set things up."

Michael managed to look puzzled. "Then what don't you understand?" he asked innocently.

Colt glared at him. "As if you didn't know! I smell a white-haired rat here. Why is it necessary for Amelia and me to pretend to be married? What part does that play?"

"It's really quite simple," his grandfather answered. "You said it yourself. We're well known around here. Our operation has gained the reputation as being strictly a family affair. If Nathan tried to set things up without some connection to the family, those men would be highly suspicious."

"So let him get some other investors," Colt said angrily, sitting back down with an exasperated sigh.

"He doesn't have the time. His unexpected trip to the hospital put him behind schedule," Michael explained, his tone patient and coaxing. "These men are all ready to go and are seeking capital. If he doesn't move soon, they'll have run their scam and disappeared completely." He fixed Colt with a serious frown. "We're his best, no, make that his only hope to bring them to justice."

This couldn't be happening. Colt had delivered

233

Amelia to her brother's room, then gone to grab a quick cup of coffee before taking off for parts unknown. He desperately needed to think. But who should he find in his kitchen but Michael, and before he knew it he was being sucked into some scheme Amelia's brother had come up with.

It was a relief to know her brother was some sort of government agent and not the hoodlum Colt had feared, but even so, hadn't they helped the guy enough already? Did they have to play cops and robbers now too? More importantly, was it absolutely necessary to pose as Amelia's husband to convince the con artists that their interest was genuine?

He sighed again. Apparently it was. And it did make sense. "All right, so that's logical too," he grumbled. "These men will know we're for real, and they'll also know we don't use intermediaries. But—"

"Well." Now Michael sighed. He looked quite forlorn. "I can't force you to do this. I've explained it to you as I promised Amelia's brother I would. And you know how important it is to catch these men. If they keep doing business, somewhere along the line one of our friends or associates will get burned." He pushed away from the table. "But you've served your fellow man enough already, I guess. I'll just go tell Nathan you have better things to do."

"It's not that, Pop. It's just . . ." He trailed off. What was bothering him? Was it that pretending to be Amelia's husband might convince him that he wanted to do it for real? Was there a chance that the role might suit him?

Then again, playing house with Amelia was an opportunity Colt found intriguing. Maybe it would be a sure way to find out once and for all if he was really falling in love with her, or whether he had simply been overcome by desire at the cabin. Still, something in him rebelled at the idea, if for no other reason than that it fairly reeked of Michael's handiwork.

Michael was slowly getting to his feet. "By the way, Gloria Clarkson has been calling. She seems quite distraught, said something about an ultimatum, I believe," he informed him in a casual tone. "I think she's about to tell you to deliver your body into her hands or forget her stock."

"Great," Colt said, disgusted with the whole world.

Gloria was a good-looking woman, but her type had never appealed to him. He was prepared to do anything he had to do to get those shares, except take her into his bed or marry her. Although he liked a woman to have a mind of her own and go after what she wanted—as his grandmother had—this was an entirely different situation.

"It looks like you're going to take your lumps on this one," Michael continued. "If you don't fool around with her, she'll fool around with that company until even the stock you already have will be worthless."

Colt nodded. "I know. I was hoping I could find some way to put her off until she got in such financial straits that—" He stopped, looking at his grandfather with grudging admiration. "You've outdone yourself, you wily old fox."

"I'm sure I have no idea what you're talking about," Michael said with a wounded air.

There was a lot of manipulating going on here and Colt knew it. Sometimes, however, his grandfather was too smart for his own good. Colt saw an opportunity to take care of two problems at once: he might be able to get Gloria's stock without sacrificing himself to the vamp of Austin, and work through this love nonsense at the same time. All he had to do was go along with Michael's plan, and even that could be thoroughly enjoyable.

So what if he played the matchmaking game? They would have to make this mock marriage look good, wouldn't they? It would provide him with ample time to enjoy more of the passion he had shared with Amelia during the last few days. In the end no one could force him to propose.

Colt grinned. "If I pretended to get married, Gloria might give up the battle."

Michael's eyebrows shot up in surprise. "Why, I never thought of that. Pretty good thinking, my boy."

"You can tell Nathan I'll do it," Colt said, not fooled by his grandfather's innocent act for an instant.

Michael left the room whistling. He hadn't put one over on Colt. He hadn't really expected to. But he had seen the way his grandson and Amelia looked when they arrived home, with a relaxed glow that was a sure sign of recent intimacy. Their relationship had changed. If they weren't falling in love, they were well on their way. Whether Colt knew it or not, this little push would put him right over the edge.

Nathan quickly hid his gun under the pillow when his sister arrived. He also managed to conceal his growing feeling of excitement at being back in the game again. It felt good to be doing something, even if it was pulling a fast one on your kid sister.

"Amelia," he said with genuine fondness. "How are you?"

"I'm fine," she replied, taking his hand and squeezing it. "You're looking much better, awake for a change. I was beginning to think you were going to sleep your life away."

She hugged him gently, then sat down on the bed, careful not to shake it as she did so. He did look much better, his color strong and natural, the lines around his eyes less pronounced. Still, she was worried. How long would he stay healthy this time?

"I've had enough of sickbeds to last me three lifetimes. You look wonderful. Just what have you been up to?" he teased, enjoying the pale pink blush tinging her face at his words. Michael Colt had been right; she looked like a woman in love.

"Never mind me. You're the one who keeps falling to pieces. When are you going to grow up and get a real job?" she shot back affectionately. She was actually quite serious. "One you can tell Mom and Dad about?"

Nathan grinned. "Hold on to your socks. I

might have found one," he informed her. "Same firm, but a desk job."

"You're kidding!" Her eyes rounded into saucers, her disbelief evident. "My brother behind a desk? I thought that would only happen if you were physically roped and tied to a chair each day."

"So did I." Nathan still wasn't so sure this job wouldn't be slow, agonizing torture. "But it has to happen sometime. They've been working up to it for a while, giving me more responsibility, letting me do more planning and such. If I succeed on this next assignment, I'll get a promotion and the desk job that goes with the rank."

Amelia was looking at him intently. "Why do I get the feeling you're less than thrilled at the prospect?"

"You're right, I suppose." He shrugged. "But I'm not getting any younger. Either the bullets are getting faster or I'm getting slower. There comes a time when you have to admit that it's time to leave the fieldwork to others."

"Nathan, are you sure?"

He sighed loudly. "No. I imagine I'll be the kind of supervisor who takes a more active role, but I think that will make me even better at my job. I guess that's what my superiors think too."

Inside, Amelia was yelling with joy. However, she strove to appear calm and give him the wise counsel he seemed to need. "If it's what you want, go for it. You've never let anything stand in your way before."

"True. I went twelve years without a serious injury. But I've been shot twice in as many years, and that tends to make one take stock of one's life."

She patted his hand. "Well, if there's anything I can do to help the change go more smoothly for you, just ask."

"As a matter of fact . . ." He trailed off, apparently doing battle with some inner problem.

"Tell me," Amelia encouraged.

Nathan felt like a first-class heel, dragging his sister into this mess. Michael Colt had better be right about her relationship with his grandson. He'd never seen her look happier, but part of that could be her joy at seeing him put out to pasture. Of course, that joy was what he was counting on to make this plan work.

"The people who put me in this condition have been caught, but by taking me out of action all this time they really put a dent in another case I was working on."

Amelia frowned. "Surely there are other—"

"No," he interrupted, "there isn't time to set up another man and establish cover. I'm it, but if I want to finish this thing and get that promotion, I'm going to need help. The moment I found out about the Colt family and their business ventures I got an idea, but . . ."

"Go on."

"It would involve you, Amelia," he said with a frown.

She didn't even stop to think. "Of course I'll help you. All you have to do is ask."

Suddenly, a mischievous twinkle appeared in his

eyes, one she remembered quite well from their childhood. Amelia gazed at him warily now, realizing he was up to something. She had learned the hard way that she always seemed to end up in trouble when he got that look on his face.

"What exactly do you want me to do?"

"Remember, you've already said yes."

"Out with it, or I'll lean on your ribs," she warned.

"Teri!" he yelled. "This woman is threatening me!"

His nurse poked her head through the doorway. "Good. It serves you right," she said, then smiled at Amelia and disappeared again.

Amelia was laughing helplessly. "You clown!"

"That's one character I've never gotten to play."

"What a shame, you have such natural ability," she said sardonically. "Now, quit the stalling, brother, and tell me what I won't like about this."

His words rushed out like lightning, with the same shocking effect. "I want you to pretend to be married to Colt, so I'll have an inside track to represent the rest of the family as investors."

"You what?" Amelia jumped up and stared at him. "Tell me you're kidding!"

He shook his head. "No."

"How did you find out about Colt and me?" she asked, then held up her hand to cut off his reply. "Never mind! I knew I smelled a rat."

"What rat? Is there a problem?"

"Not the kind you mean," she muttered.

Blast Michael Colt and his interfering ways! When he approached Colt with this plan, which he

240

was probably doing right this minute, Colt would feel exactly as she didn't want him to feel. Trapped.

She had planned on very gently luring him into her web, using feminine guile and their mutual desire. Now Michael was trying to hit him over the head with a hammer. If Colt didn't agree with this plan she might never see him again. She had a feeling that he was quite capable of disappearing.

Plopping on the bed beside Nathan, she looked at him thoughtfully, ignoring his grimace of pain. She wanted to see him in that desk job, and if that meant going along with this, so be it. And the more she thought about it, the more she wondered if it might not work after all.

Michael could be very persuasive. He could probably convince Colt to join this game, and she could still go ahead with her own plans. Colt would be putty in her hands.

She grinned at her brother and asked, "When does this loving charade begin?"

His eyes sparkled, and she realized that he viewed his job exactly that way. His career was a game, one in which he got to play many diverse characters. Amelia suddenly felt more than a little excited herself.

"Next week," Nathan told her. "Providing Colt was as easy to convince as you were."

"Why, you! Shall I fix your other ribs for you?"

Nathan yelled for Teri to come save him again, but it was Michael who stepped into the room, smiling like a Cheshire cat. "Colt has agreed to his role in our little play," he announced. "Hello,

241

Amelia. May I say you look particularly glowing this afternoon?"

Amelia scowled at him, irritated by his knowing grin and perturbed by his words. "Colt agreed? Just like that?"

"As a matter of fact, he seems positively enchanted by the idea," Michael assured her.

Her frown deepened. If he was enchanted, something was wrong. Either Michael was lying—a fair possibility—or Colt had some scheme of his own in mind. Amelia suddenly felt much less sure of herself. Would she end up playing the role of the sculptor, or the clay?

CHAPTER FOURTEEN

Amelia walked into the study and threw the newspaper's society section across the antique desk at Colt. He arched an inquiring eyebrow at her. She looked positively delectable in her russet-colored lace dress. A satin underslip of the same color cut straight across her breasts, leaving her throat and arms bare. Her thick shining hair was swept into a loose knot on top of her head, a few curling tendrils escaping.

"Another eligible Austin bachelor bites the dust, captured recently by a very enterprising woman." Amelia clenched her hands in rage. "Where do they get such . . . such drivel?" she demanded.

Colt felt his lips twitching as he struggled not to laugh. Her outrage appeared to be very real, and he wondered which part of the gossip columnist's article bothered her the most. He had agreed that the story needed to be planted, for more than one reason. The men they were after would be looking for it to confirm Nathan's connections to the Colt family. Gloria Clarkson would see it too. He would give anything to see her face when she did.

"Are you upset because they didn't use your full

name?" he asked, scanning the column. It only referred to her as Amelia, the mystery woman.

"You . . . You . . . Oh!"

"No?" Colt scanned the impressive list of women he'd been linked with. "Then it must be because I was considered so eligible?" He shot a quick glance at her mutinous face. "Or didn't you like the way they referred to you as a very enterprising woman?"

"Colt, you are walking a very thin line right now," she warned. He'd had the gall to walk in on her bath earlier and take his time shaving, his eyes watching her every movement in the mirror, ignoring her request that he leave. "Don't push your luck."

"And just what will you do? Deny me my husbandly rights tonight?"

"We are not really married, so you don't have any husbandly rights to lose!"

"That didn't stop us before." Colt stood up and walked around the desk to face her. "Why should it stop us now?" he murmured, sliding his arms around her waist and pulling her close.

This was all so confusing; she wanted to be married to him for real, not playing this tantalizing game of make-believe. Then there was the burning jealousy and rage she'd felt when she had read the article. Colt hadn't really gone out with all those women, had he? Adding to her emotional upheaval was Colt's blatant sensual teasing, a week-long assault he called "practicing his part" and seemed to be enjoying immensely. At this moment his strong hands were kneading her buttocks rhythmically, distracting her train of thought.

"Colt?" As her hands touched his chest her fingers spread out on his snowy white shirt, the warmth of his skin tingling her fingertips.

He enfolded her snugly in his arms, not a breath of space between them. "Yes?"

She could feel the heat of his body melding into hers, robbing her of what little control she had left. Her hands slid up his throat to capture his jaw, cradling his face with gentle fingers as she pulled him toward her waiting lips. "Yes," she whispered, her lips breezing softly across his before settling down to deepen their kiss.

Wrapped in each other's arms, they were oblivious when Michael entered the room. Things were progessing well, he noted with great satisfaction. The last thing he wanted to do was pull these young lovers apart, but their guests would be arriving at any moment and one very important detail of their plan had been left out.

"Nice to see you newlyweds so engrossed in each other," he announced loudly, grinning from ear to ear.

Colt sighed, disgusted. "What now, Michael?"

"We almost left out a very important detail. Your wedding rings."

"Our what?"

Michael opened a small jewelry box. "It is customary to exchange rings along with vows, and these people will expect to see them on your fingers. These belonged to my dear parents. Try them on," he requested, though he was certain they

245

would fit. It had taken a bit of behind-the-scenes research, but he had gotten their sizes and taken the rings to an excellent jeweler he knew. He handed Colt a dainty gold-etched band.

Colt slipped it on her finger, arching his eyebrows at the perfect fit. His was perfect as well, and again he caught the aroma of a white rat. "Michael, I'd like a word or two with you in private, if I may," he said.

"Me first," Amelia interjected.

The doorbell rang and Michael grinned at his luck. "Fine, fine, but right now we have to go greet our guests."

He was sure that his grandson would soon see the wisdom of his actions. Amelia, too, though at the moment she was glaring at him with a dangerous light in her eyes. That was fine with him. He didn't trust good losers.

Amelia stood close to her brother, clutching the drink in her hand with a death grip. It had all seemed so easy when Michael and Nathan had explained the plan. But she wasn't an actress. Playing the loving new wife was easy, because she had finally stopped lying to herself and admitted that she was definitely in love with Colt. But the rest of this charade was nothing short of frightening. How did her brother do it?

Nathan was smiling pleasantly and seemed to be holding up fairly well, considering that he still wasn't allowed out of bed all day yet. Teri ruled him with an iron hand, and although he groused, Nathan seemed to enjoy her attentions. His

246

wounds were healing nicely. In time he would be as good as new, as long as he wasn't hurt again.

The thought of helping him get that promotion was uppermost in Amelia's mind as she welcomed their guests, the two men who would be dining with them this evening. They looked like lawyers or accountants, maybe stockbrokers. The last thing they resembled was con artists or criminals of any kind. Appearances could be so deceiving.

Colt was watching Amelia carefully. He knew that tonight was going to be difficult for her. In the library earlier he had tried to make it easier, relaxing her with his tender teasing. If they were going to pull this off successfully, he was going to have to guide her along. It was time he started playing the loving newlywed husband.

"Having fun, darling?" he crooned, slipping his arm around her waist to hug her close.

"Lovely," she replied, smiling up at him in adoration. "I have fun wherever I am, as long as I'm with you."

Was she laying it on a bit thick? Colt didn't seem to think so. He brushed his lips casually across hers, sending ripples of pleasure across her skin. Why couldn't this be real? Was Colt wishing the same?

"I like this dress."

"I wore it just for you."

Colt was eyeing the creamy skin above the underslip, her quickened breathing showing glimpses of even more cleavage. Amelia knew that look in his eyes, the flaring of desire he didn't try to hide.

Neither of them had to pretend to feel passion, that was for sure.

"Dinner is ready," Helen announced, then led the way into the formal dining room. The table was set beautifully with candles, sparkling crystal, and fine china. The room successfully exuded an air of old money. "Now, Amelia, you and Colt sit here. We wouldn't want to separate you newlyweds so soon," she said with a sweet little laugh.

So much of this wasn't an act. Helen didn't need to pretend she was happy to see them together. Michael was every bit the doting grandfather. Colt was gazing at Amelia with a very real desire, and she knew there was that and more in her own eyes. It all felt so real, so right. She wanted this dream to come true so badly she could taste it.

After seating everyone, Helen looked around the room. "What happened to that dear Mr. Cosgrove? I wanted him to sit beside me." She stood at the head of the table, looking very elegant in her pale-blue silk dress. "Someone should go find him. Our home is quite large, he could be wandering around lost," she added innocently.

"I believe he went in search of a phone," his partner, Charles Davis, explained. "Or a bathroom."

"Found both," Cosgrove said as he entered the room. "Sorry about the delay. Had to make a quick call to the family."

"How considerate of you," Helen remarked with an approving smile. With a regal nod to the waiter standing by, she gave her permission for the first course to be served.

248

"I want to hear all about your family, Mr. Cosgrove," Helen said. He quickly found himself embroiled in conversation.

"That's a lovely ring," Charles Davis told Amelia, admiring it as she picked up her glass.

She sipped her wine for fortitude. "Thank you. It belonged to Colt's great grandmother. I was so very pleased when he wanted me to have it," she answered softly, her eyes demurely lowered.

Of the two she felt the most comfortable with Charles, which probably meant he was the more deceiving. He was the elder, probably in his early fifties, a thin, dapper man with a kind face and thinning hair.

"Family tradition is a lovely thing," the man remarked casually, though he lifted his own wineglass in a silent toast to Amelia's brother.

Nathan and Colt exchanged a quick, knowing glance. "Yes, it is," Colt agreed. "It has worked well for us, both in business and in family life. Someday Amelia and I hope to have someone to pass both our success and our rings along to."

Amelia almost choked on a bite of dessert. Wasn't he carrying this little charade just a bit too far? Children were a serious matter. But she nodded and said, "Someday."

"You don't want to wait too long," Charles teased. "Have them young while you can still enjoy them."

"You sound like my grandfather," Colt observed dryly.

The other man shrugged. "When you get to be

our age, grandchildren can be a great comfort. You can't blame us for pushing you young folks along."

Colt grinned rakishly. "We're working on it."

"Here, darling," Amelia purred, placing a loaded fork in Colt's open mouth. "I know how much you like your sweets."

Helen basked in the glow of the compliments she received for having orchestrated such a fine meal. Michael allowed her the pleasure for a few minutes, then decided it was time to get the ball rolling.

"Shall we adjourn to the library, gentlemen?" he asked.

They all concurred, and thanked their hostess again as they filed out of the dining room on their way to Michael's study. Helen smiled throughout, but turned to Amelia as soon as they were gone.

"Isn't it terrible?" she complained. "Some men still think women don't have any place in business, as if the poor dears could get along without us. It's absolutely disgusting!"

"You're right," Amelia agreed, although she was quite relieved to be offstage for a while.

"Come along, let's relax in the sitting room while the caterers finish cleaning up."

On their way through the kitchen they discovered that Teri had been nearby all the time, doing her duty as bodyguard. Her eyes were wide and wary. She started to say something, but Helen cut her off.

"Have you eaten?" she asked, eyeing her suspiciously. "I know you haven't, you're always forgetting little minor details like food. I'll never put any meat on your bones this way. Now, take a seat at the table and I'll fix you a plate."

Amelia and Teri exchanged glances and burst out laughing. "She never changes," Teri said. "It's useless to swim against her current, so you might as well go with the flow."

"What's so funny, girls?" Helen asked, setting a loaded plate in front of Teri.

"I'll never be able to eat all this!"

"Well, just eat as much as you can. I'll get us all a cup of tea and we'll keep you company."

"You really do spoil your help, Helen," Teri said, then put her finger to her lips.

They approached her curiously. She pulled a piece of paper from her pocket and showed it to them. Amelia felt her stomach do a somersault as she read the startling news.

Cosgrove has bugged the house. Be very careful about what you say and keep the conversation light.

"Take a seat gentlemen," Michael offered when they all had a drink in hand. "Let's get down to business. First of all, I want to thank the newest member of my family, Nathan, for bringing this interesting proposal to our attention."

"You're welcome, Pop," Amelia's brother said.

"But I want to hear more about this newly forming company before I commit myself or my family."

Cosgrove and Davis nodded. "Certainly."

What they wanted from the Colt family was financial backing for a new business. In exchange the Colts would receive shares of stock in a start-up company that was forming with the sole purpose of producing and marketing one product. The testing of the product had gone well. But in actual day-to-day use its results were yet to be proven conclusively.

That made the risks very high, too high for a bank or other formal lender. So high, in fact, that Colt couldn't imagine anyone seriously considering investing in the deal. And yet they already had investors committed for millions of dollars. It never ceased to amaze him how many people there were who were willing to risk it all for a quick buck.

This was the chance to get in on the ground floor, the men informed them, in the production of a new, breakthrough automotive product. But it wasn't even in production yet, let alone proven effective. There were way too many holes in this plan, holes plainly evident to an experienced investor.

However they were mainly building their capital on a grass-roots level. Getting the Colt family interested was a windfall, one for which Davis and Cosgrove were no doubt effusively grateful to Nathan. If the scam worked, which appeared likely with or without the Colt family, the two men would have the cash and be long gone before any of their less astute investors suspected a thing.

They were slick, but just greedy enough to risk approaching a more experienced source of funds such as Michael Colt and his family. It would be their undoing, Nathan hoped, if they didn't get spooked. He had already warned Michael not to appear too eager.

"The books look good, gentlemen. As you know, however, this is a family affair. We'll discuss this and give you a decision within the next few days," Michael announced, thus ending the meeting. He showed them cordially to the door with reassurances that they would hear from him soon.

"Well, I'll tell you one thing," Michael said as he walked back into the study shaking his head in admiration, "those two have more—" He stopped. His mouth dropped open.

Nathan was holding up a small black disk for him to see. He gestured for Michael to keep talking and then bent over the briefcase he had on his lap, fiddling with something inside.

"Where'd everybody go?" Michael asked in a bewildered tone, nodding his understanding. "Oh, well. I'll just grab myself a quick nip while Helen isn't looking."

He clanked a few liquor bottles together, pouring a shot of whiskey into a glass. Colt was tiptoeing around the room, carefully checking the spots Nathan pointed out to him using the detector in his briefcase. The only listening device they found was the one that had been attached to Michael's phone.

Nathan left the room and returned without the disk. "All right. This room is clear now. So much for Cosgrove's considerate call to his family."

"These boys mean business," Michael declared.

Nathan carefully sat down in an overstuffed armchair. This night had wiped him out. His hands were beginning to shake from weakness and there was a pale sheen of perspiration forming on his brow and upper lip. Teri had been right. He wasn't nearly as strong yet as he'd thought he was.

Gathering all his strength, he pushed himself out of the chair. "They mean business, all right. Let's find out what other surprises they've left for us. Keep talking."

As they left the study, Colt picked up the conversation. "We'll discuss this tomorrow. I want to think things over before we put our heads together," he said. He had taken note of Nathan's exhaustion and wanted to give him an excuse to retire early.

Michael looked at him in surprise, then followed the direction of his grandson's eyes, understanding immediately. "Fine with me. I'll toss you for the biggest piece of dessert," he offered.

"Shouldn't we offer it to our guest?"

"Heck no, Nathan is family now and it's every person for themselves in this house. Come along, let's go find the girls."

Colt sat down in the chair next to Amelia at the kitchen table. Everyone watched in fascination as Nathan carefully checked the kitchen with his bug-detecting device. He discovered one bug and escorted it out, then declared the room clear.

"How about the rest of the house, Teri?"

"The bedrooms are all bugged, along with the living room and sitting room. He really made the rounds."

"You followed him around the house?" Nathan

was staring at her in disbelief, his anger clearly evident.

"I was very discreet, he didn't see me."

"But he could have!"

"He didn't see me," Teri snapped. She stood up and went to his side. "Look at you. Grouchy, sweating. You should be in bed."

"I need to check the rest of the house first."

"You're through for the night, buster, and you don't have enough strength to fight me either."

He started to object again, but his sister's voice came through loud and clear. "Nathan, you need to get some rest."

Her worried tone seemed to take the last of the fight out of him. "All right. You've done well, all of you. I'm sorry to have to tell you this, but the charade has to go on now, all night and all day, until they're hooked."

Colt looked at Amelia and grinned. Her eyes went wide. "What do you mean?" she asked uneasily.

"We can't remove any more of the bugs or they'll get suspicious. If you need to talk privately, use the kitchen or the study. Otherwise, just act like normal." He smiled weakly. "Like one big, happy family."

"They get the idea," Teri said. "Come on. I'm putting you to bed right now."

"I'll see everyone in the morning." He left the room leaning heavily on Teri. His exhaustion was obvious, and he grinned weakly at Teri. "Don't say I told you so."

A smirk curved the edges of her lips. "I don't have to, you already did."

Amelia watched them go, refusing to meet Colt's wicked, speculative gaze. Go on with the charade? Surely he didn't mean they had to share a room? It had been different when they were alone at the ranch but she didn't much like the idea of performing upon request.

Colt yawned elaborately. "Come on, wife. Time for all newlyweds to hit the sack." His eyebrows bobbed up and down.

"Didn't I see a room with two single beds?" Amelia asked Helen, her words tumbling over each other.

Helen gave a guilty little jump and informed her, "I'm afraid there's a bit of a problem there, dear."

"Oh?" Colt asked warily. He had planned to tease Amelia unmercifully before suggesting that room—not that he intended to stay in his own bed, naturally. But it appeared his grandparents had already made plans of their own.

"I'm in the middle of redecorating the rose room. There aren't any beds in there," Helen explained.

"Then what about our old rooms?"

"We had to give them to Nathan and Teri, so she can hear him if he needs help in the middle of the night."

Michael finished the scheme for his wife. "Besides, we've already moved both of your things into the silver-and-gray room. After all, you are supposed to be married."

"What?" Colt asked, suddenly angry. He had been quite willing to take advantage of the situation, but it irritated him that they had taken control like this. Besides, he had been looking forward to surprising Amelia in the middle of the night. "I don't believe this!"

Amelia agreed. "Neither do I."

Helen and Michael stood up at the same time, ready to make a quick exit. "It's late, we'll let you youngsters lock up."

Colt wondered where they'd managed to hide two single beds. Not that he minded much, now that he thought about it. It simply meant he would have to fight Amelia head-on instead of seducing her out of a sound sleep. It was a tough job, but one he felt equal to. He grinned.

Amelia glared at Colt, shooting little daggers at him with her eyes. "Did you have anything to do with this?"

"Me? I'm as mad at them as you are," he said, but he was laughing. "You've got to hand it to them. They cover all the angles." He went to lock the doors.

"Peachy," Amelia grumbled.

One big, happy family. Machiavellian grandparents, listening devices in the bedrooms. And here she was cleaning up the kitchen while her make-believe husband locked up the house. How perfectly homey.

Colt came back quietly, waiting for her to blow. She didn't say a word, just flipped off the light and walked out of the room. He followed her up the stairs, admiring the way her dress softly swished across her rounded backside.

"Where is it?"

"This way." He led her to a room at the opposite end of the house. "Remember the bugs," he whispered softly in her ear before opening the bedroom door.

The room was resplendent in shades of dark gray and light silvery tones. Amelia smiled grudgingly. "I do like this room."

His voice was low and sexy. "So do I, especially when we're in here together, alone at last. I thought that dinner party would never end. How about you, dear?"

Amelia scowled at him. "I'll be right back, *dear.*"

With barely concealed anger she opened the door closest to her and shut it sharply behind her. Groping, she found the light switch and groaned aloud. She'd made a wonderful exit—except, instead of entering the bathroom, she had entered a walk-in closet. And now she had to walk back out and face Colt. She could hear his smug laughter.

"Admit it," he was saying. "You like to undress in front of me. Every exhibitionist has to come out of the closet eventually."

Resolutely she opened the door and walked out. Colt was sitting in one of the dark gray armchairs, his amusement apparent. "Don't worry," she hissed at him, "your turn will come."

"Oh, I hope so," he returned, between peals of laughter.

Amelia had had enough. She removed her shoes

and threw both of them at him, then scampered into the bathroom, locking the door behind her.

Colt chuckled quietly as he began searching the room for bugs with a smaller detection device he had borrowed from Teri. He found only one, under the bed. Carefully, just as Nathan had done, he removed the black disk. If the men were listening in, he thought they'd had enough of a show for one evening. Of course, he wasn't going to let Amelia know he'd removed it. That would be his little secret.

Entering the closet, he pried back a piece of the carpet in the back corner and slid the disk underneath with the microphone side down. That would muffle it so they couldn't hear, but it would still operate. They'd probably think it was simply malfunctioning. Too bad, guys, he thought, no party tonight. At least not for them. For added measure he placed a pair of shoes right on top, then started to take off his clothes.

Amelia located her contact case and cleaned her lenses, then removed her makeup, dawdling. She realized she couldn't stay in the bathroom all night, but it was tempting. This was supposedly what she wanted, to use her wiles to convince Colt he couldn't live without her. Now that the time had come, however, she didn't think her wiles were in working order.

"Darling, I need in."

Amelia closed her ears to the double-entendre in his words, confused by her conflicting emotions. What they had shared at the cabin had been wonderful. She wanted Colt desperately, but she wanted it all, permanently. Just when she had finally decided what they really needed to do was talk, that stupid bug in the bedroom had ruined everything.

"It's all yours, Colt." She swept by him without a single nearsighted glance, but her hand brushed across the muscled hardness of his bare chest, conjuring up evocative mental images.

The sound of running water interrupted her thoughts and the quiet of the bedroom. Amelia breathed a sigh of relief as she struggled with the zipper of her dress. He was going to take a bath and leave her muddled emotions alone. As long as her mind didn't start picturing the sensual image of him sprawled out naked in the sunken tub, she would be fine.

"Here, let me help you with that zipper." He was standing right behind her, his hands already touching her heated skin.

She felt the warmth of his hands on her back as he unzipped her dress, his lips trailing down her spinal column till they met her panties. "Colt!" Tingling shivers were dancing up and down the length of her.

"Have to put on a good show for the bug," he whispered in her ear, then raised his voice. "Your breasts have been teasing me all night, this russet lace tantalizing my senses as it played hide-and-seek with my eyes."

"Colt, what are—"

"Ssh!" He placed his fingers lightly on her lips. "I want to see what my mind could only imagine," he continued, sliding the dress off her shoulders, helping the satin underslip rustle loudly as it fell to the ground.

"They expect newlyweds to make love every night," he murmured, his tongue dipping into the well of her ear, his hands cupping the fullness of her breasts. "All night."

"Aren't . . . aren't you going too far?" His fingers were caressing the tips of her breasts, teasing, tormenting her unmercifully.

"It wasn't my idea to play this charade. I'm only trying to live up to my part, and I've barely just begun."

Amelia tried to pull away from him. "If you think for one moment you're going to make love to me on such a flimsy excuse . . ."

Colt wedged his muscled, hairy thigh between her soft bare ones and pressed gently, stilling her words. His lips were leaving a trail of liquid fire across her breasts as he blazed toward new, undiscovered paths. She moaned, deep in her throat, an almost puzzled sound that spoke of her confusion as well as her desire.

"That's right, love, make those soft silky sounds I love to hear." Her panties joined the rest of her clothes.

Love? Did he know the meaning of the word after all? "Colt!" she cried when he swung her up in his arms and entered the bathroom. "What are you doing?"

He stepped into the almond-colored tub, lowering them into the rushing warm water. "This will help us relax." The tub almost overflowed as they

261

sank to the bottom, and Colt deftly shut the water off with his big toe.

"I've already had my bath today." But there wasn't much force to her objection. The slick feel of his flesh against hers robbed her of any will to protest his actions.

"Not one like this," Colt murmured, his hands gliding over the slippery wetness of her body. He handed her a sliver of soap. "Wash me."

Amelia held the bar between her palms, automatically beginning to rub the soap into a foamy lather. The temptation was too great. Hesitantly, her hands touched him and she felt the tightening of his muscles, the erratic pounding of his heart beneath her hand matching her own. She was past thinking, past reasoning. The only thing that mattered right now was the intimacy they had found once again.

Her hands careened over him, following the dips and curves of his well-muscled legs as she cleaned every inch of them, enjoying his uninhibited reactions to her caresses. With pleasure she soaped and rinsed each part of him with a thoroughness that left him quivering and wanting more.

"Like that?" she murmured as he jumped at her intimate touch. He moaned softly. "Is that a no?"

His eyes fluttered open, their green depths swirling with living desire. "No . . . yes . . . don't stop!"

Her caresses ranged from soft butterfly breezes to firm, demanding boldness. Colt let her have her way as long as he could stand it, then grasped her firmly by the hips, settling her on his lap. Amelia's silken thighs wrapped around him, pinning him deliciously beneath her as she faced him with sparkling eyes.

Uncontrollable sensations began flooding her body as he started to stroke her, washing over her with relentless tide. Any struggle to control her desires was lost. She leaned against him, the wild pounding of his heart beating as one with her own, fast and furious, the warmth of the water mingling with the heat of their skin as they joined.

They were so right for each other, so perfect, fitting together as if made for one another. His hands stroked her breasts, matching another rhythm deep within her until she cried out with joy and rediscovery. They could never part, not for long, they belonged together and she would make him her own no matter what. Later, as they basked in a rosy glow, she felt sure she saw that understanding, that same possessiveness, mirrored in Colt's eyes as well.

They got out of the tub and toweled each other off; then Colt lifted her and carried her to the bed, where they made love yet again in a slow, languorous rhythm. They lay side by side, Amelia's legs wrapped around him, holding him tight. Their damp, heated flesh intertwined as they took their time chasing shuddering pleasure to its breathless, dizzying conclusion.

Afterward, when the lights were all out and the house slept, Amelia studied the long, thin scar along his cheek, her fingers itching to reach over and trace the curve. She had never touched it, just as she wasn't sure she had ever touched his heart.

Every time she had come close, Colt had turned his head away from her curious fingers. She had asked him about it once and his answer was a moody silence, sparking her curiosity all the more.

His eyelashes were thick and dark, framing emerald-green eyes that never seemed to change color —like the rest of him, constant. Her gaze swept down over his chest, and wandered back up. She'd never been able to study him like this before. And Amelia knew from experience that if she gave in to temptation and touched him, he'd awaken instantly.

What was she going to do with this complex, infuriating, sexy man? One thing she wasn't going to do was trap him into marriage. It would be so easy for her to stop taking the pill and hope she got pregnant. But she knew deep inside that getting Colt that way would be no victory. She wanted all of him, from his strange sense of humor to his bad temper and sexy body, but she wanted him fairly.

When this charade was all over she was going to tell him, reveal everything, from the way Michael had coerced her to stay in this house right down to her hesitant decision to go along with the plan for her own reasons. Michael had been right; she had a very active conscience. And that meant she would have to confess. She would have Colt honestly and completely or not at all.

He stirred beside her, his hands reaching out to pull her against him. He would understand. A man with this much tenderness couldn't have a heart of ice. Wrapped in the secure cradle of his arms, she drifted back to sleep.

CHAPTER FIFTEEN

Michael Colt perused the documents spread out before him on the desk. "Are you sure this is a scam?"

"Positive," Nathan replied. "These guys are pros."

Colt was standing next to his grandfather, reading over his shoulder. "I'll say. Their presentation is really good, professionally done and concise. They could give textbook lessons with this material."

"Is there anything they've left out?" Nathan asked.

"No." Colt dropped a notebook on the desk and sat down on the sofa. "They have everything that's necessary to try to secure financing."

Amelia held up the piece of paper she'd been studying. "They even have a patent pending on their product, for heaven's sake."

"And," Michael added, "they've put together a very professional team who've raised millions already. If I didn't know better, I'd swear it would fly."

Nathan felt like a ant about to be squashed as all

eyes turned toward him. "Trust me. I know this isn't legitimate. It's a con through and through."

"Doesn't matter," Michael said with a shrug. "If by some chance your people are wrong, then we'll be in on it, and if they're right we'll eventually get our money back."

"Are you telling me you would have invested in this company, Michael?"

"Not without considerably more research." Pale blue eyes twinkled in his tanned, wrinkled face. "But I would definitely have been more eager in my younger days. I didn't have the number of contacts I have now, or a son who's a top-notch attorney."

"How about you, Colt?" Nathan asked.

He shook his head adamantly. "No. No way."

"He didn't like that accountant from the start," Michael explained. "Said something didn't feel right about him."

Nathan stared in disbelief at Colt. "You would have passed on this deal because you didn't like one guy?"

"Yes. I would have voted against this particular project on gut feeling alone. It's the way I work."

Michael laughed, looking at his grandson fondly. "And we would have listened to him too. His guts have pulled us out of just as many scrapes as my son's law books have."

Strange family, Nathan thought. Was his sister actually going to become a part of it? She had an odd, determined look about her today, as if she had made up her mind about something. He smiled, wondering what the get-togethers would be like when the Colts and the Drakes met.

"When do you want to set up the next meeting?"

"How about the end of this week?" Michael quickly suggested. He had gut instincts, too, and they were telling him something dramatic was about to happen between Amelia and Colt. A few more days of private time together, and he felt certain that he and Helen could start planning a wedding.

"Sounds good," Nathan agreed. "There's a surveillance team coming in to keep tabs on these guys once they take the bait, and that will give them time to set up. But we're going to have to do a carefully rehearsed act with a microphone in the room. We want our pigeons to know you're hooked and worth waiting around for."

With careful precision Nathan explained each of their parts in turn. "Ready?" They nodded. "Then let's get this over with."

He went out and retrieved one of the bugs he had removed last night. Amelia watched quietly from her chair in the corner of the room as they ran through their roles, so impressed by their deliveries, she felt like applauding. She kept quiet, however, until Nathan once again made the room private.

"Very nice. Especially you, Michael," she commented with heavy sarcasm. He simply smiled and took a bow.

Colt was smiling, too, but he looked puzzled.

"Nathan, why did they bug the house in the first place? I thought they trusted you."

"They do. It's you they didn't trust, in spite of your reputations. As I figured, though, they couldn't resist bilking you—if they could first be sure you were sincere," he explained. "When Michael suggested having them to dinner here and holding the meeting afterward, they must have decided you do a lot of business out of your home. So they bugged the place to see if they could catch wind of any problems."

"Besides," Michael interjected, "they couldn't very well refuse to come. If we were really sincere, that would make *us* suspicious, and after all, they are the ones seeking capital."

Nathan nodded in agreement. "It was too much money to pass up, but they also wanted advanced notice if someone was onto their plans. Hence the bugs. By the way, studies have shown that more information is leaked in bedrooms than anywhere else."

They all laughed at this tidbit of valuable information, easing the tension in the room. Amelia was looking at her brother thoughtfully. He was good at his job. She had already decided that he would make a good supervisor and was prepared to hound him until he took the job. She had the feeling just keeping track of Colt would be enough of a problem without continued worries about Nathan.

"What is it going to take to catch these guys?" she asked. "So you can get your promotion?"

He laughed. "You really can't wait to see me shackled to that desk, can you?"

"No," she answered honestly.

"It isn't easy. The two men you've met are just the brains behind this entire operation. We don't have solid proof that they've actually committed a crime yet. Right now all they're doing is acquiring funds to start a company, and until they do something illegal—and we can prove it—we can't touch them."

Amelia wasn't satisfied. "And how long is that going to take?"

"Your part in this will be over at the end of the week," he replied, knowing that wasn't what she meant and enjoying her impatient frown. "Once they've taken the bait and the Colt family's money has been transferred."

"Will you be in on actually catching them?"

"No, my part is almost over. Other agencies are already set up for when they make their move. I'm the undercover man, remember? I worked my way to the inside with them, gained their trust, and after a short vacation," he added, ruefully touching his sore ribs, "I set them up. All I'm doing now is gathering the needed proof and handing it over to my superiors. I'm just a little cog in a very big wheel."

Amelia pursed her lips. "Then how," she asked, "do you manage to keep getting these recurring injuries?"

Nathan grinned at his sister. "Sometimes I put my nose where it doesn't belong and don't yank it out fast enough."

Teri entered the room quietly and crossed over to her patient. It had been a long and busy morning. "All right, Nathan. Enough for now. If you want to be well enough to travel by next week, you're going to have to start getting more rest."

"For once, Teri, my dear, I agree with you."

Nathan made it to his feet unassisted and left the room with her. The others watched him go. Michael stood up, stretched, then looked at the pigeons who were involved in his own private con game.

"Well, kids, nothing else we can do right now," he said with a jovial air. "Why don't you two go have some fun?"

"Somehow," Colt commented dryly, "I would never call a meeting with Gloria Clarkson fun."

Michael cackled with glee as he left the room. "Watch your backside, son!"

Colt could feel Amelia's frostiness all the way across the room as she leaned against the far wall and glared at him. "A date with Gloria?" she asked.

He snorted indignantly. "Not likely. A business meeting at her company."

"Don't forget, those guys may be watching as well as listening. The charade isn't over and you're supposed to be married."

Colt leaned back on the sofa and smiled at her. "How could I possibly be interested in another woman when I have a charmer like you warming my bed?"

"Hah! Once you start drowning in that cleavage you'll probably forget all about me."

"Never. And I'd rather drown in yours."

"Fat chance." She didn't have enough for him to drown in. There was a big difference between oranges and cantaloupes.

"I'll take that challenge," Colt murmured, standing in front of her now. Gently he uncrossed her arms, his fingers encircling her wrists. "I like you just the way you are."

"Do you?" she asked seriously, trembling at his touch.

His eyes were devouring the molded curves of her breasts, outlined by a silk sweater in soft shades of copper and deep blue. "I'd like to take this sweater off and watch your pert breasts change into tight pink buds for me, but I don't have time." He struggled with his desire, for the first time wanting to put pleasure before business.

"That's not what I meant." Should she tell him right now? Spill Michael's whole plan and her part in it? "I mean, would you take me if you knew—"

He interrupted her confession with a quick kiss. "I'll take you any way I can get you. Want to come with me?" he offered, surprising both himself and her with his suggestion.

"You're serious?" He nodded his head affirmatively. She wasn't going to give him enough time to change his mind. "I'll meet you in the car. Can I drive?"

"Don't push your luck!"

Everyone assembled around the large, highly polished meeting table was staring at her, particularly Gloria. Much to her surprise Amelia man-

271

aged to stare coolly right back at her. In fact, under other circumstances, she would have stuck out her tongue. But she just sat in her chair and affected an air of regal detachment.

"Amelia has chosen, as have the other women in our family, to take an active part in our business," Colt explained to Gloria and her entourage. "Now, shall we get down to business?"

This was a side of him Amelia had never before witnessed. He was a hard negotiator, and it was evident that he didn't like playing games. When he gave them his ultimatum, it was with a cutthroat efficiency that made Gloria gasp.

"Take it or leave it."

"But that's two dollars a share less than you offered me last week!" Gloria Clarkson seethed.

Colt gave her a thin-lipped smile. "And it will drop each day, just as the value of the company is dropping without proper management." He stood up, ready to leave. "If you can get a better offer elsewhere, I'd strongly advise you to take it."

With that he nodded at Amelia, and she walked out of the room ahead of him, very worried by what she'd witnessed. Colt didn't like anyone playing around with him, and that's exactly what she was doing. And soon, very soon, he was going to have to be told about his grandfather's plans, as well as her pliant acquiescence to them. But not today, she decided suddenly, remembering the way he had just treated Gloria.

Colt turned toward her in the car a wide grin on his face. "Wasn't that fun?"

"If you say so."

272

"Where would you like to have our celebratory lunch?"

She grinned back at him. "You haven't won yet."

"Yes, I have. The fear in Gloria's eyes was easy to read. She now knows I'm not available as her next husband and she's running scared. Her advisors will inform her that I'm offering a very fair price for her shares, a price that will drop each day she delays her decision."

Amelia didn't doubt for an instant that he was serious. What horrible retribution would he come up with when she told him of her initial deception? As long as it wasn't the most horrible of all, telling her he never wanted to see her again, she could handle anything.

At least that's what she told herself, and held on to the thought desperately. The longer she waited, the worse it would be. But as she looked at him, feeling the warmth of his hand on her thigh and the tenderness in his eyes, she couldn't bring herself to open her mouth.

"Let's eat down by the capitol building," Colt decided. "There's an Italian place with the best spumoni in town."

Amelia smiled at his mention of dessert. "Do we get to eat lasagna first?" she teased.

"Only if you're a good girl."

As they bantered back and forth on their way to the restaurant, Amelia made another of her famous decisions, the easy ones that usually ended up getting her in trouble. She was going to forget about everything else for the rest of this week and savor every moment of their time together. And then she was going to tell him the truth.

Waking up next to Colt each morning was wonderful, a simple pleasure she wanted to indulge in every day for the rest of her life. Living the role of his wife, enjoying Helen's sweet attention, and even Michael's sly winks over the breakfast table, was all a dream she never wanted to end.

The last couple of days, Amelia had begun to nurture a fervent hope that it wouldn't have to end. Colt seemed on the verge of telling her a secret of his own. The way he looked at her, the way he held her after they made love, something seemed at last to have broken through the final barrier around his heart.

Had she done it? Had she won? She still wasn't sure, and even if he did return some small measure of the vast love she felt for him, the most important question remained. Would her victory stand once her tender trap had been revealed? If only the charade could go on for another week, even a few more days, perhaps she would have time to be certain of Colt's feelings.

But time had run out. The final meeting with the men had gone well. They had agreed to accept the Colts into what they called their own happy family of investors. It came as no surprise when Nathan accepted Teri's offer to go with him and continue to oversee his recovery while he directed the final phase of the operation. His promotion was imminent, and there was an unspoken bond between Teri and himself that went beyond the relationship of nurse to patient. In those respects Amelia couldn't be happier.

It meant, however, that the moment of truth had arrived. After saying good-bye to the glowing couple Amelia placed her hand in Colt's. "Let's take a walk," she said, giving him a shaky little smile.

He returned her smile, but his was warm and open. "Good idea. I have something I'd like to say to you."

Amelia felt a surge of joy, but carefully reminded herself he wasn't necessarily going to tell her he loved her. He could have anything on his mind, from congratulations on a job well done to an invitation to stay on as his mistress. Whatever it was he felt he needed to say, especially if he had fallen in love with her, she knew her confession had to come first.

She waited until they were far out into the autumn woods at the back of the property. "Colt, I have something to tell you and I want you to listen to the complete story before you say anything."

"Me first," he said, pulling her into his arms.

"No." Amelia gently drew away from him. She had to make Colt believe that what had started out as a ploy to help her brother had ended with her falling deeply and irrevocably in love with him. "Promise?"

He could feel the tension in her, radiating out across the still afternoon air. What could possibly be so wrong? "All right," he replied, bewildered.

Hesitantly at first, gaining composure as the tale unfolded, Amelia told him everything. She started

275

with Michael's business proposition and the way she had thought to slip out of it, then went on to the challenge she felt when Colt had told her an affair would be all she would get.

More than once she quieted him with her fingers on his lips as she went over the details of how this whole charade had come about. And of how, in the end, the only plan she followed was the one in her heart, a heart that now belonged to him, along with a love so deep, she was willing to risk it all rather than deceive him any longer.

Conflicting emotions chased each other across his face, from utter disbelief at the extent of his grandfather's manipulations, to a final look of outright betrayal that hurt Amelia to the core. When at last she fell silent, Colt leaned against a tree, defensive, outraged, and seething inside.

"Is that all?" he asked in a quiet voice.

Amelia looked at him bravely, certain she had done the right thing. "Yes."

"Congratulations, Amelia. Anyone who could fool me so completely has the makings of a true Colt. It's too bad you'll never be one."

He looked at her for a moment longer, then simply turned and walked toward the house. None of the endings she had envisioned had gone like this. That he would walk away without a fight hurt her more than any amount of accusations or anger. Amelia slipped to the ground, tears cascading down her face in a blinding torrent. He was going to do it. Colt was going to walk right out of her life, forever.

CHAPTER SIXTEEN

Amelia went to her room and stayed there for the rest of the day, feigning illness to avoid Michael and Helen. Actually, she was ill, sick at heart. Her tears only made her feel worse, as if she were drowning in a sea of despair that grew deeper with each passing hour.

When darkness closed in, she realized she had to stop feeling sorry for herself and take stock of the situation. Colt would have to come back eventually; the demands of the family business would see to that. And if he thought she would be gone when he returned, he had better think again.

She intended to go after that man with everything she had and then some. He wouldn't know what hit him until it was too late. And by then he wouldn't possibly be able to doubt her unending love for him.

First Amelia had to find him, and she quickly discovered a roadblock in her way. Colt's helicopter was gone from the small airport where he kept it, and no flight plan had been filed. He had literally flown off into the sunset and disappeared, as if he had disowned not only her but everything else as well.

Amelia then called his housekeeper, who informed her that Colt wasn't at his ranch and hadn't been there. His friend William hadn't seen him, and when she asked him to check for her, none of the people William called had heard from him either. Colt was gone without a trace.

With her depression threatening to engulf her again and Michael starting to ask questions, she made up her mind to sneak out of the house and go looking for the man she loved. But where to look? The answer came to her in a poignant, sentimental flash: she would wait for him at the cabin. As long as she was miserable anyway, she might as well be miserable in a place that held fond memories of the blissful passion they had shared.

It wasn't until her third day there that she began to wonder if she hadn't been fooling herself. Colt was a strong, intelligent, extremely independent man. And he felt he had been betrayed, not just by her, but by his grandparents as well. There was a possibility he would never come back. They couldn't patch things up if she never saw him again, and it was beginning to look as if that was exactly what he had in mind.

Colt had been so angry that day in the woods, he had to get away from her before he said some things he wasn't sure he would really mean. Since then he had spent too much time alone, painfully alone, walking, riding, running, struggling to sort out and accept his true feelings.

Colt had never before experienced the varying emotions Amelia aroused in him. It was a confusing jumble of protectiveness and possessiveness, a desire for more than her body. He loved to just talk with her and learn her views.

Not even Anne, the girl he'd almost married right out of high school, had made him feel this way. Their breakup had left Colt devastated at first, but soon he realized that he didn't even miss her. He'd considered her decision a lucky break for him, and had gone into every subsequent relationship with his eyes wide open and his heart locked tight. Till now.

Amelia had been the key. No matter what had happened, regardless of how that key had been turned, the lock had at last been opened. He was in love, in so deep it had felt like drowning at first. But now it was like floating in a sea of contentment.

When Colt finally came to his senses, his only thought was to find Amelia and ask her to marry him. Panic gripped his heart when he discovered she had disappeared from his grandparents' house. And when he got word there had been a fire at the cabin, his panic turned to mind-numbing fear.

As he raced there, he imagined the worst. What if she had gone to the cabin to wait for him and had had an accident? Could life be so unfair as to steal Amelia from him now?

Colt burst through the cabin door, a speeding ticket still clenched in his trembling hand, only to find he had been fooled yet again. Dizzy with relief, he climbed the stairs to the bedroom loft, smiling. There had been no fire, but he was going to start one right now.

Amelia felt warm hands touching her intimately, and struggled to remain asleep so the touch would continue forever. It seemed so real, so alive. Every single one of her nerve endings was singing, leaping with joy. She felt her body reacting to the erotic dream that orchestrated each movement she craved.

It wasn't real. Colt was gone. But still she murmured, half awake, "Oh, yes, Colt."

"Do you like that, my love?" he whispered in return.

Her eyes flew open and she saw him, smiling at her tenderly. "Colt!" With an eagerness that astonished him Amelia buried herself in his arms. "You're really here!" She rained little kisses all over him, her tears dampening his shirt.

"Hush, it's all right, love, don't cry." Colt held the woman he loved with all his heart snugly in his arms. "It took me a while, thickheaded oaf that I am. But I'm here. I love you, Amelia," he murmured softly.

"I love you too." She hiccuped and he chuckled quietly. "Your ranch was on my agenda for tomorrow. I was hoping you would come back here to the cabin, where it all began for us. But I was growing very impatient."

"Yes, impatience does seem to be one of your more endearing qualities," he teased, very secure now that he held her in his arms and knew everything would be all right. They had a lot of talking to do, but it would work out. They would make it work. "I'd love to feel some of your impatience right now."

"And I'd love to show you," she purred. Tomorrow they would talk, or the next day, it didn't matter right now. They were together. The loving charade was at last on its way to lifetime of reality.

"You little tease," he growled, joining them together, unable to wait a moment longer.

"But I got my way," she moaned, her body moving with his as they again strove to reach that pinnacle of intense, shattering emotion and sweet sharing.

"No, we got *our* way. Together, forever and ever." And they'd only just begun.

Michael was waiting patiently in his study. Colt and Amelia were back from the cabin, and would undoubtedly come walking through the door any minute to announce their engagement.

It had been touch and go there for a while. They must have had a dandy of a lover's quarrel, judging by the blind rage Colt had been in that day he took off. But naturally Michael had known Amelia had gone to the cabin to wait for his grandson. He knew because he'd followed her. And naturally he had known Colt would wind up there eventually, because he had left word at the boy's ranch that there had been a fire at the cabin.

He smiled, pleased with himself. He was beginning to think he could fix a rainy day if he put his mind to it. "What's keeping those two?" he muttered aloud, then pushed himself out of his chair and went looking for them.

When he got to the hallway near the front door, he saw Amelia coming down the stairs. Alone. She was carrying her suitcase. "What on earth do you think you're doing, girl?" Michael thundered at her.

"Leaving. I'm going back to San Antonio and my job."

"I don't understand. Where's Colt?"

"He's already gone. For good, Michael. I told him the entire story, and he has decided to say good-bye to me and disown you," she told him, her face expressionless.

Michael's mouth dropped open. "What! Why did you do a fool thing like that?"

"Because he had a right to know the truth," she replied. "You can't build a lasting relationship without trust."

He pondered that for a moment, then waved his hands in the air. "Bah! He'll change his mind. We'll just—"

"No," Amelia interrupted, shaking her head sadly. "He's made his decision, and so have I. It's truly over. Good-bye, Michael Colt." She turned toward the door.

"Wait!" He was thinking furiously. "You can't go, my dear. About your job. I told them you wouldn't be needing it anymore."

Amelia twirled to face him. Colt was absolutely right. He deserved everything he got. "You did what?"

"This is terrible," he moaned. "I sincerely thought you would be marrying Colt and wouldn't need it anymore." He put his hand on her arm. "I'll help you find another, even better job."

"No, thank you."

"Amelia, please! I'm dreadfully sorry about this!"

She laughed sarcastically. "Sure you are."

"I am!" He went to the foot of the stairs and called out for his grandson. "Colt! You mustn't do this, my boy. We can talk. We . . ."

Michael's voice trailed off when he saw Helen come wandering out of the kitchen, her face in her hands. "He's gone! Our grandson has disowned us, and it's all your fault."

"See what your manipulating ways have gotten you, Michael?" Amelia asked bitterly. She went to Helen and led her back into the kitchen. "It's all right, Helen. Colt didn't disown you, just Michael."

Michael stood there for a moment, alone in the hall. How could this have happened? He'd had everything planned so well! Hanging his head, he went after the two women. He would make amends somehow. He had to!

"Helen, I—"

They were all there, sitting around the table and smiling at him. Helen wasn't crying, she was laughing. Colt and Amelia sat close together, their arms around each other's waists. They were laughing too.

"Hello, Pop," Colt said. "Don't you want to help plan our wedding?"

"Should be quite an affair," Amelia told him.

"My parents are coming back from Europe and everything."

Helen got up and came to his side, giving him a quick hug and a kiss. "What's the matter, love of my life? Cat got your tongue?"

Michael closed his eyes and sighed. "I," he said with a mixture of embarrassment and relief, "have just been had."

"That you have," Helen agreed.

"Royally had, I'd say." Colt chuckled. "And you know good and well you deserved it, you wily old fox."

Helen led him over to the table, where he sat down and looked at them in astonishment. Amelia leaned over and kissed him on the cheek. Colt winked at him. Helen held his hand.

"You did deserve it," Amelia said. "It was Colt's plan, and I didn't want to go along with it at first, but when you told me you gave away my job! I mean, I was going to give notice anyway in a week or two, but really!"

He shrugged. "All's well that ends well?" he suggested in a hopeful tone.

"You can say that again, Pop."

Michael watched them kiss, so obviously in love, so perfect for each other. He relaxed and hugged Helen tight, knowing Amelia and Colt had found the same devotion. He beamed at them all.

"Well, then," he said, his eyes twinkling with mischief. "About those great-grandchildren . . ."

Catch up with any Candlelights you're missing.

Here are the Ecstasies published this past March

ECSTASY SUPREMES $2.75 each

- [ ] 161 **RUNAWAY LOVER**, Alison Tyler 17391-4
- [ ] 162 **PRISONER IN HIS ARMS**, Dallas Hamlin 17042-7
- [ ] 163 **TEXAS WILDFIRE**, Eleanor Woods 18780-X
- [ ] 164 **SILVER LOVE**, Hayton Monteith 17899-1

ECSTASY ROMANCES $2.25 each

- [ ] 492 **TROPICAL HEAT**, Joan Grove 19004-5
- [ ] 493 **BLACK LACE**, Grace Reid 10836-5
- [ ] 494 **DESTINY'S LADY**, Kathy Clark 11810-7
- [ ] 495 **TENDER FURY**, Helen Conrad 18726-5
- [ ] 496 **THE QUINTESSENTIAL WOMAN**, Cory Kenyon 17218-7
- [ ] 497 **KNIGHT OF ILLUSIONS**, Jane Atkin 14596-1
- [ ] 22 *BREEZE OFF THE OCEAN*, Amii Lorin 10817-9
- [ ] 24 *THE CAPTIVE LOVE*, Anne N. Reisser 11059-9